ODDBALLS

Manchán Magan is a writer, traveller and television maker. He has made over 30 travel documentaries focusing on issues of world culture and globalisation for RTE, TG4, the Travel Channel and History Channel. His programmes are shown in 25 territories around the world. *No Béarla*, his documentary series about travelling around Ireland speaking only Irish sparked international debate. He writes the "Magan's World" travel column for *The Irish Times*. He has written travel books in Irish – *Baba-ji agus TnaG* (Coiscéim 2006) and *Manchán ar Seachrán* (Coiscéim 1998) – and a novel, *Bí i nGrá* (Coiscéim 2008). His English-language travel books include *Angels & Rabies: a journey through the Americas* (Brandon 2006), *Manchán's Travels: a journey through India* (Brandon 2007) and *Truck Fever: a journey through Africa* (Brandon 2008). He has written for the *Guardian, Los Angeles Times, Washington Post*.

His play *Broken Croí/Heart Briste* was nominated for the Fishamble New Writing Award, the Bewleys Café Theatre Award and two *Irish Times* Theatre Awards. It won the Stewart Parker Irish Language Award. He has currently been commissioned to write plays for BBC Radio Ulster, the Project Arts Centre and the Abbey Theatre.

www.manchan.com

Manchán Magan

oddballs

A Novel of Affections

BRANDON

A Brandon Original Paperback

First published in 2010 by Brandon
an imprint of Mount Eagle Publications
Dingle, Co. Kerry, Ireland, and
Unit 3, Olympia Trading Estate, Coburg Road, London N22 6TZ, England

www.brandonbooks.com

ISBN 9780863224249

2 4 6 8 10 9 7 5 3 1

Mount Eagle Publications receives support from
the Arts Council/An Chomhairle Ealaíon.

Cover design: Anú Design
Typesetting by Red Barn Publishing, Skeagh, Skibbereen

One

Nathaniel was wearing his purple fleece and beneath it, as always, a tweed suit, one of five made by a Scottish tailor in New York to his exact specifications – all now scraggy and shapeless, just as he liked them. Tonight he had chosen the brown herringbone, which clashed badly with the fleece. On anyone else, it would have looked ridiculous, but on Nathaniel it seemed natural. At anti-logging campaigns, he'd dress himself head-to-toe in protest T-shirts, one worn as a kilt, another a hat, another as a cummerbund, but always he'd match them with a tweed jacket: Harris tweed, from the village of Harris itself, or at least from one of the Outer Hebridean islands. Even at rock gigs and mountain-bike trials, he wore elements of tweed – the trousers and waistcoat normally, making sure to include a pair of long woollen hunting socks to protect against the mud. He claimed it was precisely what these clothes had been designed for: rough outdoor work by gillies and crofters on Scottish estates. It was far more ludicrous, he maintained, to wear such items in air-conditioned offices. It was simply farcical, like wearing Gore-Tex to the opera.

He and his girlfriend Rachel were in their friend Cameron's house, an expansive, ranch-style home designed by Rachel's mom. They were snuggled up in a deckchair beside a floodlit pool with Rachel's nose burrowed into his armpit. She sunk herself deeper into his fleece and smiled.

A patchwork of extensive, well-maintained gardens spread out around them, making up the district of White Mountain, New Hampshire. The houses were clad in kiln-dried cedar with dark shingles on the roof that blended seamlessly with the trees behind. An owl called from a grove of mature oaks that jutted out from the surrounding thicket stretching towards Canada. There was a strict delineation between the landscape, which was allowed remain overgrown and wild, and the gardens, which everyone agreed had to be neat and well maintained, with chemically blue pools and rolling lawns cared for by football-toned sons or gerbil-eyed students from the nearby college.

Rachel enjoyed seeing the familiar idiosyncrasies of her mom's architectural style around her: the haphazardly placed portholes and knee-to-neck windows, the off-centre cantilevered ledges and their counterpoised nooks. She and Nathaniel were whispering songs to each other. He the first line, she the second, and so on until the chorus which they allowed play silently, joining in again only on the next verse. It was a trick they had mastered in social science class two years before when they were put sitting apart. They would mouth alternative lines across the room at each other. Even now, having just finished their last day ever of high school, and with the prospect of a teacher catching them and imposing detention as remote as a seal emerging from the overheated, over-chlorinated pool, their singing was so quiet that only alternate words registered, like dust brushing against the needle of an old record.

Rachel hadn't bothered changing out of her T-shirt and jeans after school for the party, or even putting on make-up. She was still of an age when the first glow from the morning shower lasted all day, and it took a really bad mood or a nasty dose of flu to wipe it out. She had that naturally sallow complexion that would never need much embellishment, especially if she kept up the cold lake dips every morning with her father and the weekend bike rides in the forest with Nathaniel.

Not only did Nathaniel dress from another age, he looked like he might possibly be from an entirely different race, an elite, alien race. He was phenomenally lanky, with jutting-out limbs that swung disconcertingly in their sockets like a praying mantis caught in a web. His hair was swollen into a sponge that would be termed an Afro if it weren't so shockingly blond. Overall, he appeared to be a glorious misfit, yet what people noticed about him first was his smile – a smile so broad and sincere, so joyfully goofy it was like a wormhole enveloping you with goodwill. Like a benevolent galactic anomaly. The first piece of him that Rachel had kissed was his mouth; she hadn't bothered with his cheek or his forehead, but had honed straight in on the shifting, quivering, funnelling hole in his face. She knew that if she didn't get to grips with it immediately it could overwhelm her. His mouth was like the crater of a volcano or the beak of one of those cartoon birds where the camera dives endlessly into the blackness of its gullet. It had a life of its own. That much was certain. It danced, even when he wasn't talking. Often he seemed locked in battle with it, wrestling it, trying to narrow it into more conventional forms; containing its intensity.

Inevitably, it had been the choreography of his face that Rachel had first fallen for. She had been lingering in the hallways between classes, on her way from room 118 to 424 in the most languorous and meandering way possible, when she caught sight of him. She had paused for a moment at a spur of photocopiers, finishing a conversation with Katy, her best friend from kindergarten days, and was just about to hang left towards the science block when Nathaniel rose up from behind the photocopiers, startling them both.

"What the hell …!" they cried.

"Apologies," he said, brushing cat balls of dust from his thighs and adjusting his lapels. "Just getting the, em …"

They were about to round on him, accusing him of eavesdropping or worse, but then he let loose a smile, one of his most elongated and oscillating, fluctuating somewhere in between a sort of gyroscopic movement halfway between a swollen laugh and a shy smirk. Rachel was immediately disarmed. She ushered Katy off into the stream of bodies flowing towards the library and turned back to Nathaniel, rummaging through her mind for something appropriate to say. It was hard to focus. She had never even imagined such a mouth could exist – as super-sensitive as cat's whiskers, exposed for all to see. She wanted to protect it, but also to possess it, to be intimate with it. Nathaniel's mouth sparked a covetousness in her that later led to a lifetime of art collecting, culminating in her acquisition of an important collection of works by young Canadian artists which she bequeathed almost fifty years to the day later to a gallery in Vancouver. She never realised that the repeated urge to possess a juvenile work, to instruct a gallery owner to put a red dot on it and set it aside, was a direct link back to her first impulse triggered by Nathaniel's mouth.

Nathaniel never got to know the degree to which girls found his vulnerability appealing. He always felt ungainly and awkward, not that he let it bother him all that much. He regarded his mouth as a badge of honour. "Cuttlefish" was what he called himself – a mollusc with its genitals around its mouth.

"What would you do if I said I wanted to kiss you?" Rachel had asked him straight out in the hallway, surprising herself as much as him.

"I'd say this isn't the best of times," Nathaniel replied languorously. "These Xerox machines are pumping out toxins 24-7 – the less opening of mouths we do here the better."

He took hold of her hand, and without saying another word, they walked towards the main door of the school and headed off down town.

That was two years before, and since then they had hardly spent a week apart. Today was the last day of school, and within a few weeks, when all their friends had scattered in various directions for the summer, they would be heading off to Europe. They had bought two inter-rail tickets that offered unlimited travel anywhere on the continent as far east as Poland and west as Ireland, as far north as Sweden and south as Sicily.

Life was about to begin.

"What would you do if you actually woke up tomorrow with stigmata?" Rachel asked him now as he stretched back on to the deckchair, pulling her with him.

"I'd bleed over you."

"Blood or cuttlefish ink?"

Today was Padre Pio's saint day, the school chaplain had informed them during their valedictory speech, the obligatory *Desiderata* speech that the students had heard a dozen times or more in teen movies. It was as boring as always, but a relief to have it finally directed at them this time. The Padre Pio theme was a new and strangely affecting angle – a final and futile stab at attracting novices, as though the chaplain hoped that the sight of the harsh world looming ahead might frighten one or two back into the fold like baby seals paddling back towards the crate when the rescue team releases them. It was kind of sad, but touching too that he still held out hope.

"I'd be bleeding daily, not monthly," Nathaniel said. "It'd be sorta cool. You'd have to put up with my moods, and you wouldn't be able to say a thing."

He leant over to kiss her, adding, "Once a month we'd bleed together."

"I'd like that," Rachel said, pulling her lips away and re-engaging from a new angle.

Nothing would please her more than the idea of becoming one with Nathaniel. Coalescing. Although her mother had been worried at first about the intensity of their relationship, gradually everyone realised there was nothing to be concerned about. This was one of the stable ones. One of those couples that seemed immutable, somehow preordained. Like hummingbirds and angel's trumpet. He was empathic and nurturing, while she was wilful and brazen. He was the zero to her one; together they were in equilibrium. It was this that she treasured most: that feeling of ease when he was lying next to her; a sort of resonance. It was what she savoured, whether queuing up in the gas station or just standing in the school cafeteria: that sparkly, tingly feeling they felt together.

The soundtrack of *The Big Chill* wafted out from inside the den. Their friends were sprawled on Pueblo Indian rugs on a terracotta floor watching a video. It was kind of a lame way to celebrate their last day of school, but it was meant only as an aperitif for the true party that would happen next week with a DJ and live bands and a marquee. One final and unforgettable bash before the summer and then college in the autumn.

"Another beer, Cam?" one of the boys, Lek Shreinerman, asked a goateed boy with Clark Kent glasses sprawled beside him on the rug.

"Like, what do you think, Shriner?"

"Pause it and I'll score some munchies too," Lek replied.

William Hurt's flared nostrils froze centre screen while Lek went out to the mini-kitchen near the pool. Cameron flexed his muscles into a push-up and looked around him, absentmindedly surveying the sprawled forms of his friends and the unused armchairs and sofa behind. He crocodiled his way towards the pool using his arms and feet.

"So anyway," he called across to Lek, who was pulling stuff out of an enormous fridge, "Jake was grinding glass, yeah …"

"Who?"

"Jake! My brother, stupid. How many times have you heard me talk about my brother? And today, on the very last day after, like, four years together, you ask me who he is?!"

"You call him jerk-off normally," Lek said.

"Do I?"

"Sure."

"Oh … anyway, see, Jake was grinding glass in the coffee maker and mom calls, "What are you up to?" and he says, "Just making coffee, Mom," and she asks, "For who?""

"Shouldn't that be, for whom?" Nathaniel calls over.

"What? Shuddup!" Cameron said and turned back to Lek, "Anyway, he says, "Oh, no one. Just, you know …" So, I go up to him later to see what he's up to, right? And he is! He really is grinding glass – you know that crushed ice sound? Like Christmas baubles smashing? And I say to him, "What the hell do you think you're doing, Jakie?" And he tells me there was this read-through of the play at school and he wasn't picked for the part he wanted, so he was brewing up this *special* coffee for Mr Lineman. He was going to bring it to rehearsals and offer it to the poor schmuck at break. I mean, for real! The boy's a freaking psycho. I've always said so."

"Big surprise – he's been playing computer games like non-stop since for ever," Nathaniel said. "Any time I've ever been to your house he just grunts."

"It's not the computer games," Cameron said. "They don't make a difference. I mean, if Pacman had affected kids, we'd all be running around in darkened rooms munching pills and listening to repetitive music, yeah?"

"Right on!" someone shouted from the den.

"That's so old," Lek said. "Look up hilarious in the dictionary, and you won't see a picture of you."

"What happened about the coffee anyway?" Rachel called in to them. "Did Lineman haemorrhage his guts?"

Cameron shrugged without interest. "Dunno."

He pushed his glasses back up on his face and turned round to pull himself back towards the television, following Lek who was laden down with beers and snacks.

Rachel heard the movie unpause itself, and she snuggled in closer to Nathaniel. It was weird – no matter how close they were, somehow they could always get closer still. Nathaniel had a way of expanding or contracting himself like a boa constrictor.

"Angela was saying to me," Rachel whispered, "you know, with her high-pitched voice and all: "Coz, you were like *soo* awesome, today!'" she said – and I'd only swum up and down the pool a few lengths! I swear she loves me, I swear she dreams about wrapping her big train-track mouth around mine – *it's like, hello! Come on! I have a boyfriend, or didn't you notice!"*

"Go easy," Nathaniel said, stroking her hair. "Who knows, maybe she does have a crush on you. Just play it cool, yeah?"

"Sure," Rachel cooed. "I don't mean it."

"I know."

The violins on the soundtrack signalled a kiss, and Nathaniel and Rachel could hear their friends shouting.

"Slip the tongue! Slip the tongue!"

Rachel pulled away, not sure if they were talking about her or the video. She glanced around. It was unlikely they could see her out here unless by a reflection in the door.

"For God's sake, Chris, get it together," someone yelled at the screen.

The two lovers fell back against each other; the effort of staying apart was almost too much. The laws of their own personal physics were stacked against them, and they snuggled in tighter before finally getting up and going inside – picking their way through the pizza boxes, sweet wrappers and empty cans and making space for themselves on the carpet with the others just as the end credits were rolling.

Rachel looked around her and realised how much she would miss these people when they went to college. She was thinking of studying architecture like her mom, but wasn't sure. Whenever she flicked through the *Architectural Digests* at home, her mind started spinning off into a world of chalk facades, glass terraces and wooden spires, creating and moulding 3-D spaces as she went. She loved buildings. But there was so many others things too. Like writing. She had been scribbling poems since fourth grade, and some of her more recent ones thrilled her even more than architecture. And then there were the mud huts. Ever since Nathaniel had brought her to a workshop in the forest last summer where they had made huts out of mud and timber, she was more unsure than ever. It seemed pointless wasting time going to college to learn structural engineering or thermal equations or whatever when all it took to build a home was the clay around you and your bare hands.

All she knew for certain about her future was that she wanted to be with Nathaniel. They would head off to Europe and hope that things felt into place from there.

"You smell salmony," he whispered to her.

"I do?"

"Uh-uh."

"My dad insisted on cooking, like, a big humungous dinner," she explained. "He even fired up the barbecue."

Rachel had wanted to tell him more. To say how, as her dad was carrying the salmon to the deck table, he had pulled out a bottle of Dom Perignon Reservé from the chill box and handed it to her. It was a 1988, he told her. He had gone straight from the maternity ward to the wine shop when she was born and bought a whole case. They had opened two at her christening, he said, and they might as well open another tonight – see what the last sixteen years had done to it; see had they made it as beautiful as they had her.

She wanted to say all this to Nathaniel, but she stopped herself. His parents were strict churchgoers and weren't keen on any overt displays of affection or ostentatious trappings, which is how they would regard salmon and champagne. Sometimes it was best not to tell him things.

"It smells nice," he said, sniffing her.

His own dinner had been difficult. There were nude photos laid out on the kitchen counter when he came home from school; beside them, a note demanding *WHO?!!!* in thick marker. The photos were on A4 paper and had that washed-out quality of computer printouts, with misaligned sections in blurred colours. They were standard porn shots, women with strained smiles and apathetic eyes. He had ignored them at first, walked by and headed upstairs, not wanting to think about who owned them or what they were doing there. At dinner his mother had set them out in front of them all again and asked him and his dad and his younger brother the same question. Whose were they? She had found them in the My Documents folder on the computer. It was awkward; especially for his mother. He could see how uncomfortable she was.

She regretted having ever told the folks at her church meeting about them, but she knew in her heart that a sin shared was a sin halved. Her pastor had reminded her that if she turned her back on the problem she was as guilty as the sinner, possibly more so, as it was conceivable that they didn't know better. She had tried to say that she would rather do nothing about it this time, to look the other way, but the pastor had looked aghast and asked her to reflect on whose side she was on, Jesus' or Satan's. There was no in-between. Someone in her home was in thrall to bad vices. A bud of deviance had sprouted in her family; it needed to be pruned right away. If not, it could spread through the whole community. She was being tested by God, they told her, and they assured her of their complete support.

This encounter had been on her mind all week. She had postponed it numerous times. Each afternoon when the boys were at school and her husband was at work, she'd lay out the photos to await them when they got home, but before long she'd lose her nerve and gather them up again. Tonight was the weekly church meeting; there was no more time left. The congregation would want a report. To help her through it, she had taken a small drop of bourbon before dinner, and now, standing at the head of the table, she felt a bit light-headed.

"Just tell me whose are they?" she said, a dew of sweat rising on her nose.

Nathaniel had thought of owning up just to get it over with, but his curiosity as to who really owned them got the better of him. His brother, he presumed, but there was an uncomfortable strain around his father's eyes. Nathaniel was amazed that she hadn't asked her husband separately beforehand. Somehow it must have been easier this way.

The way she was looking at Nathaniel made it clear he was the prime suspect. Unless someone else owned up, he would be blamed, and his parents might refuse to pay for his ticket to Europe as punishment. Withholding money was what the pastor always advised. Money was at the core of most things for him. They sat there in silence for an uncomfortably long time. His mother kept glancing towards the oven clock with increasing anxiety as the meeting time grew nearer. Eventually she had no choice but to get up and leave, and as she did, Nathaniel's brother Garth winked knowingly at him, patting his chest proudly.

"Mom," Nathaniel said, as she was walking out the door.

"Yes?" she replied with relief.

"I think Garth has something to say."

His parents turned towards Garth, but he just shrugged back innocently.

"No," he said. "Nothing."

Their mother left the house with the speedy stride she used when anxious.

Lek got up to put another video on, and Rachel snuggled herself in closer to Nathaniel.

"You know, Rachel, I've been thinking, your hair is holding you back," her friend Katy, who was lying beside her, said.

"Huh?" Rachel said.

"Your hair. It's sending out all the wrong messages, you know? Curtains haven't been in for aeons, particularly blonde. People'll think you're on some retro trip. How about I dye it for you? I mean seriously, purple or something?"

"Purple is cool," Cameron chimed. "You reckon, Nathaniel?"

"Dunno," he said. He was still thinking about his mother.

"Anyway, like my Mom is really gonna let me," Rachel said.

"You're free now, girl. You can do what you want," Katy said.

"I'll drink to that," Lek said, slugging back a beer.

It was morning before they went home. They had gone for a walk across the golf course at dawn, their eyes blurry from too much TV and their gait unsteady. The golf course had a surreal quality in the early light, with the fairways lit up olive and a mist rising from the ground. They had all hugged each other, promising to remain friends for ever, and Nathaniel had taken off his jacket and twirled it around him like a dervish until he grew dizzy and began to wobble and fall, and they all copied him.

Nathaniel had insisted on driving Rachel home. They hardly talked, just happy to be together. It had been a good night. Rachel leant over and rested her head on his shoulders. They passed a rabbit standing on its hind legs looking around inquisitively, and Rachel stared back, turning around and patting down the mound of sleeping bags in the rear so she could watch it as long as she could. Just before they drove out of sight of it, Rachel noticed the rabbit twitch, as though sensing something fearful. She shivered too, and instinctually her fingers found Nathaniel's hair, his curly mop, and began rooting through it, winding the curls like she used to with her dolls.

"Purple?" she said. "What do you think?"

"I like blonde."

"We could both go purple in Europe – it would suit your tweed."

It was then she saw the eyes looking in at her, dark and opalescent, urgent with fear. They appeared through the trees; a trick of light seeming to bring them closer and in focus. She reached over to show Nathaniel. It was a deer she realised. But before she had even opened her mouth to say anything, it came at them, and seconds later she felt the thud of the undercarriage hitting something and bits of fur come flying up from the road. It was as though her brain had edited the sequence, cut a few stills from the film projector running before her eyes. Somehow the deer had got from behind the trees to beneath their jeep without her actually seeing it. Nathaniel had his foot pressed hard against the brake and the jeep was skidding to a halt, pulling the animal along with it. They had almost come to a standstill when a second deer, a young fawn, came racing out from the trees. Its forelegs hit the bumper, sending its feet buckling under and its torso lunging forward on to the hood. Its tiny antler buds came to rest just in front of the windscreen. It was alive, writhing and flailing on the bonnet, its forelegs battering the radiator grill for grip. Rachel sat there transfixed as the fawn pulled itself up, fell down again, and then dragged itself back on to the road with its hind legs. It was only then that Rachel had looked over and noticed Nathaniel was sitting at an awkward angle. He looked strangely calm; glaring out the mucus-spattered window like an Action Man.

"Nathaniel," she mouthed, but her voice was dry.

A small branch fell from the trees overhead, and a crow squawked as if affronted.

"Nathaniel?" she tried again, more urgently this time.

The engine had stopped now, the fan ticking over, triggered by the strain of braking.

"Nathaniel!" she cried.

He didn't move. On his forehead was a bruise, turning darker by the second. Suddenly Rachel remembered his head lurching forward with the first jolt, hitting against something and ricochetting back. It had been so quick she had hardly registered it, and he had sat up again straight away; somewhat sluggishly she now recalled. A pattern of redness was rising from the bruise – the indentations of the steering wheel picked out in dark blotches. That endlessly equivocating mouth wasn't moving – his smile gone. She reached out to touch him but couldn't bring herself to and instead began clawing blindly for the door handle.

Two

A tear rolled down Colm's cheek, drying instantly in the gale that blew in off the Atlantic. He was cowering in a shepherd shelter above Reek Head, an old stone hut with a corbelled roof, an ancient place that might have been built two hundred years ago by someone wanting to clear the field of stones and create some shelter, or by pilgrims two thousand years before that as a place of rest along the route from the landing site beyond the pier up to Cnoc Ciarán. The locals claimed it was a hermit's cell in the time of St Brendan – the knowledge had been passed down through the generations.

Colm was crouched on his hunkers, rocking back and forth, watching strands of dirty white fleece blowing across the grass towards the cliff edge and trying not to grind his teeth. The bits of wool seemed to hesitate a second before disappearing over.

I want to let my heart be bare, he thought, *that's what I want, bare and open and fully alive. Simple.*

And up here it was that simple, yet down below it got muddied. Up here he knew who he was. He could taste it. He could feel his soul inside his tall, thin sixteen-year-old body. Everything glowed up here: his thoughts, his hopes, the world around him, even his mousey blond ringlets trailing towards his shoulders. He ran through the basic facts once again, the things that seemed hardest to conceive of down below.

I want to shine. It's simple, just shine. Why can't I remember? I'm the lighthouse – that's what I need to keep telling myself. I love you!

A parabola of foaming waves charged in from the west, bringing with them a drifting crayfish pot with a metal buoy trailing behind it. The cliff seemed to swallow it, and it disappeared from view until Colm heard the clang of the buoy smashing against the rocks. The next wave sucked it back out again just beyond the line of the cliff edge before another brought it back twice as hard and the clang sounded ever louder. It was caught in a loop now, and kept going back and forth, clanging each time until the thin batons of the hazel basket were in pieces and only the lead-grey buoy remained. The hazel pieces were like tiny kayaks too light for the waves to grip on to, and they escaped, surfing back out on the current. Colm envied them their sudden stay of execution, their fresh chance to return to the world as something new, free of encumbrance, no longer with an agenda to trap life. It was their lightness that had freed them from the waves, their fragility. He was determined to keep this in mind.

Something about the sight of them sparked the familiar rush of endorphins that he had been waiting for, the reason he had come up here in the first place. A sense that the world was OK, that he was loved unconditionally by something or other, part of a flow rising up into the sky and down deep into the ground. He smiled. It was becoming increasingly hard to find this feeling, and it tended to leech away ever more quickly. Over the following days, it would drain away gradually until he was left with nothing, and he would have to come back up here, to shout at the wind and waves again until clarity returned. He knew he had to be more patient with himself. He needed to be kind to his thoughts, to nurture them and allow them the freedom to wither and die, so they could be reborn again with renewed vim.

Brushing the earth from his knees, he pulled his dark blue

smock down over his thighs and set off back down the cliffs towards the town, striding purposefully in his well-worn boots. The smock was old and made for someone far bulkier, but it had been a gift from a Breton who had spent the summer here catching lobsters, and he was fond of it.

In town, he noticed people looking at him with their usual mix of concern and resignation. He ignored them, retreating into his habitual pose, with pale eyes sunk low behind a fringe of curls and hands deep in his jeans. In his sixteen years of living in Reek, of being alive on the planet, he could probably have counted the number of times he had actually looked a stranger in the eye. It just was something he preferred not to do. On the few occasions he dared look, he was always saddened by what he saw: the judgement, the unease. His brother, Dónal, wanted him to become more outgoing, to socialise, even just a little bit, especially now that he was no longer at school. Dónal had encouraged him to come to the pub with him a few times, but he rarely got further than the car park. He liked the car park. The sodium light gave off a pleasant glow that made the place seem other-worldly. It was the only sodium light in Reek, except for the one at the very end of the pier, and he loved the way they both made the world seem like a stage set. They brought a sense of unreality that Colm imagined was in fact truer than the reality that he normally saw. The car park had the added attraction of Taytos, a vixen he had befriended the previous summer, who now allowed him feed her milk and out-of-date Tayto crisps that Bridie, the publican, gave him. He could happily spend all evening there, which he frequently did, waiting until Dónal came out at closing time and they would walk home together.

Today he had come to town determined to buy some building materials, which was a big step considering he had never before been through the doors of Daly's hardware shop and pub.

He had always waited outside while his parents or Dónal went in. But today he knew he had to confront the issue head on, and nothing was going to stop him. It was why he had taken a detour up to the cliffs, to fuel his courage.

Outside the shop he took a deep breath, closed his eyes and sidled determinedly in through the narrow doorway, finding himself on opening his eyes again in a wood-panelled vestibule with two doors leading off it and a staircase leading upwards. His attention was immediately drawn to the fuse board above one of the doors – an old and intriguingly complicated-looking one. It was enchanting, and he knew he could have spent happy hours examining it thoroughly with the phase tester that he always kept in his back pocket, but it was important that he keep focused on his goal. Steeling himself, he pushed on through the door like a gunslinger entering a saloon. He had chosen the door on which the paint was most worn, and it had proved the right one. He now found himself in a low-ceilinged room that was both a hardware shop and pub, with a tiny bicycle repair stand located at the back wall. There were two curly brown fly-strips hanging from the ceiling, both equidistant from the central bare light bulb which looked like it had more flies stuck to it than either of the strips. The words "Hardware & Bar" were written in neat Gaelic script above the window.

The room's interior startled him. Not a single ray of the bright afternoon sun penetrated the semi-shuttered, condensation-muddied window. The room was dark and cold. Colm paused with a shiver, allowing his eyes to dilate in the darkness. From the half-light of a murky corner, he noticed a sudden movement, a ponderous rising. A hulking form steadily levered itself up from a perch by the back wall and advanced awkwardly towards the counter like a bear disturbed in hibernation. The figure stepped into a thin shaft of light seeping through an air vent above the window, and

Colm saw it to be a man of indeterminate age who now leant against the tarnished bronze cash register and raised his eyebrows questioningly.

"Bollix, what is it I want?" Colm said brightly.

The man raised his eyebrows a fraction further.

"I can't for the shit or the hell remember it now that I'm on the spot, as you might say," Colm continued.

The man squinted at him. Colm was pleased with how things were going. He tossed the froth of curls from his forehead and consciously made eye contact just for a fraction of a second. He had already managed to use three curses, which his brother had been telling him were the oil that lubricated easy conversation. Dónal had explained at length the vital role they played, helping put people at their ease and lending an element of spontaneity to general chat. This was all news to Colm. He had heard curses and swear words all his life but had never understood their purpose. Now he was keen to try them out as often as he could. They might help him fit in a little more, Dónal had said. Every day he repeated a few new ones to himself until they sounded as natural as any other word.

Holy shit. Holy shit. Holy shit.

Dónal had advised him not to focus on the meaning of the words, but instead to think of their dramatic potential. He said it would be especially useful in talking to people his own age and people he met in the pub, if he ever got around to going inside. Dónal warned him that there were some people he oughtn't to use curses with – priests and teachers specifically. Colm decided hardware shop owners were unlikely to be in that category. This man ran a pub after all, and he had even seen him in Bridie Brennan's bar occasionally, so he guessed he was safe enough, but made a mental note to remind himself to ask Dónal at some point for a more comprehensive list.

"Concrete, that's the bugger!" Colm said ecstatically, starting to sway back and forth on the soles of his feet. "That's the bugger, to be sure."

"You want concrete?" the old man said warily. "What kind?"

"What do you think yourself, ya big langer!" Colm was excelling himself.

Langer was a new word, and although he wasn't quite sure how best to use it, surely it was good to make an effort. He had a list of curses that he had collected from dictionaries, from novels and from overhearing people talk, and over the weeks it had built up into quite an arsenal ready to be launched at will. He was eager to make good use of them now.

Of course, the man recognised Colm; he knew his father and had seen him often enough hanging out behind Bridie's pub down at the quay feeding the fox. He knew that it was pointless being hard on him, the lad didn't know any better, but still the man felt obliged to say something.

"You mind your tongue, lad," he said at last.

"I assure you I do," Colm said. "I take very good care of it. You know that white grimy stuff it gets on it in the mornings? I always gulp back tea really fast until it's gone. Sometimes I even use my toothbrush to scrub it."

"Huh?" the man said.

Colm stuck his tongue out.

"You say you want concrete – cement, is it?" the man said impatiently. "For your dad?"

"I want plaster powder that'll stick things together. I want to make blocks stand up and stay standing even through a storm."

"We've Portland, ready-mix, skim-coat, bonding, white cement, mortar mix, board render – which?"

"Sure fuck it, how should I know?" Colm said.

The man's eyebrows knitted angrily, and Colm guessed he

might have gone too far. He was getting gradually better at judging such things.

"Sorry," he said with a winning smile, deciding that he had got more than enough practice in for one day.

The man harrumphed.

"Regular cement sounds like just the job," Colm said. "Can I have ten bags. No, 20 bags … You better make it 25."

"What's it for?" the man asked.

"Can't say," Colm replied. "It's not for dentures or for icing sugar or anything small. It's for a big job."

"Do you want elasticiser?"

"Do I want elasticiser?" Colm repeated. "Does that make it elastic?"

"Makes it more malleable."

"Sounds good. Sure I'll get some bags of that too."

"It comes in bottles."

"Well bottles so; two of them."

"Gallons or five gallons?"

"Gallons, please."

"Are you putting it on an account?"

Colm looked at him with surprise.

"I can if you want to," he said hesitantly. "Where do you want me to start?"

"Huh?"

"Counting. From one? 1, 2, 3 …"

"I don't want you to count," the man said irritably. "I asked, do your parents have an account?"

Colm could feel the man's impatience and decided things weren't running as smoothly as they should. He made it a rule, if at all possible, never to be around angry people; it only added to his sense of confusion. The fingers of his left hand began to flick instinctively; going from thumb through to little finger and back again, over and over. This helped him stay focused. He decided it was time for evasive action, and without saying another word, he turned abruptly and walked out of the shop.

He wasn't disappointed by how things had gone. Not at all. He had achieved a lot. He had guessed that things might turn messy at some point; they usually did. Dónal was always warning him about the misunderstandings that can arise when dealing with strangers; it was just something one had to factor in. The only thing that was troubling him was the fact that the man had seemed so intolerant. Dónal said that some people who were polite to you when you're with them could be rude behind your back, and Colm now wondered if the opposite was also true: if people who were taciturn might turn charming later on. He hoped so, as he would need this man on his side if his building plans were to have any success. Time would tell. For the moment, things had got a little bit complicated, and he decided to put it all behind him and return to practising his curse words.

Fuck you, fuck you, fuck you, fuck you.

As the repetition soothed his mind, Colm felt the familiar worm rising inside him. As usual it wanted to get out. It was tricky because he knew he couldn't just cough it up. He had tried that before, and it wouldn't come. It got caught in his throat, or else it came out in bits and created an awful mess which he was then left to clean up. The best solution, he knew, was to go off for a walk by himself again. Often he just walked the roads, pounding the back lanes until the urge to let it out, to express the sense of love and abandon and excitement inside him got the better of him. He'd then let it free, sometimes by simply making a noise in his throat, a long, plangent note that lasted as long as his breath would allow it. That's all it took, and he would be OK again, free to continue as before, hidden and ignored. What he always strived for was to get it out in one go, not to leave any messy residue stuck inside. The hope was that he could just open his mouth or his heart or his mind or all his pores and let everything free.

What exactly was it, this worm? That's what he most wanted to know. He even went to the doctor once to find out, but that hadn't gone well. When Colm mentioned the worm the doctor had asked him if he ever fingered dog pooh without washing his hands afterwards. Colm had wanted to be honest, and had answered that yes occasionally he did, but he knew that had nothing to do with it. He wondered had the doctor never heard of metaphor before – could it possibly be that in all those years spent in medical school nobody ever bothers to take you aside and explain the concept of metaphor? Often it was simple things that brought it on, a deep yearning, vague and indecipherable. Other times it was more wrenching, more profound, an acknowledgment of some greater force, something he couldn't fully conceive of. More often than not, it was simply loneliness, the feeling that came from realising he was living life to a different tune, his mind was circling on a different orbit.

Colm walked along the main street, past the one shop in Reek that had an aisle in it, an aisle which you walked up and down, picking things off the shelves and dropping them into a basket that was yours only for as long as you were in the shop. Once you reached the counter, you had to surrender the basket. This struck Colm as odd, because it was precisely when you were going home that you most needed it. Dónal had tried to explain to Colm that it was really only a device to encourage people to bring more things to the counter; the shopkeeper didn't care what you did with the stuff once you had made it past his till. That was the whole game, to coax people into bringing as much as possible for him to ring up. That's why he went to all that trouble scrawling those garish two-for-one signs, to fool people into putting more into the basket than they actually wanted. He might give you a sheet of paper to wrap a bottle in, or a plastic bag for the tomatoes that was so thin it was translucent, but these were mere empty gestures. The truth was that getting the produce home was none of the shopkeeper's concern, and certainly there was no way he would let you leave with one of his shiny, wire baskets. Colm knew this for certain because he had tried.

The shopkeeper smiled indulgently at Colm as he passed, but Colm's eyes were on the road and he didn't see him. He kept them there not only because he wasn't comfortable greeting people but because he knew he wouldn't recognise them even if he did look up. He had a problem identifying people by their facial features. Unless he made a huge effort to remember something in particular about a person, everyone seemed alike to him. He needed to latch on to some element of their clothes, their gait, their voice, the particular colour of their eyes, if he was to have any chance of recognising them.

He walked out of town along the only stretch of road in Reek where two cars could pass easily, the only bit that wasn't a windy, rosary bead lane funnelled between stone walls. It was the main road out of Reek to the rest of the world, to hospitals and colleges and even larger aisle shops where the baskets were on wheels and you had to push them along and there was no counter at all, just little toll booths with moving table tops. As he passed the school, Colm was surprised to see his brother Dónal cowering behind the lavatory block wall. He was about to call out to him, but something made him pause. He realised Dónal probably didn't want to be noticed. He had that look about him. Colm could understand how he felt and bent his head down and continued walking.

Three

Many times in the six months since the accident, Rachel had wished things had been different – primarily, that she had died with him. Or, and this was what she wished most often and what she was most ashamed of, that he *had* in fact died. She never admitted this last wish to anyone. That her strongest desire of all was that Nathaniel Ash wasn't lying washed and sterile in a coma in St Rita's Ward of White Mountain Psychogeriatric Hospital. That his inanimate body wasn't hooked up to four different white boxes on wheels, and that she wasn't sitting there beside him on a polypropylene chair listening to the burring and bleeping, absentmindedly fingering the lank ball of hair and rubbery hands that were now little more than a network of blood vessels, skin and bone, wired up to monitors.

She wanted to be spared all this, and to have Nathaniel back, or else to be immersed entirely in the role of grieving lover, being cared for and cosseted by the community, being encouraged to accept the loss and move on. Guiltily, she imagined herself dressed in black and walking behind the coffin, throwing a handful of dirt on top, and feeling that shiver of censure as she caught herself checking her appearance while stepping out of the funeral car dressed in Donna Karan.

Her life had been reduced to sitting on the chair staring at his chest, his nipples to be precise. It was what she had been doing for six months now. She couldn't bear to look at his mouth, that once flirting, flickering organ that was now a vegetative leer. She had never even liked his nipples all that much; they were too broad and dark, like walnuts. Now they took on the role of a barometer of her hopes and fears, and in the infinitesimal changes of their colour and texture she imputed grave significance.

For everyone else life had returned to normal. Her friends had grieved together for the summer and then been convinced by their parents to head off to college in the fall as planned. They had left her, giving her big hugs and kisses and telling her how much they loved her and how she was to promise to call any time. Her parents tried to convince her to go off to college with them, but it was no use. Even the effort of getting out of bed in the morning to go to the hospital was barely manageable; there was no way she could have concentrated on something as irrelevant as architecture. Nathaniel's parents and brother had retreated to their church, and although they had welcomed her in at first, in time both she and they came to accept that she didn't really belong. Christ the Redeemer had never figured in her life before, and she couldn't make herself care much about him now. So, most mornings it was just her, roaming the corridors of White Mountain Psycho-geri-atric Hospital for the ten minute spells that it took the nurses to turn or bathe him.

It was no place for either of them to be, that much was certain. It was the thought that struck her the hardest and the most fre-quently. Like a mantra circling in her head. *We should not be here.* It was a psycho-geriatric hospital for God's sake, a place for old people with confused minds. Nathaniel, as far as anyone could tell, mightn't even have a mind any more and he definitely wasn't old. His parents had known someone on the board and had got him transferred here from ICU in Burlington to save them the thirty mile drive back and forth every day. It was bleak.

Nathaniel's mother had warned her not to expect much beforehand: it was an old military hospital, and although the nursing staff were excellent, the building looked decidedly shabby. Nathaniel was hardly going to notice his surroundings anyway, his mother had added.

Rachel hoped she was right, that Nathaniel wasn't aware of the lab-like, lime-glossed room he was in; that he couldn't hear the fluorescent buzz overhead or see the sad corridors rolling out in each direction, or the washed-out patients who occasionally passed by – haunted-looking figures who had long ago surrendered their lives to the cocktail of drugs the ward nurse doled out in paper cuplets, like sweet wrappings from expensive European chocolates. The only distraction these patients had was the occasional arrival of the blue bus delivering a new patient to the hospital, who they would then fuss and fidget over until he or she looked and smelt exactly like them. They had tried doing this to Nathaniel too, taking possession of him like a spider mummifying its kill, but Rachel had seen them off. It was one of the reasons she spent so much time here, to make sure they never got their feeble, enervated grasp on him.

She knew she wasn't really being fair to them, or the place, or the staff, who were in fact pretty caring. It was just that however she looked at it she couldn't help feeling that these people, this place, ought to have no part in her life. The building was from a whole other century – a piece of history built for Canadian soldiers during the First World War; a gesture of goodwill by New Hampshire to its neighbours across the border.

At first the cutting was accidental – a once-off reaction to a stressful event that had occurred earlier in the day. She had been getting from Nathaniel's room to the car park along the uncertainty of the public hallways, which always took a certain resolve. It wasn't just that the corridors reminded her of school and all the happy moments she and Nathaniel had shared between classes, but more that she had to steel herself against possible encounters with patients along the way. For the most part, they were genial old wrecks who shuffled along, never raising their eyes far from the ground and happy with the merest nod as they passed, but some were more unpredictable. It was these that Rachel dreaded. She just didn't have the strength to deal with them. They required a resourcefulness that had long dissipated. She was living on empty, which is exactly how she wanted to be, and it worked just fine as long as no one demanded more from her. The corridor was the only point in her day where she might encounter somebody who might require more. Rodney, for example, an old butcher with a peaked cap and bloated gut, who frequently came tearing down the corridor pushing a tea-trolley or medicine tray or wheelchair, or anything else that had wheels on it: IV drips, commodes, even beds – it seemed the whole place was on castors. Rachel would press herself against the wall, hoping he didn't stop to talk; wishing that she wouldn't have to force herself to understand his stroke-damaged mumble while suffering the shrapnel of his last meal landing on her face. Another old lady was prone to sudden bouts of hyena laughter into her ear. These two were not the worst, but the most frequently encountered.

On the day that Rachel first began to cut herself, she was coming around to thinking that the corridors weren't so bad after all. She was proud of herself for showing this new positivity. The only patient she had met was Ruth, a beady-eyed Serbian woman with acute osteoporosis who was sitting as usual in her wood-and-vinyl armchair smiling beatifically.

"Laugh at the world and the world laughs with you," Ruth had cried as Rachel approached, and then fallen silent until she'd gone by.

Rachel got as far as the double doors at the other end of the corridor before Ruth piped up, "Weep!"

She had looked back, startled to see Ruth basking in a crimson ray beaming down from a forgotten stained-glass window high above. Her mouth was gaping open and her neck jutted out, lit by a glow that gave her the appearance of a Venus flytrap.

Ruth remained frozen in that position, staring at Rachel for a moment before quacking,

". . . and the world weeps with you."

"Yes, Ruth," Rachel had found herself saying with surprising conviction. She understood precisely what Ruth meant, and her heart leapt. *These people aren't frightening*, she thought to herself. *They're not mad; they're just old.*

Ruth had shrugged dismissively and turned back towards the light, and inexplicably Rachel found herself gladdened by the experience, sanctified. She strode onwards along the next corridor with a trace of spring in her step, the first in many months. She raised her eyes and looked around her at this alien edifice that she normally tried so hard to block out: the lingering mildew in the ceiling corners; the pearly pendant lamps dropping down; the brilliant red fire-extinguishers chained to the lime-green walls. She found herself enjoying the fire-extinguishers, basking in their bold brilliance, their heroic ambition. She saw Madeleine, an Alzheimer's patient, in her room and waved to her, saying how beautiful she was looking today. Madeleine came shuffling out, whispering that she wanted to sing her a song, and although Rachel hadn't encouraged it, the prospect didn't frighten her completely.

Madeleine began,

> "One day at a time sweet Jesus
> That's all I'm asking from you …"

Rachel had smiled at first, but soon began to feel a bit

discomfited. It was all a bit boisterous. Too much too soon. Her face froze in a rictus smile, and she looked about her for a nurse. Madeleine was a large, heavyset woman, and she wore a flower-print dress which roughly matched the curtains. Her hair had been washed that morning, and her drug-puffed face looked twenty years younger than her 65 years.

"Just give me the strength
To do every daaaaay what I am having to doo-oo."

Madeleine was waltzing around the corridor now, her slippers allowing her vast body to slide gracefully on the polished floor. Rachel forced her mind to string together a compliment as she waited for the song to end, but it showed no signs of ending. Instead, Madeleine began singing faster and louder and more distorted.

"Oh! One daaaaaay at at at a timmmmmmmme.
Strength-to-keep, Ooooo-ne day! One daaaaay!"

Rachel backed away, but Madeleine grabbed her arms and started swinging her across the corridor. She was easily able to throw her about, and when Rachel let out a scream, Madeleine stopped in horror and seemed frightened by what she had just been doing. She pulled Rachel in to her, hugging her close to her for reassurance. Rachel found herself being pressed ever closer to Madeleine, so that it became hard to breathe. She tried pulling away but Madeleine's grip only grew firmer, and the dancing began again as a means of soothing them both. Finally the singing became so loud that the nurses were alerted and came running, wrenching the two of them off each other and sticking a needle into Madeleine's arm. By this stage, Rachel was so panicked she fell to the floor in tears.

"That's a lovely song, Madeleine," she had heard the nurses say as they led her away. "You in singing mood today, are you? Isn't that just lovely."

They had found a stool for Rachel and sat her down, asking did she want a cup of tea with them in the nurses' station, but all she could think of was escape, and she had run out to the car as quickly as she could. It was when she got home and was examining the bruises on her arms that the cutting started. She was sitting there on her bed staring at the changing shades of purple beneath her skin, and suddenly she found herself with a safety pin in her hands, dragging it along the flesh until it pushed through. On the first sight of blood, she dropped the pin immediately, pulling back stunned, appalled at herself. But even stronger than the shock was an overwhelming sense of release, and a natural desire for more. She retrieved the pin, pressing it through the skin once again and wriggling it about so that the hole grew bigger, big enough to stick her fingernail in. The blood began to flow freely, and it was this that finally stopped her, made her jump up in the hope of not dirtying the bedspread. She managed to stem the flow until she reached the sink.

It was the unexpected sense of elation afterwards that most surprised her. Suddenly she was aware of feelings again, real feelings, for the first time in months. The pain, the shock, the unexpectedness. It all felt agreeably novel. Better still was the rush of excitement. This was too much to hope for – a sense of euphoria. It was as though her body had bypassed her mind so as to show her a way out of the morass that she had been trapped in all summer. But unfortunately, these feelings didn't last all that long, and by evening she was back in the hole again.

After that it had become routine. In the mornings she'd go to the hospital, sitting with Nathaniel, or with whatever bit of him was still present – his body, his breath and the odd shiver which the neurologist insisted wasn't fear or surprise, just transient neural anomalies – until mid-afternoon when Nathaniel's parents would arrive. Then she'd sneak off home, heading straight upstairs, locking the door and grabbing the peroxide and her *blood rag* – an old tweed shirt of Nathaniel's. It would start all over again: she'd light a candle, turn on some Enya or a Cuban salsa compilation that Nathaniel had made for her, and she'd sit on the floor in her room with the shirt on her lap. She always went for a few test cuts first to get her in the mood, slashes that weren't too deep. Then she'd start picking at the old wounds she had carved out before on her sallow flat belly in the shape of letters spelling out *Nathaniel* and *God*. God above the navel and Nathaniel below. God had hurt the most as there was less flesh there. Her slight belly had cushioned the pain of Nathaniel somewhat.

Of course that was still the early days when it hurt; by now all she could feel was relief. Her body had switched off the pain receptors in the area – or perhaps she had carved them out. On her calf was a third wound – a haphazard arrangement of lines and angles. Each had to be excavated in turn, starting with Nathaniel and ending up on the cat's cradle on her calf. She was always waiting for that moment when her body was triggered into panic, tricked into emitting its sweet intoxicants. But even if it came sooner than expected, it was by then too late to stop the cutting. There was a sequence that had to be followed – every wound had to be reworked freshly each time. All had to be of equal depth with the words properly legible. When she was done she'd lay aside the razor, out of harm's way, then sit back, staring into space, occasionally marvelling at the beauty of the colours of her seeping blood (the rich purple leaving her heart and the washed-out yellowish stuff returning) until Nathaniel's shirt was soaked right through. She'd then manoeuvre herself carefully to the sink to wash out the rag and tape up the wounds, allowing herself a square of Garibaldi's 70%-cocoa chocolate as a reward for a job well done. The rest of the afternoon would be spent lying on her bed, hugging herself until the tingling died down and the reassuring glow flowed into every cell. At some point she'd invariably fall asleep. It was often the only sleep she got, day or night.

Other than these sessions and the bedside hours staring at Nathaniel's torso, life had become largely meaningless for her. A series of bodily functions: eating, sleeping and washing. Snatched conversations with people: her parents, the nurses and Nathaniel's family mostly. It was about all she could manage. Often she could handle only one proper conversation a day, which then played itself back over and over in her mind, keeping other, more unwelcome, thoughts at bay.

About a fortnight after the cutting began, she found herself caught short by something Garth, Nathaniel's brother, had said to her outside the men's lavatory in the hospital.

"We gotta keep him alive, you know?" he'd said, and she couldn't decide if it was meant as an accusation or not. Was that not exactly what she was trying to do? Wasn't it why she turned up at his bedside every bloody day, running the gauntlet of those terrible corridors. It was what lay at the heart of her cutting too: an attempt to shock her body so that it in turn might shock his back to life in a sort of chain reaction. She had read of a trial in which dozens of mousetraps were set in a room one by one, until a point was reached when one more trap would set all the others snapping in unison. It was what she was hoping for.

Garth had waylaid her as she was passing by on her way to the car. The lavatory door was open, and she had caught sight of him staring into the mirror, crying, his body bent over the washbasin with a hand on either faucet. When he saw her passing, he came storming out, running right into her chest, clinging to her blouse.

"We gotta keep him alive, you know?" he cried, while she pretended to listen. "I always think of the great times … when he tipped over the canoe, remember, and mud wrestled those kids? Or when him and Lek and Cam all put their clothes on backwards and inside out after the bike race. He was the only one who kept them like that the whole rest of the day, 'member? Or when he used to stick quarters up his nose – that was so cool, and he didn't even have such a big nose either. I'm still wondering how he did that."

Rachel had stroked his face absently and muttered something reassuring. She heaved her chest out so he could feel its soothing plumpness, in case that was what he really wanted. She tried to find words to make it all better, but all she could think of were the nude photos Nathaniel had told her Garth had put in the My Document folder. She wondered what had happened at the church meeting. An image of the pastor in his natty grey suit and ostentatious crucifix, down on his knees with Garth, shot through her mind; both of them with their hands down their pants ogling the grainy printouts. She didn't doubt she was cracking up; in fact, the grief counsellor had advised her it was healthier to lose control for a while, so that she could regain it later on – that was, if she ever wanted to.

But his remark had suddenly made her question herself.

We gotta keep him alive, you know?

Was she thinking more about hurting herself than making Nathaniel better? No one had ever told her that grief could be so complicated, could feel so much like fear – the same fluttering in the stomach, the same restlessness, wanting to hide, being immobilised by torturous cramps and a pounding headache with the realisation that you're completely alone.

She had just got home that day and was laying out the tools – the knife, gauze pads, antibiotic cream, and the blood rag with its curious starched feel like a sail on a frosty morning – when she heard a ring at the door. She cursed loudly, hating to have this moment of release, of endorphin surge, delayed by anything. The urge to escape reality was too strong to delay it even by a minute. She needed this – to ride the chemical rush, to close her eyes and tense her toes and squeeze every last blissful ounce of intensity from it.

She thought about not answering, but then worried it might be one of her parents having mislaid their keys, and she didn't want them coming back later surprising her in mid-flow. Already they were beginning to get suspicious. They still hadn't spotted the words on her belly, but her Mom had noticed the cuts on her calf the week before when her trousers had scrunched up in the hammock, and it had been hard to convince her that they were just bramble scars. With an inventiveness that surprised her, she had managed to string together a long, drawn-out story about being on a walk in the forest and tripping on an old root and getting badly scratched, and her mother had seemed to swallow it. The outside chance that her daughter might be taking walks again and might have regained an interest in something other than her grief was too attractive for her to question it more closely.

But her trouble didn't end there. A few days later, Rachel had found herself unable to staunch the "G" in God and had to drive herself to the emergency room in a hurry. The admittance nurse had spotted exactly what Rachel was up to and had started asking awkward questions and enquiring about her parents' contact details. Fortunately, a Code Yellow was called and the nurse had to rush away; the young doctor who did the stitches was overworked and didn't have the time to be interested in her or her injury. She knew she'd have to be more careful from then on.

The doorbell rang again. Cursing furiously, Rachel threw a dress over her tools and traipsed downstairs. She flung open the door, ready to send whoever it was packing, to be as rude as was necessary. But when she looked out there was nobody there. She searched up and down but could see no one – not a car nor any sign of anyone lurking in the bushes. She closed the door again, double-locking it just in case, and went back to her room where she lit a candle and some incense in an effort to recapture the mood, turning her mind to the job at hand and preparing herself for the possible pain if she touched a fresh nerve. Like an avuncular surgeon, she playfully explained to herself what would be involved in the procedure; cooing the words in a honeyed slur; focusing her spiel more on the delicious release that would invariably follow, rather than anything that might come before.

"It's quite harmless, sweet-pie, we'll just make a slight incision here, and then run it along as far as …"

When totally prepared, she grasped the incense stick and used it to stroke the "N" in Nathaniel. Its tip warming the scar, making the skin glow until it began to smoke. And while the smell was unpleasant there was no pain, even when the scar had burnt clean away and the wound lay revealed and slightly molten. This part of her body had come to accept the abuse and had shut down its nerve receptors. Even the blade didn't make her flinch – her receptors had recalibrated themselves to only sense pleasure, the rush of endorphins flooding from the brain.

Once the incense had burned out, she reached for the craft knife, snapping off its blunt edge to reveal a fresh-tempered piece, and then paused for a moment to anticipate the impending pleasure – the period of release ahead. She had just dabbed moisturiser on her belly to bring up the lettering on *God* when the doorbell rang again. This time she ignored it, focusing her attention determinedly on the G, carefully picking away the scab, musing over its crispy texture. When it rang a second time, she breathed in to steady her resolve and reached out for the remote control to turn the CD-player right up. Part of her wondered who it might be, but she wouldn't give in. This was too important. Whoever it was – the pool cleaner, the delivery boy from the wine merchant's, a raffle ticket seller – would eventually go away.

She had sliced open the horizontal centre stroke of the G just as the bell rang a third time. This time, long and urgent. It was then that she saw it for what it was, a battle of wits between her and some outside force. She would remain strong. She would triumph over it. Laying the rag to one side, she got up and popped open the CD mouth, flicking away the disc and choosing another, something louder, something that would drown out all interference. She wavered for a second between Rachmaninov and Smashing Pumpkins, finally choosing the latter and squatting back down again contented. Carefully, she picked open the inverted moon of the G, thrilling as the first sweet sight of blood crept to the surface. It was at that moment that a handful of gravel came spattering against the window. This was simply too much – an outright violation of her privacy. She cried out in frustration, throwing down the blade and lurching across the room to the window, with the rag wrapped around her arm and pressed hard against her chest to staunch the flow, blood dripping on to the carpet in spite of her best efforts.

Standing on the gravel beneath the window was a middle-aged woman, her hair curled up under a thick woollen cap. She was wearing a dirt-coloured hoodie with an oak leaf inscribed on it and had a jovial, bustling air.

"What the hell?" Rachel muttered to herself.

The woman was staring up at her, one hand over her eyes trying to peer through the glare. In her other hand was a blue dinosaur wearing a backpack, dangling loosely, almost touching the ground. She shouted something, but Rachel couldn't hear it above the noise. She cast about looking for the remote control, but couldn't find it, so instead reached for the window key and wrestled with opening the latch while keeping the rag around her arm.

"Would you open the door, child," Rachel heard when she finally got the window open. The woman spoke with a pronounced twang. "I've been waiting here for I don't know how long now."

"Huh?" Rachel yelled confusedly. Her sudden rise had disorientated her, made her unsteady.

"Come on, now, hon, get a move on," the woman said breezily.

"Go away!" Rachel cried. "Get out of here."

The woman put her hands on her hips and stared up. Her rosy cheeks struck Rachel as an admonition of her own ashen features. She stepped back from the window and thought for a second, then realised she had no option but to go down and deal with the woman. She wiped the wound roughly with the rag and pulled her jumper down over it.

The moment the door opened, the woman lurched backwards a few feet, as though repelled by some invisible force emanating from Rachel. She threw her hands to her face, only daring to peak out between them.

"Oh, my gosh!" she cried, letting her fingers run down her fleshy cheeks watermarked with broken capillaries. "Oh my, oh my gosh! Look at you, child! Rachie, Rachie, Rachie!"

She reached her arms excitedly forward, but Rachel's glower was enough to make her pause and drop them again.

"Would you look at you!" the woman cried again. "Oh my!"

Rachel was mulling over what to do. Her instinct was to press the panic button beside the door, but she hesitated. It was possible this woman was one of the patients from the hospital and that they did in fact know each other. She rattled her mind trying to recognise her, but it was no use – as far as she knew she had never seen the woman before.

"Where's your *rian*, child?" the woman suddenly cried. She was a bundle of hyperactivity, sparking and fizzing like a cartoon character. "Why in the name of God's breath are you not wearing it? Huh?"

She sounded anxious; her jollity suddenly switching to concern at the absence of some crucial item.

"My what?" Rachel cried, "What are you selling? How do you know my name?"

"Is it on your neck?"

Rachel frowned. This woman's vitality was exhausting, and it was clear that whoever she was, she wasn't about to leave until she settled whatever was bothering her. The woman came lurching forward on to the step trying to pull at Rachel's neck, apparently checking if the thing was there. Rachel dodged her head sharply backwards, batting the woman's arms away while at the same time trying to shut the door on her. But the stranger was well-built and wasn't going anywhere.

"Get away from here," Rachel screamed. "This place is covered by surveillance, OK?"

She nodded to a camera in the corner while shoving the door again.

The woman was taken by surprise and reeled backwards, staring at Rachel open-eyed as she backed out over the threshold. Despite her great size, she was quite agile on her thin sandals and managed the feat of reversing at full speed without tripping, then stood stolidly on the gravel without any trace of animosity or disquiet apparent on her face. In fact, if anything she appeared lost in wonder.

"Get out, d'you hear," Rachel cried, suddenly both angry and frightened at the same time. "You're from the hospital, right? You better be real careful, lady. You can't come turning up on people's doorsteps. Now, just grab your bag and get the hell away. You're lucky I'm not calling the cops."

Now that Rachel had regained the upper hand, the woman appeared to become more cowed. She picked up her duffle bag reluctantly and turned away, brushing down her combats and breathing a long sigh. Rachel went to close the door, but the woman turned back around, this time with a wide grin across her face that soon worked its way into a laugh, a loud belly laugh.

"Oh, baby," she said, "this is funny. Now this here, this is truly funny. You gotta hand me that. This you couldn't make up in one of them movie tales."

Rachel glowered.

"You don't recognise me, do you?" the woman said. "Huh? Not even a twinge? Well, wow-wee! That's something. I never even thought to say, I just presumed you'd … It's Charlotte, girl. Charlotte."

Rachel made for the panic button, but as she was about to press it something clicked insider her.

"Charlotte," the woman said. "Remember?"

Rachel stepped back, suspicion etched across her features. She knew the name. She just couldn't remember how. It was somehow familiar. It provoked a spark, a hazy sense of love within her.

"Who the hell are you?" she asked.

"Charlotte Francis, silly! Auntie Charlie."

"I don't have an Auntie Charlie," Rachel spat. "I don't have an aunt, period!"

"Sure you have – I'm her."

"Look – I do NOT have an aunt. I sort of remember that name, but I don't know you and I don't know what the hell you're doing here."

"I just stopped by – that's all. It's been long enough, eh?"

Rachel fell quiet for a second. Perhaps she was mistaken and she didn't know the name after all.

"Maybe we should call you a doctor," Rachel said more kindly. "The cops too. Look, I don't know you, OK? Now, you've got to get away from here."

"Silly, silly," Charlotte laughed. "Why would you remember, I suppose. You were so young. It's just that I thought we had something special, you and me. I *know* we had something special. But I suppose it's been a long time. It's OK that you don't remember."

She smiled magnanimously. Rachel just blinked, hoping the whole thing would go away.

"Did your mom never talk about me?" Charlotte said. "I thought she might have said something, that's all. Silly me, hoping too much as usual."

She turned back around and took a few steps along the drive.

"I'm sorry, child," she said, deflated, "real sorry for frightening you. I didn't mean anything by it."

She swung her duffle bag over her shoulder and, looking down, noticed the dinosaur still dangling from the other hand. She lifted it up to her helplessly then dropped it again.

"I brought you ..." she said, then stopped, noticing a stain begin to seep through Rachel's jumper. The exertion had made the blood begin to flow again. "Good God almighty, girl – you're wounded!"

Rachel put her hand over the stain guiltily and turned away, while at the same time still pushing the door with her shoulder, but Charlotte rushed forward and managed to get her arm around Rachel's chest and clasped her to her. It was with a certain blustering tenderness, but invasive, nonetheless. To her surprise, Rachel reacted totally instinctively, and rather than feeling panic as she had in the hospital with Madeleine, she found herself unexpectedly, and quite to her horror, giving in. Her body slackened.

She was still aware of the threat the woman posed, but was no longer prepared to resist. She hadn't the energy. She suddenly realised that she was exhausted; a wave of great weariness broke over her and she became aware that there was something about being close to this woman that felt natural. Maybe it was her slightly grassy smell or the softness of her well-worn clothes or simply the relief of having her secret, shameful habit observed by someone else. Despite all the woman's ebullience, there was an air of serenity about her that Rachel felt herself reaching for.

The profound sense of release that arises from giving in came over Rachel. Her breath began to slow down almost in spite of herself, and her body gradually unwound. She became aware of the vice-like tension in every joint. She felt as spent and weary now as an animal at the end of its annual migration. She had been roaming through difficult territory for too long.

"You're bleeding," Charlotte said again. "Look – you are! We've got to get you sorted out. Come inside and we'll see what we can do."

Rachel allowed herself be led indoors. She stood under the chandelier and stared dumbly ahead as the woman craned her neck examining the wound and then began looking around, wondering where she might most likely find a cloth and some water. In her dazed state, Rachel found herself sort of trusting this matronly stranger who was growing gradually more familiar. Charlotte went bustling off, trying to locate the kitchen for some water. When she got back, Rachel had vomited all over the carpet and seemed so disorientated that she hardly noticed being led into the living room and having her top pulled off so that Charlotte could tend to the wounds.

For the first time in weeks, Rachel felt pain as the woman carefully dabbed at the letters of God. Her wincing was prompted by relief as much as pain.

Four

"Oh, chicken," Charlotte said, compassion welling in her eyes, "what have you done?"

Rachel hung her head, feeling the woman's words like a salve.

"You do remember, don't you?" Charlotte asked, stroking her cheek. "You remember?"

Rachel stared.

"Your mom and I were sisters, yeah? I mean, not birth sisters, but ... your gran was my godmother, she adopted me. I was seven and your mom was nine. She had her own life, her own friends. I think she sort of resented me – whatever, we weren't all that close anyways. But you and I were, right from the start. It brought me and your mom closer for a bit. Every week I'd come over and mind you – Tuesdays and Thursdays, yeah? We always had such fun. Going for walks along the old towpath by the river and heading into the woods when it wasn't wet. Your dad never liked us going 'cause of the bears, but seeing as he was away so much he didn't need to know. Anyways, he shouldn't have worried, I wouldn't have let anything harm a hair on your head. No way. And sure, them bears were on our side, remember?"

Rachel was so tired she had trouble following the words. Even keeping the woman's face in focus was hard. All she was really aware of was the hand coming out towards her, dabbing at her belly, causing her pain.

"Is it ringing any bells?" Charlotte continued, raising her voice a little to combat the Smashing Pumpkins upstairs. "I used to tell you stories. You and I, pet, we'd both make them up together … about the otter catching salmon, and how he could never get the scales off his claws, remember? And how he had to go to the Sahara to find the right sand …"

Rachel looked up at her with squinting eyes, trying to place her, searching for some hint of familiarity. There was something about that voice, the way she said "pet", but it was impossible to pinpoint any closer. The grassy smell was familiar too. She had always known that smell. It wasn't so much grass as straw or maybe leaves, semi-dry autumn leaves. Then it came to her what it was: cannabis – the sweet, musty smell of cannabis leaf. A distant memory of something to do with otters rose up in her mind too, and she could picture the animal sweating in the desert with its sticky feet and the stinky smell of salmon festering in the heat. But none of this was the same as actually recognising this woman, remembering who she was.

"It's a shame," Charlotte concluded.

Rachel found herself not entirely disagreeing.

"Have any younger brothers or sisters come along?" Charlotte asked, looking around her for the first time at the upholstered armchairs and equestrian prints.

Rachel shook her head.

"What age was I?" Rachel asked cautiously, in the same way as a child asks about the tooth fairy – not sure whether the issue was too ridiculous to query further.

Charlotte paused to think, reaching down to rinse out the dishcloth before starting on the crusted lines of *Nathaniel*.

"Just turned three when I left," she said. "I've been away a while."

Rachel nodded, then turning to face her, she asked, "Why did you ...?"

Charlotte shook her head and looked down at her hands in silence. She was crouched on her hunkers, and she shifted herself now, shimmying from foot to foot to avoid a cramp, careful not to spill the bowl of pinkish water beside her.

"We had a fight," she said at last, looking up into Rachel's eyes. "Your mom and I had a fight."

Rachel shivered as a bead of water ran towards her thigh.

"Yeah," Charlotte continued reluctantly, "your mom was fine about it, but when your dad found out that I was teaching you all the *stuff,* he freaked out. Like, really freaked. Said I was a devil worshipper trying to steal his child from him. I tried explaining, but he wouldn't listen. You know, I didn't mean any harm. The opposite. I never even wanted to teach you anything. It was you who started. You wanted so much to know it all. You kept at me. You were wonderful, so special, so open to it ... I've never seen that before – or since."

Charlotte fell quiet and looked away. She seemed lost in thought. Rachel had no idea what she was on about.

"None of us had ever seen a child like you before. You lapped it up, all of it, and kept coming back for more. You would have been doing your own spells by the time you got to school if we'd continued. You used to hurl your milk away, and your soother, and even your diaper; anything and everything until I agreed to show you more. You were a natural. You even somehow convinced me to give you a pentacle of your own. You called it the *rian,* and you wouldn't go to sleep without it. I was so proud of you. At every circle, you always knew where to place the candle, where to lay the salt. Like you had a map of the universe hidden inside your head and could just tell where everything should go. None of us had ever seen anything like it."

"Are you telling me you're some sort of witch?" Rachel exclaimed. "Some kind of Wicca nut – you must be kidding?"

Rachel knew enough about this sort of thing to know it was ridiculous, something only the losers and Dungeons and Dragons freaks at school bothered with. She had a friend from kindergarten days who was now Goth-obsessed and semi-Lesbian and worked as a waitress at the mall, spending all her money on Wicca stuff. She even tried to give Rachel a talisman once.

"You reckon you're a witch, is that it?" Rachel scoffed. "Was that what you were looking for under my shirt – a crucifix or something? The sign of the devil – 666?"

Charlotte wasn't listening; she was lost in the past, her face gradually darkening.

"He said I was trying to hex you – your dad!" she said coldly. "And that I would make you a loser, like me."

She reached into her pocket, pulling out a neck chain, a silver star with a turquoise circle in its centre.

"This is it," she said handing it to Rachel. "Of course I knew I had it all along, but I thought you might have got your own by now."

Rachel took it from her, turning it over carefully in her palm, feeling the undulations of the ivy engraved on the rim. She realised she recognised this trinket.

"I suppose I was just being foolish," Charlotte said sadly.

It was like being presented with your first rattle or your baby shoes.

"I wear it myself now," Charlotte said. "I just took it off because of work. When I arrived last week I got a job as a cashier in one of the stores downtown, and the manager made me remove it. He was fine with it at first, but a customer complained, saying she had given her credit card details to a woman wearing the sign of the Antichrist. She was freaking out that I now had all her info and knew where she lived. I was lucky she didn't get me sacked straight off."

Rachel handed it back, and Charlotte started to put it back on, then paused.

"It's yours after all, maybe you want it back?" she said.

Rachel shook her head, and Charlotte seemed relieved.

"You feeling any better now?" Charlotte asked.

"I dunno," Rachel said quietly. "Still a bit weak."

"You look bad," Charlotte said and bent down to rummage in her duffle bag, pulling out various things: a dog-eared book, a bag of apples and a jiffy bag of chopped up vegetables. "I think I have something here that will help."

She found a half-bottle of bourbon and a tiny brown phial of ointment. After swallowing a few gulps of the bourbon, she began dabbing drops from the phial on to the now-bloodied cloth and lay it against Rachel's skin. She added another few drops of ointment to a glass of water and told Rachel to drink it.

"I can hardly hear myself think with that music blaring," Charlotte said. "It's gotta be turned down."

Rachel shrugged.

"Hold steady there, and keep the cloth pressed against the wound," Charlotte said, scooping up her bottles and bag and heading upstairs while Rachel collapsed back in the chair. The blood had begun to clot by now and there was no more pain, but the cloth felt strangely reassuring. She could feel the area around her navel relax for the first time in months, as though her taut, traumatised skin were sighing and easing itself into the fleecy strands of the fabric. She had that same hazy, blissed-out feeling that bleeding gave her – not quite as intense, but more sustained. She was musing dreamily over the situation when Charlotte came back, wavering a little, wading down one step at a time, one hand on the banister, the other on the wall as though picking her way over rocks.

"Are you OK?" Rachel asked.

"Fine," Charlotte said breezily. Her cheeks were now as flushed as Rachel's were pale and Rachel could smell the bourbon from her.

"We've got to do something about that room," Charlotte said. "It's a mess – like you've been summoning daemons in there. Full of darkness and negative shit. A right little Beelzebub's den. We'll have to flush it out … Look, these goose pimples came from just being there. It's despair central. You're going to have to help me, OK? Are you up to it?"

Rachel felt rooted in the chair. It was safe here, protected. She had no wish to face the remnants of her scattered world just yet.

"Help with what?" Rachel said.

"To get some light going on in there," Charlotte declared.

Rachel shrugged dazedly.

"Give me that rag a second," Charlotte said, grabbing it from her and folding it so that the bloody bits were inside and a dry corner lay facing out. From a tiny cedarwood box in her bag, she sprinkled white powder over the cloth.

"Hold this up to your nose and breathe deeply," Charlotte said. "It'll make you feel a whole lot better."

Rachel did as she was told and almost immediately felt a surge of adrenalin rushing through her, peppering her mind, making it bristle. She jumped to her feet, looking around her as though she had just woken from a dream. The room seemed brighter than before, more harmonious, and she found she was suddenly able to appreciate what her mother had been trying to convey in its avant-garde design – the high white windows and limed floor. It was luminous.

The two of them headed upstairs to Rachel's room, where the candle was still burning and the open window was beginning to clear the smog of incense that had infiltrated every thread of fabric over the past few weeks. Looking at the room now with this stranger, Rachel felt suddenly foolish. She couldn't bear to look at the blades and tape all neatly laid out, and the blood rag, Nathaniel's lovely shirt, now smelling of rancid meat. She bent down to kick it out the window, but Charlotte stopped her.

"Excuse me, young lady, we're going to need that later on," she said, picking it up and dropping it delicately in the corner. The smell of it stirred up in the room a nauseous odour.

"First off we need a broom," Charlotte announced, "I presume you have one, right?"

"A witch's broom?!"

"No! Just a broom, for heaven's sake."

"We have a vacuum cleaner."

"Is it an upright?"

"Bagless."

"Bagless …! That's no good. What about a mop?"

"Yeah, Rosita keeps one under the stairs, I think. Let me check."

Rachel headed downstairs with determination and searched about until she found Rosita's mop and bucket.

"That's more like it," Charlotte said, jittery now with the growing excitement that always preceded such work. "It's only for symbolic purposes anyway, something to represent the phallus … Now, where's your wand?"

Rachel stared at her.

"You haven't lost that too?" Charlotte cried.

Rachel just blinked.

"Oh, come on! How could you?" Charlotte scolded, sighing. "It was such a pretty one too, and you were so proud of it. We'll have to get you a new one. Any whitethorn or ash in the garden?"

Rachel shrugged.

"Rowan, even?"

"I dunno, there are a few different trees," Rachel said.

"You don't know!" Charlotte shrieked "What's happened to you?"

Rachel glowered.

"Put on some shoes and follow me," Charlotte said.

Rachel reluctantly followed Charlotte outside, and they walked up and down along the herbaceous border with Charlotte shaking her head dismally.

"It's all bloody bamboo and creeping conifers," she complained. "Don't you have any real trees or shrubs? Even a vegetable garden?"

Rachel shrugged, "Dad's in charge of the garden. Although it's really Rosita's sons who do all the work."

"Look, we need to find some proper trees," Charlotte said. "An oak, a hazel, even a cherry – as long as it's not variegated or creeping or dwarfed."

"There's some fruit trees in the neighbour's garden," Rachel proffered.

"What kind?" Charlotte snapped.

"Apples, I think, maybe pears too."

"Perfect," Charlotte said, hurrying over to the fence.

She was just about to leap over when an Alsatian came bounding towards her.

"Careful!" Rachel screamed.

"You could have warned me!" Charlotte said. "Does he know you? Is it safe for you to go in?"

"He knows everyone, but he hates us all. I'm not going near him."

"This is important, honey. We need a wand. We can't leave your room in that state."

"Don't you have your own?" Rachel said, growing impatient.

"Sure, but I'm not going to carry it around with me, am I? That'd be just asking for trouble."

Further along the fence was the neighbour's greenhouse and Charlotte went over to it, sticking her nose up against the glass to look inside.

"Who owns this?" she asked.

"The same neighbour."

"Does the dog have access to it?"

"Don't think so. His kennel's on the far side."

"Good," said Charlotte, smashing a pane of the glass with her elbow, then using her bag to clear away the glass.

"What the hell are you doing?" Rachel cried.

Charlotte hauled her upper torso in through the greenhouse window, taking care to avoid the jagged edges.

"There are a few things in here that look hopeful," she shouted back.

The Alsatian was barking wildly, battering the latch and scratching at the glass to get in.

"Jackpot!" Charlotte cried. "I think we've struck it big-time!"

"What?" Rachel said with mounting concern.

"I'm almost sure this one is a plum," Charlotte said, handing out a little potted sapling to Rachel. "*Prunus japonica.*"

She pulled herself awkwardly out again, unpicking stray shards of glass from her hoodie and shaking herself down. She looked around with a triumphant expression.

"What this place really needs is a medicine garden," she mused. "With all the trimmings: a full array of herbs, roots, rare barks and berries." She bent down and rubbed the soil through her fingers. "It's perfect for it."

The Alsatian was still barking as they made their way back into the house where Charlotte rummaged around for her reading glasses before bending down to examine the buds on the sapling.

"It's definitely a *prunus*," she concluded, "and I'd put money on it being a *japonica*. Either way we'll give it a try. Have you got a knife?"

Rachel pulled a Swiss Army knife from her pocket, and Charlotte grabbed it, giving her a withering *I need hardly have asked* look.

She cut the sapling off at the root, allowing the little plant pot fall on the floor, scattering potting compost all over the kitchen.

"You'll ruin the blade," Rachel complained.

"What? You planning more surgery?"

Rachel leered at her, and Charlotte set to work stripping the leaves and side branches off. Once it was bare, she lay the branch against Rachel's arm to judge the length, slicing the leader shoot to cut it to size and then whipping and whirling it through her fingers to skin the remaining bark. Then, having checked it again for size – it stretched from Rachel's elbow to her index finger – she handed it to Rachel, thickest end first.

Rachel took the wand, giving it a trial tennis swing.

"Stop!" Charlotte bellowed, grabbing her hand firmly. "For God's sake, be careful with that."

"Ow!" Rachel exclaimed. "That hurt."

"Just be careful. It's not a toy. And we don't have time for messing. When are your parents home? We've got a lot of work to get through, and I certainly don't fancy bumping into your dad today."

"What am I meant to do with this?" Rachel asked, giving the stick another short swing.

"I told you to be careful!" Charlotte said, grabbing for it again. "Don't do anything until I tell you. This isn't a magic show; this is *magick* with a K."

In the bedroom Rachel immediately sensed how creepy the place felt. She wondered how she had never noticed before. There was a darkness to it, a sadness. The blood on the carpet spoke volumes. She didn't know how things had ever gotten so bad. She remembered learning in biology class about how birds occasionally pulled out their feathers when stressed, stripping themselves completely bare. Maybe that was it. She had wanted to feel something – anything, and the fact that she bled red like other mammals was a consolation. It was proof that she was alive, that it wasn't all a nightmare; that even if she couldn't cry or couldn't feel or couldn't even bring herself to care at times, at least she could bleed like everyone else. The memory of blood, so pure and vital, had been a source of hope in the suffocating, sterile, monastic atmosphere of the hospital.

Charlotte now became business-like, pacing back and forth, surveying the room like a builder assessing a quote.

"This is where it's at," she said. "It's all centred here. We're going to need water – three buckets at least and a cauldron as well."

"A cauldron?"

"Well, whatever you have – a pan or a skillet or something."

"Will a basin do?"

"No, it won't," Charlotte snapped. "It's got to be metal, but not aluminium. Even non-stick is better than aluminium. And I'd prefer if you don't call me Charlotte when we're working – it's Akasha."

"What?"

"How can you have forgotten? It was you who gave me the second part of the name. You called me Sha because you couldn't pronounce Charlotte."

"You're Sha?" Rachel cried. "Really?"

Charlotte nodded.

"I thought she was a pretend friend. I used to talk to her until I was seven. I didn't know there was ever a real Sha. You're her?"

"Just go get the water. The energy in this place is giving me migraine."

When Rachel got back with the buckets, Charlotte was taking a sniff of powder from the cedar box. She put the box away hurriedly and began scattering handfuls of earth she'd brought in from the garden all over the carpet; grinding it in with the heels of her sandals while uttering incantations.

"What the hell are you doing?" Rachel exclaimed.

Charlotte ignored her, concentrating on the job at hand – spinning on her heels to embed the dirt as deeply as possible. Rachel looked on anxiously.

"We're getting there," Charlotte said, when the carpet began to tear.

"Wait, this isn't such a great idea," Rachel said with a gasp.

"Come on," Charlotte said dismissively. "Are you going to help me or not?"

Rachel stepped tentatively forward and Charlotte put her arms on her shoulders.

"Don't worry," Charlotte said, "this isn't voodoo – you're in no danger, at least no more than you were with your knives. It's run of the mill stuff, especially for someone of your ability. I can't help it if you've forgotten who you are ... It's like riding a bicycle, you'll soon pick it up."

She grabbed the buckets of water and flung them across the room.

"For God's sake!" Rachel screamed, the mud turning to sludge at her feet. "The sitting room is straight below – it'll pour right on to the furniture."

"Can't be helped," Charlotte shrugged, taking up the mop and swinging it back and forth a few inches above the floor. "This has to be neutralised one way or the other ... Now bring me all those horrible things, the blades and pads and stuff.

You've given your power away to them – you need to take it back."

Rachel handed over her various tools and Charlotte threw them on the floor.

"Do you have any liquor in the house?" she asked.

"Only wine," Rachel replied.

"Wine?" Charlotte scoffed. "That's no good. We need something stronger."

Rachel just looked at her, wide eyed.

"Guess I'll have to use my own supplies," Charlotte said, grudgingly taking out the bottle of bourbon. "But you've got to pay me back later."

She took a quick slug before pouring the rest over the pile, then pulled out a box of matches and handed them to Rachel.

"You do this bit," Charlotte said. "It's important. I saw those burns on your skin. You've made fire your enemy, now you gotta bring it back to your side again. Take back control."

"Are you out of your mind?" Rachel cried. "I'm not burning anything – not here. This is my room."

"You should have thought of that before," Charlotte said impatiently. "This is where you gave away control. I can't help if it's messy."

Rachel stared defiantly at her.

"This is serious," Charlotte explained. "I mean it. There's no fooling around …"

Rachel sighed, and making a determined effort not to think about what she was doing, she lit a match and stepped back.

The room exploded into flame, blackening the ceiling straight away and making the pendant light above her head spark and fizz. Within minutes the cutting tools were engulfed in a mass of flames that raged towards the bed frame and duvet and blew the power in the rest of the house. Only when the sprinkler system cut in did Rachel fully realise what she had done. Her house was on fire. She was about to run out the door when Charlotte caught her by the arm and dragged her back.

"You've got to see this through," she said. "It's important you witness the whole thing."

As they stood there watching the flames struggle with the foam, which was pouring down from the ceiling, Charlotte reached around and squeezed Rachel's shoulder reassuringly.

"You did good," she said.

The sodden carpet was acting like a barrier, stopping the flames from spreading beyond the bed. Charlotte took up the blood rag and used it to flap at the bed frame until the flames on it were extinguished. She then picked up the burning duvet by its corners and flung it out the window.

"Good work," Charlotte said, picking foam from her hair. "You still have it – you just need to practise."

The fire was down to a low smoulder when Charlotte turned and led Rachel down stairs. It was then they heard a car approaching, Rachel's mother driving up the avenue.

Five

Dónal Long was sheltering from a gale behind the old toilet block of Reek national school. He didn't look much like his brother except for the gentle blue eyes. He was dark with bushy black eyebrows while Colm was blonde and fair-skinned. Although older than Colm, he was a bit shorter and somewhat less lithe, less graceful. He was waiting for Gráinne to finish class, but he didn't want her to see him. In fact, he wasn't particularly eager to see her either, but he knew that she was the only one who could stop the pounding pressure in his head. His brain was suspended in a specimen beaker under the control of a malevolent scientist, who by turning a dial could increase or decrease its pressure – at least that's how it felt. Only through great resolve could Dónal match the pressure of his brain to that of the beaker and thereby avoid a catastrophe. He had been drinking for three nights straight and it hadn't helped. Gráinne was his only hope. She might provide some relief; even just as a release valve. It had got to that.

The school door opened, and children came spilling out, tumbling recklessly into the rain.

"*Ná déan ar bhúr gcótaí!*" he heard Gráinne shout, and a few of them turned on their heels and went back inside to fetch their coats.

Dónal coughed.

"What are you doing here?" she called over to him, above the heads of her pupils.

"Miss, I left my boots inside," a rose-haired girl said.

"*Bhuel, téigh isteach agus faigh iad,*" Gráinne tutted, before turning back to Dónal. "Why have you come?"

There was no use in telling her he was trying to stop the pressure jars, trying to stop the mad scientist driving him insane.

"Sheltering," he managed at last, looking up into the dark sky.

Gráinne was too busy watching the children to take much notice. Her eyes scanned each in turn, checking that their coats were zipped up against the cold and waving goodbye as they scattered right and left along the road towards home – blotches of dull brown and navy along the road brightened by the harlequin satchels braced to their backs. When the last child was through the gate, Gráinne turned back inside and signalled to Dónal to follow.

The honey-glossed oak and iron desks and lacquered wardrobe were just as they had been in his time and his parents' time, as was the Virgin Mary on her plinth above the red flame and the soaring sash windows that looked out over the bay. The one thing that was new was the heavy electronic typewriter on a pedestal at the back where the nature table had been. The typewriter was Gráinne's innovation – to teach the children computer skills.

Dónal slunk in, squeezing between the ribs of a cramped desk, waiting while Gráinne cleaned up, stacking copies and peeling modelling clay from around the inkwells. She had a fair idea what Dónal was doing here – why he had finally turned up after a week's absence – but she couldn't decide how she should react. With compassion or anger? She had heard that he'd been drinking hard since the skipper laid him off a few days before. There was no place on a trawler for someone in his condition, he had been told. Dónal had inherited a taste for drink which he normally managed to keep under control. The last week had proved too much for him, with first his mother taking off and now losing his job. He had been told not to bother coming back until he sorted himself out.

Gráinne went to water the flowers on the May altar, brushing Dónal's shoulder as she passed. He grabbed her and pulled her in to him.

"Dónal!" she protested, but then relented and allowed herself be reeled in. She gave him a brief kiss before pulling back. This place always made her uneasy. They had first met here fifteen years before when their classes had come together for Holy Communion instruction. Gráinne had been teased by one of the boys because her mother, Mrs O'Tuathaigh, was the teacher and Dónal, although he didn't know her very well, had intervened. It wasn't so much out of gallantry as because they were cousins, and he knew if his mother heard back that he hadn't protected her, he might get a clout. Now, twelve years later, Gráinne was the teacher, the third in a continuous line of the same family who all provided the same basic grounding in maths, songs, spelling and prayers.

Dónal looked up at her now, his eyebrows hanging wearily low, and she was moved to lay aside the water jug and let her fingers run through his hair, kneading his scalp as far as his shoulder blades. His eyes closed with pleasure.

"Things are tough?" she said.

He nodded.

"Will you be OK?"

"Can we go somewhere?" he asked.

She shook her head.

"Jesus, Gráinne!"

"What?" she said. "I'll help, but …"

Dónal extricated himself from the mousetrap desk and pushed Gráinne against the wall, kissing her forcefully on the lips. Gráinne's mouth opened impulsively, and her arms linked tentatively around his neck. He leant a cold, damp hand against the wall and with his free hand stroked her hair and the length of her back. She arched towards him instinctively. Their heads veered and pulled stiffly from side to side, like the kissing one sees at late night bus stops, or dogs feeding.

A rhythmic bellowing was coming from next door.

"*Seacht faoina seacht: daichead a naoi. Seacht faoina hocht: caoga sé. Seacht faoina naoi? Éinne? Seacht faoina naoi?*"

The master was pounding the seven-times tables into the older children. Dónal recalled his years under him – a stiff, preening man who still yielded his big stick, as a throwback to the days before corporal punishment was banned.

"Can we get out of here?" Dónal said. "To the lighthouse?"

Gráinne shuddered again, but agreed. She felt bad for Dónal. His mother had left yet again. She was for ever packing a few carrier bags and hauling them on to the bus when things got too much. Her nerves would get at her, sparking a need to get away, to Dublin or further afield – sometimes Liverpool; she had a cousin there. She always told them not to follow her, that she'd make her own way back when she was good and ready, and Dónal's father seemed to accept this. Invariably, a few days later she'd turn up, exhausted, but noticeably more relaxed, more at home in her skin. This time, Páid, the bus driver had spotted her and tried to get her to stay, but she had caused a scene. Some of the neighbours had noticed her too, seen her hauling the bags down the hill towards the crossroads, but they knew better than to intervene.

On previous occasions Dónal's father had taken up the slack, cooking meals for them in the evenings and getting a local girl in to do a bit of cleaning. An aunt had come by to put on a wash every few days. But this time things seemed more serious. Their father hadn't been the same since his stroke the previous autumn, and he didn't seem able to cope this time. When Gráinne called by Dónal's house as she always did the evening his mum left, she found a dish of cauliflower spread across the floor and Dónal's younger brother, Colm, unscrewing all of the light fixtures in the house. Colm told her that Dónal had gone to the pub, and looking around, she noticed their father, an active and gregarious man until his stroke, slumped in an armchair by the fireplace, staring fixedly ahead, one hand sunk in a hole ripped through the armrest, the other gripping the elbow of the buried arm, as though restraining it from burrowing deeper. Clumps of matted horsehair – the chair's innards – lay scattered about. She had knelt down beside him and asked would he like a cup of tea, and after a long pause he nodded sadly.

On trying to boil a kettle she found that Colm had taken the front plate off all the electrical sockets. He was sitting on the ground, dressed in a tight woollen jumper and flannel pyjama bottoms, with three screwdrivers and a cheese grater, smiling up at her.

"I need to boil the kettle, Colm," Gráinne said.

"Yeah, but I'm just in the middle of something," he replied. He had only recognised her when she came in because she turned up every day at the same time. She and Dónal had been going out together for years and would undoubtedly get married at some point, despite the fact that they were cousins, yet Colm still found it difficult at times to recognise her. He was never totally sure of anybody until he actually heard their voice or smelt them. When Gráinne was in the house with his sister Máiréad and his mother, it could take quite an effort to tell them all apart. Colm had prosopagnosia – although no one had ever told him there was a term for it. He could normally manage to differentiate between his family, but if they changed something about themselves, he'd have to concentrate all the harder. Once when his father grew a beard on a pilgrimage to Knock, Colm hadn't recognised him, and it had taken him a few days to adjust. Likewise whenever his mother got tanned in summer, he'd have to make an extra effort to come to terms with the new person. That was on a one-to-one level; it was even more difficult to recognise people in a crowd. He would often come upon his brother and sister somewhere around the town where he hadn't expected them to be or wearing something different and wouldn't recognise them. His family had noticed the problem early on and merely presumed that it was a sign of low intelligence since no one had ever told them it was a medical condition.

"You're in the middle of something?" Gráinne asked him, looking down at the sockets and screwdrivers. Often she had trouble grasping what he was trying to say and thought the best idea was to repeat his words back to him.

He was freeing electricity or, at least, seeing whether it would affect the feeling in the room in any way if he exposed all the wires at once. But he knew enough not to tell Gráinne this. She wouldn't understand or even want to know, and instead he said, "I'm assessing equilibrium."

Gráinne sighed. She never knew what to make of Colm, how to engage with him. He tended not to say much except when he was really excited, and then he went overboard. She had had him as a pupil for a year when he was twelve; he was obviously clever in ways, but it was hard to get him to focus, and she had been slightly relieved when he had dropped out of school soon after, saying it bored him. That was four years ago, and he had been just hanging around at home ever since, reading mostly. In other places, the authorities or some interfering state agency would have been after him, but in Reek people tended to leave well enough alone.

"Well, can I boil the kettle?" Gráinne asked.

"It's 2,400 watts," he said. "Isn't it?"

She shrugged.

"Check below," he said.

Gráinne turned the kettle upside down. "It says 2,000," she said.

Colm banged his fist against his head.

"Oh yeah. Stupid me. Of course, 2,000! 2,000. 2,000."

"Well?" Gráinne said.

"We'll unplug the fridge and something else to compensate," he said. "Just wait a second. "

Colm busied himself screwing and unscrewing various wires, then flicked the fuse and said, "There! You can suck as much power as you need."

She made the tea and sat with Colm's father for a while. He didn't much want to talk. As far as he was concerned, there was nothing left to say. They had all noticed the gradually ratcheting sense of nervousness or alienation in his wife over the weeks. It was bound to come to this. It always did.

"*Más cuma leat, a chroí, b'fhearr liom bheith im aonar,*" he said, and she tried not to be offended.

She had done as he'd asked and left them in peace, going off towards the pub to find Dónal. She wanted to find out why his mother's departure was so much more serious this time, but when she came upon him, propped against the bar in Bridie's, he too had been reluctant to talk, and she ended up going back to her parent's home alone. That was a week ago, and she hadn't laid eyes on Dónal again until just today. It was her father who had told her that he had lost his job on Con Crawley's trawler. Now, he had come to her, and it was important that she try to help him. If he was asking her to come to the lighthouse with him, then she would have to go. She owed it to him.

They passed the warning sign at the bend before the lighthouse, a large black circle with the words BLACK SPOT written above. As usual Dónal wondered who it was aimed at. Most likely the tourists, but they could hardly be expected to decipher its meaning. It was there to warn of danger, but it did so in as unintelligible and abstract a way as the Celtic markings on standing stones. Possibly, the council had erected it as a reminder to locals that tourists came heltering around the corner at full speed, mesmerised by the heather-covered headland plunging down to the sea and largely oblivious to the road ahead. There was something so alluring about the mercuric grey waves and the old lighthouse in the background that they appeared incapable of maintaining control of their vehicles and frequently ended up in the ditch, or smashing their shiny little rentals into the dry stone wall just beyond it – which was kept loosely built on purpose by the farmer who owned it to ensure a compensation payment after each little bump.

The lighthouse was a squat limestone heap with none of the elegance normally associated with such buildings. It was damp and cold even on the hottest days and could easily be mistaken for a slightly taller version of the fish-gutting barns that jutted out on either side. In even the slightest mist, the top two storeys with their narrow band of glass were obliterated. It had been built a hundred years ago when there was a thriving herring industry here, with men landing, gutting and salting fish from dawn to dusk and barrelling it through the night. Now since the lighthouse had been automated, the place was abandoned, other than for the occasional Gore-Texed foreigner following old Ordnance Survey trails.

"What now?" Gráinne said, looking up at the dour casket that had diminished even further in stature since the last family moved out. It had no real purpose now, other than as an outer casing for the salt-resistant computer and thousand-watt beam churning away inside. Dónal smirked at her, crouching down behind a pallet of fertiliser sacks and pulling out a large brown key eaten through with rust. He brandished it proudly, and she tried to smile. They had often talked about finding somewhere they could be alone and had considered the lighthouse the ideal spot, if only they could get the key.

Dónal now stuck it into the thick-painted door, its rivets bleeding with encrusted rust, and it screeched as the salt and sand crystals crushed in the hinges. Inside smelt of rats and seaweed, and Gráinne was overcome with a sense of nausea. It reminded her of the time Dónal had brought her to the trawler hold and wanted to kiss there. The walls were weeping with damp, and the hum and flicker of the computer made it seem like the building was on life support, ticking over until sundown when the hundred separate beams would jolt to life, forming their collective beam of deliverance.

"I asked the girls to draw their favourite memory of the summer," Gráinne said, needing to distract herself from the situation. "Laoise drew eight lines and two circles, and when I asked her what it was, she looked at me as though I were stupid, saying, "*Sin Daideo ar a rothar, agus féach ansin Seán Óg ag piocadh miongán agus mise ag déanamh iarracht an stuif a bhaint don charraig le scian.*"

Gráinne paused, but Dónal hadn't heard her. It was gradually dawning on him that this was all a bad idea. The last thing he needed now was Gráinne and her stupid stories, her false brightness.

She looked over at him and noticed he was crying.

"Dónal," she said, putting her arm around him. He tried to turn away, to curl in towards the wall. His hands buried into the pockets of his donkey jacket, as though they were digging their way out of this world to somewhere better. The dial on the specimen jar had spun to its highest setting, and he didn't trust himself any more. Gráinne hugged him to her, and instinctively he began pushing his groin against her.

"Dónal," she cried.

"Are you going to help or not?" he muttered.

He pulled at her blouse, squeezing her breasts, but her face turned so miserable that he ended up pushing her away, shoving her a little too hard so that she fell on the floor. Waves of self-pity flooded through him. He should never have brought her here. Gráinne was crying now. She made her way uncertainly towards the half-light at the door and left.

He could hear her shuffling steps retreating, and he collapsed to the ground and lay there until he grew numb. He should have heeded the black spot warning, not have been tempted by her grey, mercurial attractions. He got up and began half-consciously feeling his way around the walls, exploring their smooth calcified surface that coiled upwards to a butt beneath the lantern. The building was like the shell of a giant sea mollusc and he imagined that at any moment the slug might return, squelching him into obscurity. The only light came from a crack above the door, and as he felt his way around, he was surprised to come upon various protruding objects: bulging brass instruments, glass-covered gauges attached to rotting wooden boards and a large barnacle-covered stop-cock. Over time the building was being absorbed back into the coastline by the surrounding plant and animal life, like a pacemaker being knitted into a body.

Rickety steps led up to the lantern room, which was double bolted. This was where he had always most wanted access to, but the lifeboat coxen who had told him about the key of the front door hadn't trusted him with this upper key. Through a chink in the oak slats, he saw the battery of lamp batons, a dozen bulbs on each. Somehow they gave him hope, that a light could be so powerful as to cut through the murkiest fog, the deepest darkness.

The door below creaked open and Gráinne stepped back in.

"I want to help," she called up.

"Gráinne …" he tried to sound gentle, but realised it was futile and so he fell quiet.

"I love you," she said.

He came down the steps towards her.

"You don't," he said, trying to keep his voice steady. "You don't know what it means."

"It'll be OK, Dónal," she said. "Trust me."

He put his mouth to hers to shut her up and found his hand slipping under her sweatshirt. He knew she would give in this time. She would do anything. But the thought of this sent the pressure rising again in his head and he pulled brusquely back.

"For Christ sake," he said. "Don't let me!"

She began to cry.

"*Teigh abhaile*, Gráinne – just fuck off home!"

She pulled her coat over her and walked towards the door.

"*Is* bastard *ceart tú, a mhac!*" she said as she left.

He broke into a frantic laugh, running towards the door and shouting after her, "That's my girl!"

He shuffled back inside and threw himself on the ground, staying there until he was woken by the noise of the motor switching on and the lamp beginning to carve its way slowly around Reek Head and out to sea. Below him he could hear the cry of nesting gulls and a gale hurling sea spray up at them. He remained on the floor, his mind falling into rhythm with the light, its warmth burning through him, lulling him into merciful oblivion. Each time the light went round, the pressure inside lessened.

Six

"Why now?" Rachel's mother, Lucy, said to Charlotte. "Why after all these years did you choose to come here now?"

They were alone, sitting in a bare concrete room in the Concord Police Department, with Charlotte's right hand shackled to a chair. Charlotte could see the animosity burning in her sister's eyes. Bitch. *Fourteen years and she doesn't even ask me how I am*, she thought. *Some sister.*

It had always been like this. Lucy had resented Charlotte ever since she first arrived, aged seven, with two enormous suitcases as her entire worldly belongings. Her mother had succumbed to leukaemia the previous spring, and when her father couldn't cope, he had begged Lucy's mother to take her. She was Charlotte's godmother after all, and with his drinking spiralling out of control, he couldn't be responsible for anyone. Lucy's and Charlotte's mothers had been close since college, but even as toddlers the two daughters never got on. Suddenly Lucy was forced to accept her as her sister, but deep down she resented it.

It hadn't helped that after Charlotte's father remarried he began sending her extravagant presents out of guilt. Each birthday, his sudden pangs would bring something ever more excessive, culminating in a six-week stay at an elite sailing school in Chesapeake Bay when, aged twelve, she had expressed a passing

72

interest in sailing. With each new present, Lucy's simmering resentment of her "sister" had increased. When Charlotte's father sent a yacht long after she had lost all interest in sailing, the very year Lucy had been refused the pony she had craved for eighteen months, her patience snapped, and at the first hint of provocation had physically attacked her sister.

"There must be a reason," Lucy was persisting. "Are you still strung out? Looking for money? I thought you might have got the message by now: there's no statute of limitations on what you did, you know? No kissy-kissy, let's make up."

Charlotte knew what Lucy was referring to and winced at the memory of it: the evening she had overdosed while babysitting Rachel, falling unconscious and leaving Rachel drawing pretty shapes in the coke dust scattered on the table. It had been the last in a long line of incidences, which had included arrests for burglary, assault and drug dealing – although the dealing had been a case of mistaken identity; she had never actively been a pusher. After the overdose, Lucy and her husband had forbidden any further contact between Charlotte and their daughter, which in practice meant any contact with them too. Charlotte knew this stemmed more from their guilt at leaving their daughter with a drug addict than any rational wish to protect her, but she had accepted it as penance, a way of alleviating her own shame.

"Please, just tell me, why?" Lucy was crying now. Her memory of that moment of finding her little Rachie innocently fingering the white powder had grown more intense if anything as time went on and she came to realise how frail her grip on her daughter really was, and how close she had come to losing her.

Charlotte had come to see Rachel, of course, but she didn't say that to Lucy. She just kept her eyes down, towards Lucy's sequined yellow plimsolls. She had loved Rachel more than anyone else in the world. And despite fourteen years absence, she loved her as much now as ever. All she wanted to do was say goodbye. That's all. She realised of course that her sister would never want to lay eyes on her again, and if the situation was reversed she might well feel the same. But surely Lucy couldn't stop her saying one last goodbye? For fourteen years, Charlotte had respected her wishes and kept away; didn't that count for anything?

At first, Charlotte had planned to just call by the house, say her piece and leave again. *Hi, I'm sick, very sick. I love you. I'm sorry. Goodbye.* That simple. She was going to take the night bus up to New Hampshire, head out to the house after breakfast and then catch the last bus home again. But it hadn't worked out like that. Her wallet had been stolen when she was asleep on the overnight bus, and she had turned up in Concord, New Hampshire, without money – no way of buying breakfast, or even a ticket home again. She didn't want to turn up after all these years and be in a position where she had to ask for money again, so she had booked into a hostel and taken a job in town for a week in a local supermarket, nervous the whole time in case her sister or her husband or Rachel might walk in. What would she say?

Hi, Welcome to CostCo! How can I help you today?

The shop manager had kindly (or naively) given her an advance on her pay cheque, but she had still worked out the week, which showed how much she had changed. This was the new Charlotte – more mature and responsible, and aware that she couldn't afford to be leaving any more bad karma behind – getting away with things now just meant having to deal with them in a future life.

At the end of the week, she had got her cheque, bought a dinosaur and made her way out to the house. She had given herself two hours – enough time to say what she needed to say and be back in town for falafels in the diner she liked before catching the night bus home again, this time with a holster-style pouch securely fastened around her neck.

She had thought about this moment for so long, considered everything, steeled herself that Rachel mightn't live at home any more – that was why she had bought the dinosaur. She had written a letter to stuff inside it's little backpack and was going to leave it for her if needs be. She knew she wouldn't get a second chance. Once her sister knew she was back, she would somehow arrange it that Rachel was sent far away out of her reaches.

It's hard to over-estimate quite how taken aback Charlotte had been to find Rachel standing there at the door looking out at her, with the same scrunched up little mouth and delicate eyes, but now wan and weary, drained of life, of blood. At that moment Charlotte realised all her plans had to change. Just seeing her little girl there, standing in the porch of the big house, looking so wounded and scared, was enough to cut Charlotte's heart in shreds. Her beloved little thing had turned into a blank-eyed, haunted woman. It was too much to bear. Charlotte knew she couldn't walk away now. No way. Even if her sister had come out with a shotgun and baseball bat, still she wouldn't have moved an inch until she knew Rachel was OK. Something was very wrong, and she needed to find out what.

It hadn't taken Charlotte long to put the facts together, and immediately she realised that she would have to do something, something big, something to get through to the girl. But what? Her Wicca instinct, if she had one, would have kicked in now, guiding her wisely along. As it was, she just had to fend for herself, reacting blindly, first to stop the bleeding and then …

Well, her next step, even she would admit, had been a bit excessive. She certainly didn't mean to burn the place down. She got carried away. She just wanted to get through to the girl, and she couldn't think of any other way. If Charlotte hadn't turned up when she had, who knows what would have happened to Rachel? Certainly her parents didn't seem to be taking proper care of her.

Eventually, Lucy realised Charlotte wasn't going to talk to her, and she left the police station. An officer with intricate facial topiary came and, after unshackling Charlotte, led her to an office where she was processed and medically examined, before being brought to a cell where she spent a largely sleepless night. Next morning she was released without charge and escorted to the bus station; Lucy had decided not to press charges, despite her husband's urgings. She wanted to get Charlotte as far away from her family as fast as possible. They had been able to use their influence as local liaisons for the neighbourhood-watch committee to have Charlotte driven to the bus station and cautioned not to return.

Rachel herself escaped without punishment on condition that she agreed to seek help, to start seeing a counsellor twice a week. She had asked her parents a lot of questions about Charlotte, but neither of them was willing to say much. The family moved into a short stay apartment, and things returned surprisingly quickly to normal, although Rachel felt herself under constant surveillance by her parents. She started going to the movies in the afternoons after her daily visit to the hospital instead of hanging around in her room, and twice a week she drove across town to the counsellor who gushed at her with fawning platitudes.

By the time the builders had finished renovating the house and they moved back home, her parents were relieved to notice that Rachel seemed to be a bit more open, more resigned. They weren't to know it was a façade – a hard-achieved ploy to counter the threat her counsellor had made about the possibility of hospitalisation for a few weeks if things didn't begin to sort themselves out. They had discussed the accident, over and over, just as she had with the police and her parents, but the counsellor still felt there was something more, something Rachel wasn't telling her. She constantly asked her to relive the experience, which seemed to Rachel a form of cruelty. The hospital break would just be to help stabilise her, the counsellor had assured her, and to work out a medication regime that really suited her. The fear of it was enough to kick-start Rachel out of her funk and paste a perma-smile across her face. After a while, it froze itself into a rictus requiring almost no effort at all.

She knew she had to get away from the counsellor but couldn't think of a way of doing it, until finally she hit on a brainwave: she went straight home to her parents and told them she was keen to start college. Her parents had been so delighted that her father immediately took a few days off work to drive her around the nearest good schools. She had feigned interest in all of them and applied immediately for the ones furthest away, buying pretty clothes for the interviews and practising her presentation skills. She accepted the first college place she was offered. Her mom was so delighted she bought her a little mauve sports car so she could get home at the weekends to be with Nathaniel.

College turned out to be no better or worse than life at home – just a different lie, but without the cutting and bloodshed. She was careful to hide her misery in public, in particular in front of the chaplain and student liaison officer. She wrote enthusiastic emails home about new friends and fascinating lectures – all fiction. She tried to make herself believe them, but the truth was that she rarely summoned the energy to go to lectures, and she hardly talked to anyone. To keep the darkest thoughts at bay, she began running in the evenings. The sheer mind-numbing drudgery of it appealed to her: hammering her body against the hard asphalt, going around in futile circles and causing pain in the process. The track and field coach noticed her and asked her to join the team, but she laughed in his face. She didn't mean to be rude; it just seemed so crazy that people would actually value the torture regime she was inflicting on herself, that it might be prize-worthy.

She hoped to waste the four years of college like this: hidden away, pounding around the track and driving down to see Nathaniel at weekends, waiting for him not to wake up. But just before Christmas break, her freshman adviser called her in to talk about her grades. She hadn't handed in an assignment all term and rarely appeared at classes. He warned her that he would be forced to call in her parents if she didn't show some improvement, and so she resolved to do just enough work to keep them off her back. She cracked open her books for the first time, trying to summon up some interest in them, but nothing they contained seemed of any relevance. She read each one from cover to cover, but none of it stayed in her head. She knew she would end up failing and being kicked out unless she could think of some plan. After looking around her, she realised the only student who got away with doing less than her was Tabitha, a girl from Alabama who was star of the swim team. So Rachel went back to the track and field coach and asked to be put on the running team. She won her first race a few weeks later and kept on winning throughout the season. Nothing more was said about her grades. As long as she kept winning and her parents kept paying the fees, she was safe. The competitions felt crass and inane to her, but the running began to feel OK. She grew to enjoy the way she could suspend all thought during it, losing herself in the pain and exertion. And, just occasionally, a waft of exhilaration would surprise her as she stepped over the finishing line first. She even took part in some weekend trials, which meant giving up her vigil at White Mountain. It was around this time that she began to accept that she was no longer running simply because it caused pain, but also because it made her feel good.

In the middle of March, a letter arrived for her, addressed to Rachel Bean, the AWARD-WINNING RUNNER, Sandler College, New Hampshire.

It read:

Hi Rachel,

Is that really you? I've been Googling you for ages but no luck. Suddenly a long-distance runner with your name who came 2nd at the Boston heats sprang up out of the digital ether. Is it you? I hope so. I need to see you.

Congrats on the running, b.t.w. Are you all blistered? Try Echinacea, just mix it with some camomile. You need to mix up a tincture of just the right blend … Maybe I should come up? Write me and tell me if it's you. And be careful with those blisters. In the past, you know, they were seen as the devil's mark – especially the ones with pus coming out. Teats for nursing daemons. You'd have been dunked in the river for yours, you know that, don't you? I'm not messing here; I'm trying to inform you. It's why we're all so addicted to makeup now, we want to hide the blemishes. None of us want to get drowned, so be careful. It's a terrible way to go, but maybe very relaxing too. Never let them see the suck marks around a zit. You're one of us, Rachel, no matter what you think. They'll smell it off you. Did you never wonder why you cut yourself? You didn't feel pain, did you?! I know that.

I'm not doing so well myself, now. Feeling a bit lost. Why do we always find ourselves on a boat floating down the river with a waterfall on the far end, why is that? There's always a waterfall and no one gives us a map and no one survives. There's always another waterfall, and you and I know what's at the bottom, don't we?

I'm planning to go away, that's why I'm writing. I got some insurance money from a fall I had – in a bowling alley, actually. Oh yeah, your auntie is a serious bowler, so suck on that! And I'm taking a trip to Europe. It's important we start activating the old energy portals again, you know? There's sacred power in Mother Earth that needs releasing right now. Are you willing to help me? I sure want you to. Will you? What else have you got? Your boyfriend has gone – face it, he's just a husk, like when summer's over and the swallows leave and the clover dies. That's your boyfriend. Sorry if that sounds cruel, but it's true. He's just the afro-head on a seeded dandelion. Let him go become something else.

You and I are both alone. It doesn't mean we can't hold hands as we float down the river, right?

Your loving Aunt,

Sha

Rachel crumpled up the letter and put it straight in the bin. She had a big race later that day and was determined to give it her full focus. She wanted to cut time off her previous trials. She had performed better than ever in the heats and felt that today was the day. She was now proud of her role in track and field; theirs was the most successful team in a decade. A lot of expectation was riding on her, but she didn't mind. In fact, she had even invited her parents up for the weekend. It was the first time they would get to see the place properly. She had done a full workout the day before, even aqua-jogging with weights, which she hated. And the night before at the fancy restaurant her dad had insisted on bringing her to, she had eaten only pasta. She didn't touch a drop of the Dom Perignon Reservé her dad ordered – the same vintage as he had at home.

She was in good condition; her strides were getting longer and faster. Out on the track during the warm-up, she felt her quads tighten a little, but they eased out gradually as she began to nimble up, and once in the starting blocks she felt fine. She thought of Nathaniel. Just having him there with her in her mind made her feel safe.

Her body judged the starting pistol perfectly, and it sprang out of the blocks easily and settled into a good pace early on. A twitching nerve in her toe distracted her in the second lap, but it disappeared by the fourth, and she felt herself slipping into the zone. A Dutch girl passed her 1,000m in, and she was able to tuck in right behind her and just not think for a while, while she was pulled along at pretty consistent 47's. (She hated it when people did this to her, but it was the other girl who had initiated the move.) Just over a mile into it, she felt sure she could outstrip her opponent, and so she picked up the pace a bit, passing her and two others and feeling that rush of euphoria that made it all worth while. She knew now why the coach worked her so hard. She was capable of so much. She was glad she had relented and allowed him bring some scouts along. She was proud of herself.

Just as she was coming out of the bend on the final lap, an image of Nathaniel came to her. It was like he was hovering somewhere overhead, and the thought struck her, What was he doing up there? Why wasn't he back where he was meant to be? Where was he off to?

Suddenly Rachel knew the answer, and as if to prove it, she saw at the back of her eyelids the rabbit standing on its hind legs, twitching like it had that morning. She blinked and it was gone, but in its place was the most chilling sensation, and a shudder ran up through her. It ended in a dry gasp in her throat that she couldn't seem to clear. She heard a cracking noise and realised that it had come from inside; something shattering. At first she thought she might have been shot, but that was silly. She tried to focus again, to regain the pace, but something wasn't right. Her great striding legs weren't kicking as they should. Her mouth opened, and her gasping became a scream. She found herself on the ground, her hands out in front protecting her face, the grit digging into her fingertips. Her face twisted in anguish as she realised the pain was coming from her hamstring. It felt as if it had been hacked away with a blunt knife. She kept her head down as the other athletes raced by. She could sense a steward approaching carrying a stretcher, and other officials were following behind. This infuriated her so much that she got back on her feet, ignoring her nerve sensors that were roaring in pain, and she kicked her leg out in front of her, hobbling one step at a time towards the finish line. She thought of the fawn hoofing and kicking in a path of blood across the median line. Screw them, was all she could think. Screw them all. She was determined to finish the race, even if her hamstring ripped right off her bones and out through the skin.

From among the mêlée beyond the finishing line, her father came running out.

"What's wrong?" he was screaming.

She ignored him, there was no point. She knew Nathaniel was gone. Tears washed down her cheeks.

Her coach ran up and held her against him.

"What happened?" he asked.

"He's dead," she managed.

"Who?"

"Nathaniel, you idiot," she cried.

"He's not," her father said. "We told you, we were at the hospital yesterday before we drove down. He's fine."

"He's dead!" she screamed.

The medic tried to examine her leg.

"Leave me alone!" she cried. "Where's my bag? Coach, I need my bag!"

The coach retrieved her bag, and she pulled out her phone

"See," she said, pointing to the screen. On it was a flashing voicemail message. She clicked on it and the words *Nurse-station, Whitemountain* flashed on screen.

"I knew it," she said resignedly.

She shoved the phone at her father, and he pressed the call button.

"You have one new message," the automatic voice said. "Message one, received 3.44 p.m. …"

There was a pause and then a beep that segued straight into a timid voice saying, "Rachel? It's Francis from White Mountain. Could you give us a call as soon as you get this. It's urgent."

Her tone said it all.

"Well?" said Rachel to her father.

He nodded sadly. "It looks bad."

Rachel collapsed to the ground again, refusing to allow the medic to take her to first-aid. A nurse came out to her and gave her something to dull the pain, and she conked out right there on the track and was carried to the first-aid tent. Sometime later, she was woken by a stirring curtain, and looking around her, she saw a head peaking in through the entrance flap. A burly, big-haired woman in sweatpants and a sleeveless T-shirt. The thick woollen cap was what Rachel recognised first.

"There you are!" Charlotte said. "Didn't you get my letter?"

For Charlotte this had proved to be a fateful day – possibly one of the most fateful of her life. Settling herself down on the bleachers that morning with her sandwiches and flask, she could never have conceived things would turn out as they had. Yet the second she saw Rachel fall to the ground, her legs literally collapsing under her, she knew everything had changed. Charlotte had cried out at that moment, in unison with Rachel. Not out of pity or concern, but relief. For she finally saw her purpose in life. Her sacred role. She always knew she and Rachel had a special bond, an indelible cord, and now this amazing coincidence of arriving once again at precisely the time she was most needed was a validation of so much. The synchronicity of coming to Rachel's house at the moment she was butchering herself with craft knives had not been lost on Charlotte, and now, once again, turning up at Rachel's greatest moment of need, was a clear validation of everything she believed in – most of all, of her clairvoyant abilities.

Charlotte had been waiting for a sign like this since she first turned to Wicca as a teenager. The rest of her friends all had more innate spiritual ability than her. They were more psychic, more intuitive, better able to visualise and prophesy. This had always been Charlotte's problem. It seemed to her that everyone in the world was more spiritually gifted than she, but few of them were half as passionate about it. It was only while in prison that she had begun to seriously study Wicca. It was there that she became part of a coven – before that she had always practised alone. The rest were mostly muscle dykes, obsessed with the whole warrior aspect of witchery, but it was still nice to be part of something bigger, to have a support group. It made the rituals more meaningful. The Killeen Coven, they called themselves, after the old Gaelic word for cell. She studied a lot, and she knew reams about the theoretical side and the history, but it seemed there was always some show-off ready to show up her practical limitations.

Her factual expertise gave her some kudos among the dykes, but she would much rather have swapped all that for just a drop of innate *magick*. It wasn't like she was hoping to transmogrify stuff or traverse space and time; just now and then to get a vision or an incidence of crystal-clear knowingness. After all these years, it seemed the least she could expect. She had given the Mother Goddess so much of her attention and time, wasn't she due something in return? No matter how many spells and cures she learnt off or lineages of minor deities she could recite, it never did her any good. She longed for power, yearned for it. It was why she started injecting herself in the first place. Heroin gave her that feeling of omnipotence. It practically guaranteed it; even if only for a short while. None of the extortionately priced residential workshops she had taken in Hawaii, or the 3-day intensive forest ritual in the Everglades, or the seven-part audio-visual course with optional telephone tutorials that she had paid for by selling her car had ever done that.

If it was a competition between heroin and Wicca, heroin won. She blamed her entire drug problem on the goddess entities. They were surely taking the piss. She and her friends used to joke about how every two-bit wand-waver was given a more profound mystical side than her. When she had started babysitting Rachel, her friends had said that even the baby was probably more spiritually gifted, and they had set out to prove it with ingeniously devised tests involving hiding the pentagram or offering the baby a choice between it and her rag doll. Sure enough, baby Rachel did occasionally seek out the pentagram – scurrying deliberately across the floor towards the shiny, star-shaped jewel. They used to pretend she was an oracle and could answer any question they posed. They would ask something abstruse and then set up Lego blocks representing each answer and getting her to pick. It was uncanny how she always chose the wisest option. It used to astound them. Of course, their minds were so blasted most of the time that reality was a malleable entity, and they were never sure quite what they were saying or doing, but it certainly did seem as if baby

Rachel was connected to a higher source. One night they thought about reading auguries in her diapers, but they came to blows over how best to decipher them.

The moment Charlotte had set eyes on Rachel that morning at the track, bent forward at the starting line, tensed like a vein before shooting up, she could tell straight away that the cutting had just been replaced by another obsession. No doubt Rachel had now adopted an intense training schedule, as strict as a junkie's daily routine. Rachel was barely functioning in life; that much was clear. She was as dead to everything in the world beyond the track as Nathaniel was in his hospital bed. Charlotte was sitting there on the bleachers wondering how she might get through to her when she saw Rachel fall and heard her cry echoing up through the stadium. If she had had any doubt at all about her role as a human angel, it disappeared at that point. She had been reappointed. She could feel the sword of an archangel come down upon her shoulder, and she looked up into the sky and breathed in his majesty, assuring the spirits that she would not be found wanting.

Again, of course, the problem had been to know exactly what to do. Her intuition only went so far. Beyond that she was left to forge blindly ahead and hope for the best. She knew she couldn't do the house burning trick again. She needed time to think. Then it came to her – a journey. She remembered that she had written to Rachel about a fanciful journey she intended to go on. There was no real basis to it; it had just been a carrot to entice her interest. Now she would actually act on it. Why not? A trip to Europe would be fun. The problem, of course, was where to go. On a whim she had decided England because of her interest in King Arthur and she had heard tickets to Heathrow were cheap. She went straight to the campus travel agency and bought two tickets with her brand new (and first ever) credit card. From there she went straight to the first-aid tent.

Seven

"Where are we staying, anyway?" Rachel asked as the overhead lights brightened in the cabin and the air steward told the passengers to fold away their tray tables and raise the seats to the upright position.

"With a lady called Mabel," Charlotte said, blurredly. She was exhausted by her fear of flying and the rather vitriolic fight she had had with Rachel earlier on.

It had been largely Charlotte's fault – she recognised that. She hadn't been able to resist quizzing Rachel on her Wicca instincts. She had promised herself not to bring it up, at least not until they had got to London and were settled in, and then only tentatively, but all her best intentions came undone as soon as the familiar panic arose when the aircraft left the runway. She needed something to distract her, something reassuring to talk about, and what could be more so than witchcraft?

"Rachel honey, I was just thinking," she said with faux-innocence, "have you ever felt an inclination to speak to a tree or give thanks to the moon?"

She was gripping the armrest for dear life; she couldn't really turn to check Rachel's reaction, as she was certain that if she took her focus away from the cabin door for even a millisecond, the pilot was liable to send the aircraft plunging into the sea. The lives of all these passengers were in her hands. She was anxious about the ominous silence from Rachel. She feared she might have already gone too far, but couldn't help herself now.

"Or even to pick a certain leaf and bring it home?" she rambled on.

"Don't start," Rachel had said, but the tension was already beginning to play havoc with Charlotte's body, her ankles were beginning to swell, and she could feel a twinge in her base chakra that was in danger of throwing all the others out of alignment.

"Don't *you* start," she had snapped back irritably, her solar plexus already beginning to spin in the wrong direction. She wasn't used to young people, how they can tinker with your chakras as easily as those plate-spinning men who keep entire solar systems in orbit using only sticks.

"What did you say?" Rachel said with icy indignation, in a tone that any mother of an adolescent would have known meant *back away* – as clear a sign as an elephant's rapidly flapping ears.

"I said, don't start, child," Charlotte snapped back. "Seriously. I ain't your mom. This trip is the best thing that could have happened to you and you know it."

Rachel had swerved around in her seat. At this, the elephant hunter would have been back in his Land Rover heading back towards camp, but Charlotte was smiling broadly and counting down from one to five on the tips of her fingers. She had long ago withdrawn her focus from the pilot, and he seemed to be managing just fine.

Rachel breathed in deeply, the better to fuel the impending tirade, but suddenly she found her throat catching on a tide of tears that swept in from nowhere. It had been happening more and more often of late, and she was powerless to stop it. The realisation had suddenly struck her that Charlotte was right. She really did have no other choice but to be here, with this crazy woman, heading to God knows where. The man in the aisle seat cleared his throat awkwardly, and Rachel hid her face and tried to calm herself, staring down hard at her runners and at Charlotte's bulging ankles. She was frightened of the force of her moods, how all that anger had suddenly changed to despair, and how Charlotte had seemed to know it would.

"Sorry to do that to you, child," Charlotte said, leaning in close to whisper, "but I do not *do* tantrums. I've come too far in life to put up with stuff like that."

Rachel tried to stop crying, but she couldn't. She tried holding her breath and pummelling her eyes, but it was no use.

"Look, it's good to cry," Charlotte said. "It's good to mourn, but let's make this the last time. Get it all out of you now, and we can move on. Onwards and upwards!"

Neither of them said anything more, but Rachel continued whimpering on and off as the internal display showed the plane tracking at tortoise-speed towards Greenland.

"OK, that's enough now," Charlotte said in a reasonably kind tone after a while. "No more tears. Let's draw pictures."

"I don't draw."

"Sure you do."

"I don't bloody draw, I told you," Rachel said through her teeth.

"And I'm not asking," Charlotte said in a slow and insistent way, "I'm telling you. Now, draw your hand."

Charlotte pulled out some sheets of paper and a pencil.

Rachel did nothing.

"I can't draw," she shrugged.

"Of course you can," Charlotte said breezily. "We all can if we try."

She took the pencil from Rachel and snapped it in half, handing the sharpened end back to her.

"Now just look at your hand really closely and copy the lines down on paper."

Seeing there was no way out of this, Rachel eventually took up the pencil, gripping it hard between her fingers, and tried her best. She was concentrating so hard that the lead tip snapped off, and they were then left with two blunt stubs.

Charlotte pressed the call button immediately and sat back until the steward appeared.

"I need a knife," she said, brandishing the pencil.

"Knives are not permitted on board this aircraft," the steward said patiently.

"Well, a parer so," Charlotte said.

"We don't carry parers," the steward said.

"Look, I'm not being awkward here, I'm not asking you to perform a tracheotomy or anything, I just want to sharpen my pencil. Can you organise that?"

"I'm sorry, but this airline ..." the steward began to reason.

"This girl here is in urgent need of a drawing tool," Charlotte interrupted. "Do you understand? She buried her boyfriend a week ago, and now all she is looking for in this big bad world is a sharpened pencil. Are you going to help her?"

Rachel was crying again. The man in the outside row was staring intently into his lap.

"Maybe you can put out a call over the intercom," Charlotte suggested. "Anyone onboard with a parer? Huh? Would that be a good idea?"

The steward tried to say something mollifying, but Charlotte just pushed the two pencil pieces towards her, saying,

"Please, just have them sharpened."

She turned away and stared out the window. The steward had no choice but to leave.

"Couldn't you have summoned up something with your wand?" Rachel said bitterly.

"You just stay calm there, baby cakes," Charlotte said calmly.

Rachel guffawed, then fell sternly silent, staring ahead until a few minutes later the air steward came back with a pack of children's colouring pencil.

"Will these do?" she asked as brightly as she could.

"Perfect!" Charlotte said delightedly. "You're such a sweetheart … Now Rachel, let's get down to drawing."

Rachel didn't dare refuse, and they spent an hour quietly drawing their hands.

The flight had continued more or less peacefully, and now, as the plane was descending towards Heathrow, Rachel wanted to know a bit more about this woman Mabel with whom they would be spending the night, but Charlotte wasn't forthcoming.

"She's a kindred spirit," was all she would say.

"A witch?" Rachel said.

"She practises Wicca, I think," Charlotte said stiffly, "if that's what you mean. She cares about the natural world."

"How do you know her?"

"An online message board," Charlotte eventually replied through gritted teeth as the plane bounced twice before settling on to the runway.

They took the Tube to Hampstead and were given directions from there by a traffic warden to the grey Victorian terraced street where Mabel's flat hid behind a key-cutting shop.

An illuminated lottery sign marked the shop entrance. Mabel's door was set into an alcove to the side decorated with Moorish tiles and lit by a dim energy-saving bulb. A small laminated notice in a tasteless cursive font read:

Multi-Dimensional Healing, Karmic Clearing & DNA ReCoding. Empowering you to remember who you are, why you came and accelerating movement in your missions.

The doorbell chimed exultantly, and a wizened, beige-toothed woman in her sixties opened the door with the chain securely fastened.

"Are you Mabel?" Charlotte asked, and the woman's teeth widened into a full smile.

"Charlotte?" the woman said, closing the door to pull aside the chain. "Merry Meet! You found me. The sign is a give away, isn't it?"

She pointed to the lottery sign bolted above the key shop door. It showed a closed hand with a thumb pointing encouragingly upwards.

"When I saw that, I knew this was the place for me," Mabel gushed. "And what's more, the landlord is called Oakley – my favourite tree!"

She hugged Charlotte and Rachel, talking non-stop about the frantic day she had spent organising her dolphin campaign.

"Well, no, not just dolphins, that's classist of me, I mean porpoises too," she said contritely. "You've probably heard about the latest crop circle, yeah? Things have been mad here ever since. I've been sending out bulletins and trying to fax through to the Naval High Command in New York. I got through about eight times, but then they switched off their fax machine, the rotters … In fact, now that I think of it, I really ought to tell the others. Would you forgive me a moment while I …"

She crouched on a stool by her computer and started hammering out emails, turning at one point to say, ". . . and then maybe we can all have a nice cuppa?"

Charlotte and Rachel looked around the pokey room, which had pictures of whales and dolphins on every wall – photos, drawings, cartoons and murky, impasto sketches. The window frames were stained blue-grey with condensation and had diamond-shaped glass pendants hanging from the mullions, providing handy anchor points for the spider webs. Charlotte looked to Rachel and blinked conspiratorially. Rachel turned away. She was becoming ever more doubtful about her decision to come away with Charlotte. It just seemed like there had been no other alternative at the time. The doctor said it could take at least a month before her hamstring improved enough to train again, and even then she would have to take it easy for the next term. There was no one waiting for her in White Mountain hospital any more – she couldn't wile away the hours on her grey plastic chair. There was nowhere for her to go, nothing to do. When Charlotte had handed her the ticket to London, she had grasped at it as a life line, a way of not having to think.

"If you come away, I'm not going to let you mope," Charlotte had warned, "and we're not going to talk about your boyfriend. What happened happened. I know about the police report – his toxicology levels – but it's of no concern to me. I'm just glad he didn't take you with him. Now, you need to start focusing on life, take your mind off all that; it's killing you."

Rachel had resented her tone, but had come away nonetheless. There really was no alternative.

"There!" Mabel said with a sigh, swivelling around on her stool towards them. "Did you get to see the latest one? … It only appeared online this morning. I printed it out in case you had left for the airport by then."

"The latest what?" Rachel said. She was perched awkwardly on the arm of a sofa.

Mabel stared hard at her.

"Are you not part of the message board?" she asked accusingly.

"She's my niece," Charlotte interceded quickly. "I thought I explained that. She's just travelling with me."

"Oh, right," Mabel said uneasily. "You probably did. I'm such a scatterbrain, and it's been such a day."

Charlotte eyed Mabel and pointed in a furtive, knowing way towards Rachel. "Very Wicca," she said, in a stage whisper, over-enunciating the words like a mother discussing a child's onset of puberty. "But not fully accepting it yet, if you know what I mean?"

"Say no more, say no more," Mabel said pleasantly. "Well, *any-who,* here's the latest one. It was posted online only this morning."

She passed around an A4 printout of concentric circles cut in a wheat field with two small triangular shapes sticking out at either end.

"It's only a crop circle," Rachel said disappointedly.

Mabel chose to ignore the remark.

"You can imagine how it set our alarm bells ringing," she said eagerly, reaching out a hand towards Charlotte's knee. "The two dolphins are clearly visible, see? Surrounding the earth in a protective shield."

"Of course!" Charlotte gushed.

Rachel was scrunching her eyes trying to make out dolphins in the pattern of triangles and circles on the page.

"I can't ..." she began, but was interrupted by the doorbell chiming.

"That'll be them now," Mabel said, getting up and heading towards the corridor. "I hope you don't mind, I've called an impromptu meeting to discuss the next step."

She went out to the corridor, and Rachel took advantage of her absence to ask, "What sort of message board exactly did you meet this woman on?"

"I can't remember," Charlotte said breezily. "It must have been something to do with dolphins, I suppose, or crop circles. I post on a load of different ones – mostly it's the same people on them all."

"God!" Rachel said.

"It's a pretty crop circle, yeah?" Charlotte said.

A string of overweight matronly women filed in, accompanied by a younger stick-thin man with a ponytail. Introductions were made, but Rachel was too tired to take in anyone's name. Two of them sat beside her on the sofa, and the others perched on the ground. They were all talking at the same time about the same things.

"The timing is no coincidence," said a sack-like woman with panda make-up, pointing towards the printout. "Just weeks after the sonic testing began. The forces beyond must be trying to send us a message. If even the ETs are concerned, just imagine how serious it is."

"What's this about?" Rachel tried to whisper to Charlotte, but was hushed up.

The young man happened to overhear her and turned to stare at her chest. Mabel leant over to him reassuringly, saying she was a house-guest from the States.

"Oh, right," he said dismissively, sighing in a patronising way before turning to address her. "Well, this is about what your government is doing to the oceans."

"Now, now, Cliff," one of them chided gently, "don't let's make it personal."

"Well, it sure is personal for the dolphins," he said, pulling at his ponytail. "Know what I mean?"

"First off, there was Sydney Harbour last week, OK?" a woman said to Rachel in a conciliatory manner. "A pod of whales swam in and stayed for hours entertaining the crowds. At the same time, exactly the same number were beached off Cape Cod – most of them died. Now, what does that tell you? That we're standing on the threshold of something big – a 'choice point'."

The young man signalled the woman's quotation marks with his fingers.

"Two different worlds exist side by side," she went on, "and our emotions will decide which remains. Will the dolphins come and help us or will they die? Understand?"

Rachel nodded vaguely

"Should we tell her about the sonar testing?" the man asked Charlotte. "Or have you already brought her up to speed?"

Charlotte gave a shrug, suitably vague as to whether she had any idea what he was on about.

Nobody said a word for a while, waiting for Charlotte to respond further, until finally Mabel piped up, "Things got serious only in the last few weeks when the US Navy began testing. I can't believe your aunt hasn't told you."

Charlotte smiled benignly, bowing her head contritely.

"It's a new type of low frequency sonar for detecting submarines," another one of the women said. "The decibels are equivalent to us standing next to a rocket being launched. Even the Navy admits it can cause brain haemorrhaging in some cetaceans."

"You heard about the hundreds of giant squid beaching themselves in California?" Mabel said. "I've written to the chief marine officer outlining our concern."

"Well done," said the man. "Now we need to focus on getting the message out about the crop circle. It's clearly a warning from *pacha mama*."

"I picked up a report about some manatees having died in Florida," someone said.

"OK, but let's think about what action we should take," Mabel chided gently.

They went on talking about crop circles until Rachel couldn't keep her eyes open any longer and dozed off on Charlotte's shoulder. She was awoken from a dream about cuttlefish jumping out of a swimming pool and dying on multicoloured tiles by Mabel. It was shortly before midnight.

"Did we wake you?" Mabel said with faux concern. "It's just that we need your help – we're having a prayer in a few minutes. People all over the world are joining together at 4pm Pacific Standard Time to focus on the oceans. Just breathing gently and thinking of the whales – sending them peace. Hopefully they will feel it and decide to stay a while longer."

Rachel was too sleepy to resist and she got up shakily to her feet as the clock was chiming midnight. The pony-tailed man and Charlotte linked hands with her.

"We ask for divine intervention," he intoned, trying to infuse his reedy voice with a degree of resonance, "to awaken, heal and remember the self and the planet for the whales and dolphins, through the third eye with love and in communion with dolphin-love-light …"

As the prayer went on Rachel felt the man tugging surreptitiously at her arm, encouraging her to sway gently back and forth in time with him. This in turn set everyone else in the circle swaying. He thanked the whales and dolphins for the gifts they had given and assured them of human kind's appreciation and respect into the future, and he went on to outline the energy that he and his friends would endeavour to set for their benefit and that of Mother Earth.

Finally, after about fifteen minutes of similar ramblings, Mabel checked the computer screen and saw that the prayers were coming to a close in other parts of the world and she suggested that they wrap things up. They had done all they could for one night. She prepared a pot of geranium tea, and after a short discussion about plans for the following day, the group filed out. Mabel crouched down to turn off the computer, looking spent and exhausted.

When she unfurled herself back up to standing, she looked meditatively around the walls at her crustacean icons, saying,

"Aren't they just so beautiful? I would do anything for my lovelies." She paused and sighed before continuing, "All they want is to share their light with us. What could be more beautiful?"

She looked around her with wide eyes, and Charlotte hugged her, which was apparently what was expected. Rachel knew she ought to do the same, but couldn't bring herself to.

"Thank you for guesting us in your beautiful home," Charlotte said, looking around the dingy room expansively. "It feels so good to be among dolphin energy and especially to be in the land of Merlin and Gwendolyn again."

"Merry meet, merry meet," Mabel said before showing them how to fold out the sofa bed, and then, taking a bar of fair-trade chocolate and a jug of lemon barley water into her room, she bid them goodnight.

Next morning Rachel awoke hot and crabby, tangled up in the bed-clothes beside Charlotte, who was staring straight at her. She jerked herself away from the stale fug of Charlotte's breath and stared distractedly around the dolphin-plastered room, getting her bearings.

"What the hell was all that about?" she said, turning to Charlotte indignantly.

"Last night, you mean?" Charlotte said breezily. "I'm not sure, to be honest. I don't really follow sea mammal issues. I thought I knew Mabel from a Knights of the Round Table message board, but I must have got confused. The prayer was nice though, wasn't it? Made me feel tingly inside, and wasn't it amazing how our energy harmonised and we began swaying spontaneously?"

Rachel said nothing. All she could think about was how to extract herself from this situation as soon as possible.

"We are leaving this morning, aren't we?" she asked.

"If you want ..." Charlotte said reluctantly, but she was cut short by Mabel peeking out of her room in her nightdress.

"Hi-di-hi!" Mabel said, tip-toeing over to the computer. "Are you sleepyheads still in bed?"

She switched on the computer, opened the blinds while waiting for it to boot up, then sat down and checked some websites.

"Well, that certainly was a successful night," she said after clicking through a few pages. "There's been no reported beachings in the last eight hours – I think our prayers are really working. We'll have to keep it up … You'll come on the march with us today, won't you? We're handing in a petition."

"Well, actually, Mabel," Charlotte began diplomatically, "Rachel is keen to get to Cornwall as soon as possible."

Mabel struck a tragic face.

"She's a total Camelot nut," Charlotte continued. "All her life she's been begging me to bring her to see King Arthur's Hall."

"Really?" Mabel said, looking at Rachel.

"I guess," Rachel said hesitantly, "I love all that – Merlin and Voldemort shit. Can't wait for Cornwall, it'll be awesome, seeing the, eh … the Misty Mountains."

Mabel stared hard at her, but before she could say anything the doorbell rang. It was some of the same bunch from last night, but joined by two younger girls. They came in and began pulling the furniture back against the walls, folding the sofa bed up, literally as Charlotte and Rachel were getting out of it. Mabel sent the two of them into her room to dress, although she herself remained in her nightgown.

Once the room was cleared and the two had dressed, everyone settled themselves in a half circle on the floor with one of the girls on a stool in the middle.

"This is Rachel and Charlotte," Mabel said to the girl. "You don't mind if they join us?"

"Not at all, dear," said the girl. "The voice of Sanusara is open to all."

There was a general murmur of agreement about this, and then Mabel said to the girl, "Well, if you're ready, I'll pull the blinds?"

The girl nodded and everyone sat in silence, waiting for a few minutes as the girl seemed to fall asleep. Her head fell forward, her shoulders relaxed, and her breathing became gradually deeper. Rachel was about to ask what the hell was going on when suddenly the girl's head sprang up and she looked around her wide-eyed, making a sort of popping noise with her mouth like a goldfish in a cartoon.

"From the watery realms deep beneath the seas, we the dolphins welcome you here today," she said, in a deeper, huskier tone than her normal one. "Come, journey a while in our domain."

She paused to make more popping noises before continuing,

"Long have we yearned for this connection, water mammal to human. This time on earth is pivotal to us and our cousin-kin the whales – we send to you their anxiety in energy-word-pattern form. Listen and feel it in your hearts – from their home-world to yours. It is our gift and a source of service to you. Man is given dominion over mother-sea and earth but understands it not. He-she is forgetting to honour the worlds around him."

There were general sighs of agreement to this, and the dolphin in the form of the girl nodded smugly.

"He-she does not yet see how his-her tampering with the magnetics is leading my brethren to the beaches, confusing the depths with the shallows. It is harming my species, and we ask that you intercede, O blessed ones who are so attuned to our thought patterns. Sagely take heed and remove your noises from our seas, we plead."

"We will, we will!" a few of them interjected.

"Listen to our song," the dolphins continued more firmly, to discourage further interruptions, "and you will know that our exodus is imminent. We are in pain. Seek out the legends of the pre-civilisations, the Atlanteans, the underwater ones, and you will learn your own destiny. Tell your leaders in their white house that their supremacy is transient. The water will prevail. If you deafen us the seas will no longer sing for you. I am of the council of dolphin breath, honoured to be invited to share amongst you this day."

The girl fell quiet, and nobody said a word for a long while. Rachel was doing her best to stem a fit of giggles. Finally, Mabel got up and put on a new-age track with synthesised piano interspersed with dolphin sounds, and just as Rachel felt she could control herself no longer, Mabel nipped her gently and signalled for her to follow her into the kitchenette where they made sandwiches together while the rest continued their meditation.

Rachel was glad of the distraction and diligently spread slice after slice of white bread with tuna pâté and Stilton. She wanted to ask Mabel was it intentional that she was serving a favourite food of dolphins, and had she checked that none had been harmed when the tuna was caught, but she didn't dare. Mabel hummed little snatches of off-key dolphin noises to herself contently.

Once they had eaten lunch and drunk countless more cups of tea, they got up to make preparations for the march on Westminster. Rachel shifted menacingly in her seat and stared daggers at Charlotte until finally Charlotte was forced to get up and announce that they would have to leave straight away. Mabel tried to insist that they stay on at least for the march.

"We need the numbers," she pleaded. "The dolphins are counting on you."

Charlotte was about to waver, but Rachel insisted that she had already bought non-transferable tickets and couldn't afford to waste them.

"What's money compared to this?" Mabel asked.

"Indeed," Rachel said diplomatically, "but there's a special shaman who has travelled all the way from … from Romany to show us around."

Mabel looked impressed by this and made no further protest. She gave them both a big hug, and after a round of deep, long, meaningful squeezes from everyone else, they were ushered to the door.

"Be careful out there," the scrawny man called after them.

"You owe me, big time," Rachel said hanging from the bakelite ball and metal coil on the Tube towards Victoria Coach Station. "I don't know how I kept it together in there. Those guys were crazy."

"They were a bit full-on, I'll grant you," Charlotte said. "But that's 'cause they weren't Wicca – they're New Age. I kinda liked them."

"What's in Cornwall?" Rachel said. "Why are we going there?"

"Well, not Voldemort anyway!" Charlotte scoffed. "That's Harry Potter, you fool. Don't they teach you anything in school?"

"We're not staying with more weirdoes, are we?"

"We're in a youth hostel tonight," Charlotte said, "if that meets with your ladyship's approval."

Eight

Dónal roused himself from the lighthouse floor as night began to fall. He knew he had better go home, although he really didn't want to. He had promised Con Crowley's wife, Sheila, that he'd take part in the jigs and reels show for the tourists in Bridie Brennan's that night, and if he wanted his job on the trawler back he had better turn up. Dancing for tourists was humiliating and mind-numbing, but the money was good – not that Sheila gave him even a fraction of what she told the tour operators she was paying her dancers, but he made sure he made up for it in tips. There was a group of them who danced together, and at the end of the night, Dónal would make certain to add an extra swagger to his final hornpipe, while eyeing up the women as he did so. Then he'd go around the room with a long drawn out spiel about how recognising the rhythm in the phrase "rashers and sausages" was the key to doing a good hornpipe, and they'd all laugh and hand him a few euros. Most of the other dancers were more proficient than him, but they weren't prepared to work the room like he was, to press the flesh. As far as he was concerned, he more than earned his tips for having to endure their asinine questions and comments. Once, someone had actually asked him whether dancing had been forbidden on the Gaelic reservations during British rule. It had taken Dónal a moment to work out what the man meant, and he had to patiently explain that Ireland didn't have reservations; that although we were pushed off our prime land to the badlands of Connaught, we weren't actually corralled there. Yet, he mustn't have been clear enough or it simply didn't register, because a few minutes later the same man, a Minnesotan, pointed to Seáinín, the fattest and most agile of the dancers, and asked whether they had the same problems with diabetes in the Gaeltacht areas as Minnesota had on its reservations.

"They say it's genetic," the man said; "they just can't handle our modern foods."

Dónal took the cliff path as a shortcut home, promising himself he'd just grab some food and head back out to Brennan's; maybe bringing Colm along with him and actually convince him to come inside for once, to leave the fox to its own devices. He knew it was hard on Colm: crowds disorientated him. Whatever chance he had of recognising people on an individual basis was made impossible within the dim, smoky atmosphere of a pub. Everyone looked sweaty and red-cheeked, and the noise levels were so loud it made it hard to recognise people's voices. For Colm, pubs were like air raid shelters during a raid.

Dónal was careful to keep in from the cliff edge; the tufts of couch grass and sea pinks that hung precariously over the edge blurred the line where the land fell down to the crashing sea below. It had fooled people before – a neighbour had fallen over (or, possibly, jumped), as had countless dogs and sheep. The sea had been eating away at this place for ever. Dónal's father could point out the remnants of whole fields that had disappeared since his childhood.

Back at the house, the kitchen was fogged with vapour, and Dónal's sister Máiréad was straining a saucepan of potatoes into a colander by the sink. Swollen cumulus clouds rose up from the cool metal draining board.

"Look what the cat dragged in," Máiréad said when he

entered. "This isn't a boarding house, you know. You can't swan in any time you like."

She looked red-faced and sullen and was glancing down disapprovingly at his grubby jacket and unkempt hair.

"I was held up," he said.

She snorted.

Colm was over in the corner, cowering as though he too might have suffered a lash from her earlier. His tall angular body was closed in on itself like a scallop defending itself from attack. He was rocking himself back and forth – doing what he called 'pulsing', moving his body in rhythm with his heartbeat. It was relaxing and hard to stop once you started.

"What's up, buttercup?" Dónal said, crouching down in front of him.

Colm's face was set in stone, his pale cheeks smooth as limestone. He was wearing his favourite well-worn leather field boots and tan Lois jeans, frayed around the ankles.

"Tell me," Dónal said.

"Taytos," said Colm finally.

"Has she run away again?"

"No," said Colm. "Máiréad won't let her in the house."

"She's a wild animal, for goodness sake," Máiréad interjected.

"Not any more," Dónal said. In recent days, Taytos had started following Colm home from the pub.

"He was putting butter on his lips and trying to get the fox to kiss it off," Máiréad said.

"Were you?" Dónal asked with a laugh.

"An experiment," Colm said indignantly.

Máiréad carried a large Pyrex dish of pollock in milky sauce across to the table – a scum of scales and whey lined the edges. She set it down, doling out large spoonfuls on to each plate.

"Dada, are you coming to eat?" Dónal said.

His father, a small, barrel-chested man with tufts of side-burns sprouting by his ears, was staring distractedly at the television with the sound turned down, his fleshy, unshaven jowls masticating on a square of butterscotch. He had hardly moved from that spot in days. He even slept there some nights.

"Are you coming or not?" Dónal asked again, impatiently.

His father cleared his throat noisily and made to lever himself out of the chair. With his hands buttressed at his hips, he slowly straightened his spine with a long sigh. Máiréad pulled out the chair at the head of the table for him, and he shuffled towards it with a faraway smirk.

Dinner was acrimonious, as usual. A fight broke out over the butter dish. It was always the most insignificant of things that struck a spark in the tinderbox atmosphere of irritability and self-pity that had infused the family since their mother left, and it inevitably flared into a conflagration.

Dónal had dived for the butter and the salt as soon as he was seated – dropping heaps of both over his potatoes before passing the dish deftly over his sister's outstretched arm to Colm. Máiréad caught the snub but didn't react. She wouldn't give him the pleasure. Then, when Colm was finished, he passed it on to his father, shooting his sister a quick sneer as he did so. Again she didn't react, but it was clear she was quietly seething, her cheeks flushing even redder.

Colm loaded up his fork the way he liked it – in a mini kebab of potato then fish then potato – and had just brought it to his lips, when Máiréad started in on the prayer. It was her own subtle revenge, carefully timed to annoy everyone. She knew no one could refuse to go along with it.

They all laid down their knives and forks again, and Colm was forced to spit out a piece of potato, as chewing while praying wasn't allowed. His carefully prepared kebab was ruined.

"*Beannaigh sinn, a Dhia, beannaigh an bia agus an deoch, agus saor sinn ó gach olc*," Máiréad intoned.

They all repeated the words; even Dada managed to rouse himself. They blessed themselves swiftly, and Máiréad took up her fork again. She had just brought a lump of fish to her lips when Colm started into a second prayer.

"Thank you Lord for providing this meal and for all your mercy shown to us sinners, and please bless Taytos …"

"We've done the prayer, Colm," Máiréad said.

"Yeah, but I want a bit more."

"There's only one prayer," she said. "There's always only one. You say yours tomorrow."

"But Jesus won't mind," he said.

"Oh shut up!" Máiréad said.

"*Éistigí anois, éistigí*," Dada said, startled by the raised voices.

Dónal took the opportunity to feed him a mouthful of fish – he had had nothing to eat all day according to Máiréad, nor was he showing much sign of hunger now. He accepted the fork from Dónal but didn't bother chewing it. He was already sinking back into his reverie again.

"*An bhfaighfeá braon uisce dom, le do thoil, a chroí*," he slurred to Máiréad.

She hated the fact that her brothers were never asked to do these little chores. Máiréad was the only daughter and as such was expected to fill in for Mama in her absence; she resented it, but there was no one to complain to. Now that her boyfriend Ciarán had gone back to Kildare for army training, she was on her own. It had always been the same. If an egg broke in the pan on a Sunday morning, her mum would take it, and if a second broke it was automatically given to her. The same went for burnt toast or a disk of black pudding that had burst its skin.

She got up and fetched the water for her father, shooting him a glower on the way.

Kittens, the family cat, jumped up on to Colm's lap and attempted to lick the smell of fish from his fingers.

"Get down!" ordered Máiréad. "That's disgusting. You'll get Weil's disease."

"You're vile," Colm said, bending down to allow the cat lick his face.

"She's right, Colm – put her down," Dónal said; "they have leptospirosis. It'll make you sick."

"So there!" she said. "Even your hero Dónal knows I'm right."

Dónal sighed; the idea of dancing for drunken foreigners all night was becoming worse by the moment. He looked across at Colm, who seemed equally ill at ease. Colm was particularly sensitive to moods and tension. Dónal knew he'd get upset if the family didn't at least try to get along. He decided to suggest a quick game of pontoon before going to Brennan's. Colm loved it when they all did things together. Dónal was just about to suggest it, when he noticed Colm stretching his neck forward and picking up a fishtail with his teeth and waving it from side to side so that the fish's spine slapped from cheek to cheek. He wanted to be the joker, to make everyone laugh. He was looking around him giddily, eager to attract attention, but no one except Dónal seemed to notice. He began to bark like an otter, flapping his arms and nodding as though he were head-butting a ball.

Dónal smiled in spite of himself, and after a while Dada began to clap in time with him.

"*Maith a buachaill tú,*" he said. "*Garsún an róin – déan cleas dúinn!*"

Colm flapped on frantically until the cartilage of the over-cooked fish could take it no longer and the vertebrae snapped, sending the fish head flying over towards Máiréad at the sink.

Kittens went careening across the floor after it. Colm was left with a flaccid fish bone dangling from his teeth and silver scales like alien freckles on his cheeks. He felt good.

"You're the man, Colm," said Dónal, and his father chuckled.

Máiréad came back with the jug of water and, reaching into a plate of yellowing lettuce that lay uneaten in the centre of the table, she took a leaf and roughly wiped Colm's face with it.

"You're a messer," she said, cleaning away the gunge from around his mouth.

He smiled happily. The same lettuce had been put on the table for the last three nights; this was the first time it had been touched. It was only there because Máiréad had been taught in home economics class that every meal ought to be served with a vegetable, and she couldn't be bothered to cook any. These bitter, limp leaves were a concession. She knew no one would touch them; they were there merely to fulfil an obligation.

"What's for pudding?" Colm asked hopefully.

Dónal shrugged and looked over at Máiréad, who was already warming the teapot and cutting slices of currant cake.

Dada shifted uneasily in his chair, and Dónal noticed the smell of him, bodily and stale. He hadn't washed in too long.

Dónal felt a familiar anger rising inside him again, the glass chambers pressurising. The state of his father disgusted him. He wanted to reach out and shake him. The family was foundering, and nobody seemed prepared to do anything about it. Dónal's jaw clamped tightly shut to stop him telling his father what he thought, and he bit his tongue. The warm, salty blood filled his mouth, but he didn't let on to anyone. He didn't even wince, just took it without complaint. As soon as the teapot was placed on the table, he poured himself a cup and swallowed back a scalding mouthful to cauterise the wound. His jaw muscles ached. He could taste the strange mix of tannin and blood on the roof of his mouth, and staring down into the cup, he noticed a thin vein of blood dispersing through the liquid like a meat spot in an egg yolk.

There was no way he was dancing tonight – he was in no state to play the happy leprechaun for dimwit tourists. He pushed his chair back and stood up without saying a word. He needed to get away. Grabbing his coat, he headed out the door and off into the night, taking an old path over the hill, not caring about the brambles that grabbed at him as he passed, clawing him and tearing his skin. The moon was up. It sought out as usual the aluminium milk tankards on the single remaining dairy farm in the area. The tanks shone up out of the slurry darkness around them like inland buoys. The mounds of filament netting on the pier shimmered occasionally, their effervescent strands rippling in the wind, catching the reflected moonlight. He turned off the path into a reedy field and tramped up along the ditches over the mountain pass that led out of Reek Valley and into the world beyond. He was content for a while, going nowhere, marching into the unknown with sheets of rain pelting benevolently into his face like palms leading him on.

In a remote pub in the neighbouring parish, he dried his clothes by the fire and drank pint after pint of stout, soothed by the familiar lanolin smell of wet woollen jumpers and tweed jackets and the wonderful earwax smell of cheese and onion crisps. He settled himself at the margins, away from the older lads on one side of the bar speaking Irish, and the young ones on the far side speaking English, and the middle-aged ones in between using a bastardised version of both. The language had become yet another division in the community, now used mostly only in church, at school and by the elderly. He tried to lose himself in the constellation bubbles of golden pints around him and managed with sheer insistence not to be inveigled into joining the musicians who were belting out reels in the far corner. One of them handed him a tin whistle, but he refused to put it anywhere near his lips. All he wanted was to kill time, to watch and listen to the drunken men and women around him, blurred and emotional – to join them in their bout of temporary amnesia – a community hiding from reality together, mercifully free of any tourists.

He was the last to leave in the very early hours of the morning. It had stopped raining, and he staggered back the nine miles over the hill, which felt far longer because of the boggy ground that squelched with every step. The effort of it sobered him, and when he rounded the last bend that led to the crest above Reek Harbour and felt the sun on his back, he realised he didn't feel so bad any more. The tension had dissipated. He turned to look back at the sun, noticing with a smile that it appeared to be following him, and that he and it were rising at more or less the same pace.

By the time he reached the crest, the sun was pouring straight into Reek Valley, cutting through the mist, illuminating patches of dew and casting the first shadows of the day. Below him his homeland was a motley of jigsaw-edged fields and crumbling out-houses arranged around an eroding lump of concrete they called the pier. Only Bridie Brennan's bar appeared to be thriving, preening under a fresh coat of lurid orange paint, no doubt paid for by all the tour groups that stopped by for scones and a lavatory stop. The entire valley was lifeless at this hour except for the few cows and two lone Germans in a field by the cliff edge, shaking the rain off their flysheet and wringing out their sodden towels. No wonder the place appealed to them, he thought. Its asceticism was primeval, containing only what was necessary for human survival: crops, cattle, shelter and a pub. To them it was idyllic, a haven from their fraught lives; to him it was a rope, a slowly tightening noose. He collapsed down on a mound of heather and stared out to sea.

Back at the farmhouse, Colm was just getting out of bed, sleepily reaching over to the bedside table for his key ring or phase tester or any fidgetable item that would help disperse the agitation coursing through him. He hadn't slept much. He'd been woken again by a familiar dream that always felt too real to be a dream. He was in a balloon along with three others whom he really loved: people who understood him completely, who recognised how glorious he was. They were floating over a swathe of dusty grassland watching a leopard drinking by a steam. It wasn't the location that felt so real, but the people – their essence. He knew them. He was certain of that, but he just couldn't remember their names or whether he had actually ever met them in this life. Their love for him was clear in every word, every glance. He always felt so happy there. It was hard afterwards to have to come back – back to a world where no one understood him. Sometimes, when he was up on Cnoc Ciarán, he got a similar feeling, of being understood, accepted, except that he was awake, which made it all the better. What he wanted was a way of keeping the sense that he was loved unconditionally and was part of something bigger alive the whole time. In the dream it was obvious to him that he was so much more than he appeared to be on earth. He was vast, endless, glorious, and only just temporarily encased in this pale, rangy body, but it was hard to remember this when he was awake. The truth would gradually wane, particularly around others.

He got out of bed, leaving his keys aside and reaching for something more effective – his measuring tape, by far his favourite fidget gadget. It was important that he give some more thought to the cement problem. It was good to know that he could get it in Daly's; now he had to find a way of paying for it. Without cement, he could never make much progress on his plans to build somewhere for himself. The whole idea of building first came to him a few months before when he realised that the place he felt most at ease was in the shepherd's shelter on top of the cliff. It was because he was alone there; no one could confuse him. He was able to keep in contact with who he really was. The truth was that most people saddened him. They made him feel more isolated and frustrated. It was the awareness of their own regrets and confusion that really got to him. He could handle his own thoughts well enough, but taking on the burdens of others proved too much – especially his family's. Since they were closest to him, he felt them the strongest: his sister's frustration, his dad's disappointment and, most of all, his mother's mood swings when she was drinking – chicaning through anger, self-pity and accusation. He was coming to realise that this was what was keeping him locked inside himself. He knew he had to find some way out, and for that he needed space, somewhere he could breathe, but he reckoned his family would never understand. They wouldn't let him go, worrying that he wasn't up to living on his own. That's why he had come up with the idea of the boulder shelter – somewhere of his own, but not too far away. They'd still probably resist the idea, but he'd just have to prove that he was up to it. It was vital that he do so, because otherwise ... well, the alternative was too bleak to consider.

Anyway, how hard could it be to live on his own and look after himself? Admittedly, his attention wasn't always what it ought to be – focusing on things that didn't interest him was a struggle – but he could work on this. And if he wrote lists for shopping and cooking and cleaning he could get by – especially if he was really determined. He refused to be trapped inside himself for ever, to spend the rest of his life rocking or flipping or flapping just to get through the day, fidgeting with his measuring tape like a baby with its rattle.

Sometimes he thought of leaving Reek entirely, just setting off somewhere new, but he had no idea where. What he wanted was to find a place where others could see the light shining from people the way he did. But for all he knew there was no such place. Maybe no one else was like him. It wasn't that he saw light coming from everyone, just some people, very few actually – a glow from around their body, particularly their top half; shafts of it, radiating out from the head and shoulders and spine. In fact, Colm had only ever seen light like this coming from less than a dozen people – it was definitely rare, but hard to miss when you did see it. There was another more numerous group who had a less prominent display of a light around them; little more than a dull, fuzzy blur, but noteworthy nonetheless. He had seen quite a few like that, but they weren't half as interesting, and he could ignore them with just a little self-restraint. But the really bright ones were hard to ignore; the really radiant ones. He felt he had to respond to them in some way. Their light was too magnificent, too rare and beautiful not to. Yet he knew from past experience that many people didn't like to have it pointed out to them. It made them feel uneasy or embarrassed. Dónal had told him it was best to keep his thoughts about people to himself. But it was hard to keep such a thing quiet. It was too exciting. For Colm, the fact that people glowed was so wonderful that he wanted to be able to congratulate them. It was such a rare phenomenon that he couldn't just walk on by without saying something, without complimenting them in some way. Once or twice he had even seen people who were so bright that he couldn't look at them straight on.

The first person who responded well when he pointed out their light to them was a science student called Beatrice who had spent the previous summer in Reek studying jellyfish. She was from Oregon and had come to spend a semester in Trinity College before coming to Reek for fieldwork. She had been charmed by the remark, saying that she was honoured, and even got him to describe what he saw. He noticed she began to shine even brighter as he explained. Ever since then, she had appeared in the balloon dream with him – in fact she had probably always been there, but he hadn't recognised her before. He found that he did not have the same problems recognising someone by the light coming from them as he did by their facial features.

Colm had spent three weeks helping her with her jellyfish project. They spent the mornings collecting samples, scooping them into a net and transferring them to a bucket half-filled with seawater. When they had about eighty jellyfish stacked like pancakes in the bucket, their tentacles somehow managing not to get tangled in each other, they brought them to one of the old herring processing sheds by the lighthouse and chopped them up in a large blender. Then they squeezed the liquidised flesh through a piece of mesh until eventually a paste like gooseberry sauce came out the other side, which was frozen and sent to Dublin.

Beatrice was the first person he met who fidgeted almost as much as him. Mainly, she flapped a little when she got excited, her hands shaking from side to side, making her nail-bitten fingers do a sort of single-handed clapping. She used to be far worse, she had told him, but had learnt to control it. Colm asked her to teach him how, but she insisted that if it was a natural part of him, he shouldn't feel compelled to stop just for others. Everyone fidgeted, she said, it was just a way of focusing the mind, or dealing with stress, or excitement. "Look at any game show on TV," she said, "all the panelists jumping up and down, drumming their fingers, waving their arms." Beatrice encouraged him to notice all the different ways people fidgeted: playing with their hair, stroking their beards, swiveling their wedding rings, biting pencils, playing with earrings, cracking knuckles, doodling. "And what about smoking?" Beatrice had said, when he was still doubtful "and chewing gum. They're no different from what you do."

"Yeah, but I can keep fidgeting for hours," he said.

"Which is exactly what rocking chairs were invented for."

She told him that when she was young, she could spin herself in circles for hours without ever getting dizzy, but it had upset her parents so much that they had organised a "prayer chain" with the congregation of her local church. The whole community had taken turns praying twenty-four hours a day for thirty days until she was healed. They had held a huge party in the local hall at the end to give thanks to God, and Beatrice hadn't the heart to spin again after that. The community called it a miracle. She claimed she missed spinning every day since and that she knew for a fact that he would feel a lesser person if he lost the things that made him happy.

"Have you never heard the quote, 'The right to swing my fist ends where the other man's nose begins?'" she said. "It's an actual *right*."

It was Beatrice who first made him think of moving out, of working out a way of having a life of his own. She never said anything directly; it was just the fact that everything she talked about was so different from what people around him thought and so close to what he himself thought. He didn't know how he could ever match the two while still living at home. When she went back to Dublin at the end of the summer, he was left alone with Taytos again, and he felt lonelier than ever; that was when he started thinking seriously about the building project. He decided to take a trip up to Dublin to Beatrice to see what advice she could give, but when he rang the number she left him, her roommate answered and said she had gone back to Oregon. The man had been dismissive at first, but when he realised how downhearted Colm was about the news, he asked was he the boy who had helped Beatrice with the jellyfish project? When Colm said he was, the man said that Beatrice had suggested that they might be able to work together in the future, that Colm might collect some more jellyfish for them. Colm had been too upset by the bad news to really take in what the man was saying, but he must have agreed, as the following weekend the man turned up in Reek looking for Colm to show him what he wanted done. By that stage, Colm had got over some of his disapointment and was quite excited by the idea of a job, especially since the man had said they would pay well if he supplied them with good quality material. He needed money after all for his building plans.

They had sat in Bridie Brennan's having tea and sandwiches while the man explained the new research they were doing into the electrical pulses that created luminesence in jellyfish. Colm had no problem remaining focused on this as it was about electricity, one of his favourite topics. He found it weird that they were studying light, considering how he had first met Beatrice, but he didn't say this to the man, who was busy explaining to him that the light organs were in fact tiny black seed-shaped nodules on the underside of the outer edge of the umbrella-like body. The research team were hoping to isolate the protein that contained the energy that powered the light – a tiny charged battery that short-circuited in the presence of calcium in seawater and released light. Colm was fascinated. When he was six, he had first worked out that certain jellyfish shone all the time – not just at night – by bringing them into a darkened room during the day. He had wondered at the time why they didn't shine so well in tap water as in seawater.

In the afternoon, Beatrice's former roommate had set about showing him what they wanted done. For this next phase in their research, they were only interested in collecting the outer circumference of the jellyfish, where the light organs were. It meant cutting a thin ring around the outside edge. It was a tricky operation, as if one cut too thinly, one risked damaging the light organs, and too thick a ring provided too much extra slime and debris to make the samples usable. The man had spent a few hours showing Colm how to do it, but no matter how hard Colm tried, he couldn't keep his hands steady enough. The man had been patient at first and told him to take as long as he liked, they would pay well for each good sample they received, but the harder Colm tried the worse he got, and eventually he had to admit defeat. The man had bid him an exasperatted goodbye and driven back to Dublin, and Colm hadn't heard from him since.

The camping Germans came cycling up the hill towards Dónal, dressed head to toe in Spandex and breathable rain gear with their tent and sleeping bags perfectly backed into panniers. He couldn't help but admire them, their resilience and ingenuity. He was glad the sun was shining for them at last. They deserved it. He knew he had to pull himself together. He owed it to his brother at least to maintain a strong front. If his mother came back, she would need his support, although somehow all of them suspected she wasn't coming back this time. She had been going for longer and longer periods of late. She promised them that she would always get in touch within a month, and that they should not start to worry or contact the authorities until at least six weeks had passed. If there was something physically or mentally wrong with her, they could do something about it, but she claimed there wasn't; it was just that she needed to be away.

Dónal decided his first priority ought to be to get his job back, and he headed down towards Con Crowley's newly built bungalow to find out whether they were planning on taking the trawler out today. It was perfect weather for it – a south-westerly wind and clear skies. Dónal knew Con was under pressure to keep the boat at sea as much as possible, just to cover the interest on its crippling mortgage. He also had heard that Con hadn't yet found anyone to replace him on the crew. When it came to money, he was as mean as his wife Sheila was with her dancers: no one else was willing to work for what he paid.

The smell of wet cement was overpowering at Con's bungalow. The driveway was covered in dribbles of rock-hard slurry as though a herd of concrete cattle had just been through. Dónal rapped on Con's bedroom window until eventually Con stumbled towards the double-glazing, bleary-eyed, bare-chested and with a protrusion rising from his red tracksuit bottoms.

"Jesus, Dónal, what are you like?" Con muttered, opening the window. "You scared the hell outta me and Sheila."

"It looks good for fishing," Dónal said.

Con looked out beyond him at the sea and to the cloud line on the horizon. "Are you sober?" he asked.

"Yep," said Dónal with a dry mouth.

"It's south-westerly?" Con said.

"Yeah."

"How's the tide?"

"Middling."

Con sighed wearily, considering his options.

"Ask the fecker where was he for the dancing last night," Sheila growled from the bed. "You're not thinking of taking him on again, are you?"

Con looked irritably at Dónal, and through clenched teeth said, "I'll be out to you in five. Fill the diesel and remember the drop of oil."

As Dónal stepped away from the window, he heard Sheila berating her husband.

In less than ten minutes, Con Crowley was gunning up the rusty old pickup, dressed in the same red tracksuit bottoms with a matching top and a brown woollen cap. Dónal had the trailer hitched on, with the outboard and five plastic crates in it, stacked on top of a snake's nest of blue-green nets. They drove to a neighbour's caravan two fields in from the school.

"Go get *Seáinín*, Dónal," Con said. "Don't bother knocking. He'll never hear, just tear straight in."

Dónal charged into the caravan to find Seáinín sprawled on the bed with a Swedish student who was in the area learning Irish.

"What the hell …!" cried Seáinín, trying to cover his voluminous mass with a paisley sheet. "Get out, you mangy …!"

"Con sent me," Dónal said. "We're going fishing."

Seáinín threw a boot at him and shouted, "Go wait in the truck."

Con's eyes were twinkling when Dónal sat into the cab.

"Was that OK, so?" he asked casually.

"No problem," Dónal said. "He'll be along in a minute."

"Good man, Dónal."

Seáinín emerged a few minutes later pulling his arm through a black bomber jacket.

"Did you send that prick in?" he demanded as he fell into the back of the Nissan and cuffed them both over the head. "And where the hell were you last night, you gobshite? You were meant to be in Brennan's. I had to do the Walls of Limerick on my own with Deirdre and she smelt bleedin' rank."

Con laughed.

"How are the lessons going?" Con asked.

"With Ulrika?" Seáinín said. "She's finding the grammer awful hard."

"You just have to keep at her," Con said. "Keep drumming it into her."

"I'm doing my best," Seáinín said.

"No better man!"

Nothing more was said as they drove on and parked up beside the painters' scaffolding that still cloaked Bridie Brennan's bar.

Even as they got out and carried the oars and oarlocks down to the water and rowed out to the *Radharc na Mara*, they remained silent. It was as if the glass-flat sea and empty world demanded it. Even the birds were eerily absent; the gulls were still nesting in the far cliffs. Every slash of the oar through the sheet of water was like a violent exhalation.

Once they reached the trawler, Con squatted down on to an upturned fish crate and barked out orders.

"You get the breakfast started," he said to Dónal, lighting a cigarette. "Seáinín and I will work on the engine."

Con sat for a moment savouring the first few mouthfuls of tobacco, looking around him, wincing at the too numerous blotches of brown primer that were valiantly trying to fend off the outbreaks of rust that threatened every seam of the wheel house, the net scaffold and the engine cavity. The winches looked particularly fragile, their surfaces a mass of calloused black-purple rust, as though very little core metal remained to stop them from crumbling entirely. He sat there gloomily for a moment until the smell of frying rashers brought him to his feet and he headed down below deck. He was loath to break the perfect silence with the thrum of diesel engines, but the mortgage had to be paid somehow.

"Any ideas where to go?" he called up from below.

"Out by Valentia," Seáinín's voice shouted from the cold storage. "The Sweeneys landed a fair catch there last week – just a bit north of the wreck, towards Barra Head."

"And you believe them?" said Con. "Those bastards would lie to Jesus in Gethsemane. We'll head for Drumlish – it was grand there before. Switch on the bilge pump, and we'll flush out that hold before we go."

Nine

Rachel and Charlotte fought again on the bus to Cornwall. There was something about being holed up beside each other for long periods that provoked their mutual antagonism, highlighting their absolutely divergent characters and interests. They chatted for a while about Mabel and the night before, and then fell silent until boredom got the better of them about an hour into the bus ride. The vast mechanically shaped fields and meanly apportioned groves depressed Charlotte, and as usual she found herself returning to her main topic of interest.

"You know it kills me that you won't wear your pentagram," she said.

"Don't start," Rachel warned.

"What?" Charlotte cried. "You should be proud – these rights were hard fought for. You know, once I won $400 in a tombola raffle at the local store, and they took a photo of me to put up on their wall. They were just handing me the cheque when the manager noticed the pentagram and asked would I mind having another photo taken without 'my necklace'. I refused, of course! So I never got the prize. That's how committed you need to be."

"You're the one who needs to be committed," Rachel murmured through her teeth.

"Sorry?" Charlotte said.

"Nothing," Rachel said.

"What did you say to me?" Charlotte said, her voice rising hysterically.

"Nothing, sorry, I'm just tired," Rachel said.

"Don't you dare judge me, bitch," Charlotte said.

Rachel realised she had struck a nerve and thought it wise to back down, but she couldn't help herself.

"I was just saying that sometimes what seems normal and sane to one person can look different to others."

"You cow!" Charlotte screamed.

Rachel looked at her with a smirk, glad to have scored a point. "Maybe we both should just draw our hands for a while," she said sarcastically.

Charlotte got up and moved to another seat behind her and stared out the window, seething quietly.

They looped off the motorway into a grim industrial estate on the outskirts of a town, bumping over traffic-calming devices and growing gradually hotter as the bus's fan struggled to cope with the idling speed. At a smashed-up shelter, they picked up ten more passengers, some of whom had to stand in the aisle. Charlotte and Rachel both had strangers sitting beside them.

As the bus was pulling out of the town again, Rachel reached around and asked Charlotte for the water bottle which was in her bag.

"No," Charlotte said.

"Sorry?"

"No," Charlotte said again. "No way."

"Please."

"Not if you're going to talk to me like that."

"Oh, for God's sake!" Rachel said.

The people sitting beside them pretended not to hear. They realised they were Americans and had been on their guard, suspecting that perhaps they might cause some type of scene, as they so often did – even just something minor like gushing at the sight of an old castle or attempting to engage them over-enthusiastically in conversation.

"I mean it," Charlotte called back to Rachel, "you've got to start treating me with some respect."

A spinsterish woman pursed her lips and blushed on their behalf. Rachel reached around and tried to grab the bag, but Charlotte pulled it to her, accidentally scrapping Rachel's wrist with the front buckle.

"Ouwww!" Rachel screamed, rather too loudly.

The man beside her pulled away lest it was presumed that he was somehow involved – or that her exuberance was contagious. She sulked for a moment and then quickly reached over the seat and slapped Charlotte roundly on the head. This made the scratch on her wrist break open and it began to bleed slightly. She didn't notice at first and continued to flay out at Charlotte, who was leaning back into her seat out of range, clutching the bag safely between her thighs. Both of them were too engrossed in themselves to notice the other passengers. They didn't even seem to notice when the bus stopped and the driver got up and began to squeeze his way down the aisle towards them.

"What's happening here …" he began, but then noticing the blood on Rachel's arm, he yelled, "Oh Christ!"

"Just give me the water," Rachel was saying, still focused entirely on Charlotte.

Charlotte had spotted the driver and began to throw him imploring looks.

"Is this girl harassing you?" he asked her.

Before Charlotte could reply, Rachel butted in.

"She cut me!" she cried, brandishing her arm. "Look!"

"Do you two know each other?" he asked.

"She's my niece," Charlotte said haughtily.

"I am not," Rachel screamed.

"Look, I don't have time for this," the driver said. "You're both getting off right now."

"But we're going to Avebury," Charlotte said indignantly, "and to Tentagal to see Merlin's cave."

"Get off!" the driver said. "And make sure you put something around that wrist first – I don't want any blood on my seats."

Charlotte and Rachel had no choice but to take their bags and leave. They walked down the aisle still feeling too resentful to be embarrassed.

"Now look what you've done," Charlotte said as they watched the bus pulling away from them back on to the main road. Rachel was too upset by the sight of the blood to care.

Charlotte sighed and dropped her duffle bag on the ground wearily. She started rooting around in it, pulling out the water bottle and the tiny brown phial of ointment she had used to sooth Rachel's cuts before. Rachel smiled when she saw the phial. She found herself laughing gently.

"What?" Charlotte said warily.

"It's like we're back where we started."

"Yeah," Charlotte chuckled, "now sit down and I'll see can I clean you up."

They both sat down cross-legged on the side of the road. Charlotte pulled out her bottle of bourbon, and they shared a few sips, Charlotte's noticeably longer and deeper.

Rachel threw herself back on the grass still laughing, and said, "What now?"

"Beats me," Charlotte said. "Witches' wisdom says if one path in the forest leads to a dead end, you immediately choose another. Let's just stick our thumb out and see where the road wants to bring us."

"You mean hitchhiking?" Rachel said, getting up on her elbows. "Are you mad? We'll have our throats slit."

Charlotte looked at her, bristling at the use of the term mad, but she decided to ignore it. "This isn't Oklahoma, child. It's the land of Robin Hood and Friar Tuck. We're two fair maidens lost in the lush meadows of Avalon – some great knight of the forest will come and rescue us. Now, go stand on the side of the road and stick your thumb out – they're more likely to stop for a pretty girl than an old hag."

Rachel sighed uncertainly, but got up and did as she was told. For the first half-hour cars sped by, taking no notice of them, except for one or two middle-aged drivers who slowed to a crawl, eyed Rachel until they spotted Charlotte on the ground behind her and then pulled away. Eventually, just as it was beginning to rain, an old woman in a camper van took pity on them and pulled over.

"Where are you headed?" the pleasant-faced septuagenarian with a grey bob and girlish cheeks asked from the driver's seat.

"Wherever," Charlotte announced grandiosely. "Following the spirit of Gwenevere and Merlin."

"Right," said the old woman stiffly.

"We're heading your direction," Rachel translated.

"That's fortunate," the woman said brightening. "Hop aboard, so."

Once they got inside and saw the elderly man sitting on the corduroy bench in the back, smoking a Rothmans, it became apparent why she hadn't questioned them further. He looked like someone you'd want a break from.

"That's my husband, Jack," she explained resignedly. "Say hello to the nice girls, Jack."

He looked far older than her, more brittle and creased. His lips were dry and puckered. Rachel noticed Charlotte eyeing his tattoos, and fearing that she was going to make some inappropriate comment, she stood between them and introduced herself, offering him her hand to shake. He just stared at her, then glanced slowly forwards towards his wife.

"Oh, no, he doesn't use that hand much," she said, watching them in the rear mirror. "Do you, Jack? He had a bit of an accident, you see."

The other hand was so nicotine stained that Rachel was loath to touch it, and so she put her arm down again.

"Why don't you girls join me up here in the front," the old woman said. "Jack has issues of world politics to contemplate."

She giggled at this, and Jack gave an almost inaudible grunt.

Rachel and Charlotte squeezed themselves in beside her, perching on the edge of the narrow passenger seat, their heads thrown forward, almost touching the windscreen.

"Well, this is nice," the woman said eagerly. "And what are you ladies up to today?"

"We're thinking of heading to Avebury," said Charlotte. "And the Chalice Well at Glastonbury. I really want to spend time with the Archangel Michael's energy at St Michael's Mount. I hear it's something else."

The old lady looked at them in concern. She turned on her indicator and made to pull over on to the side of the road.

"I'm sorry," she said as she slowed down, "but we're going to Southampton – it's nowhere near any of those places. We've a boat on the Isle of Wight."

"Perfect," Charlotte said. "Don't mind me – we're going wherever you're going."

"But …?" the old woman began.

"She gets ideas into her head," Rachel said soothingly. "Take no notice – the Isle of Wi … of wherever, is exactly where we were headed."

"Oh," the woman said.

Rachel shot a threatening look at Charlotte to stay quiet.

"Well, I suppose, it would be nice to have company," the woman said hesitatingly. "Jack can get very immersed in his concerns sometimes, can't you, Jackie?"

He wheezed something before taking another drag of his Rothmans. His mind seemed to have to struggle to even coordinate bringing the cigarette to his mouth, without attempting anything more ambitious.

"We could be useful if you get into any trouble – a flat tyre, for example," Rachel said. "It's good to have help on hand."

"I suppose," the woman said.

Rachel was beginning to realise she would have to take matters into her own hands if this trip wasn't to descend entirely into chaos.

"You're probably not as agile as you used to be," Rachel said, hammering home the point.

"Well, I suppose," the woman said, slightly taken aback. "In fact, it's one of the reasons we're making the trip – we sail back to Cork each summer. Jack's people have a farm there. His nephew runs it now – the old house is a cow shed, but they've a new place with a portico and a verandah, if you don't mind! We've been going for thirty years, although I'm not sure how long more we'll be able to manage it. The boat isn't getting any easier."

"You mean County Cork, Ireland?" Charlotte exclaimed.

"Yes, County Cork," the woman said.

"Like in the Blarney Stone and Murphy's stout?" Charlotte gushed.

The old woman stared anxiously at her again, discomfited by her enthusiasm.

"I suppose," she said finally.

"Oh-my-God!" Charlotte cried in a single deep exhalation.

"That's only my favourite place on earth! I've always dreamt of going there. Cork, Ireland, has been like my fantasy since for ever. I mean … wow! And your husband is really from there?"

The woman smiled awkwardly. Charlotte looked back at the wizened form of Jack as though he were an Olympian deity.

"A genuine Corkman!" she went on disbelievingly. "That's wild, really wild."

Jack coughed up a mouthful of phlegm and spat it out the window. It stuck to the outside of the pane, smearing into an artful orb, the various grades of mucus separating into different colours from cream to yellow to deep green central globules.

"Oh, Jack!" the woman said exasperated.

"Don't you see what this is?" Charlotte said to Rachel. "It's a sign! It's exactly what we were waiting for. The spirits of the land of St Patrick are calling us."

Jack had a coughing fit, and they all looked around in concern as he recomposed himself.

"We'll come with you," Charlotte informed the woman.

"Well now, I'm not sure," she said awkwardly. "It's only a small boat."

"No problem," Charlotte exclaimed. "We're both old sea-dogs. Aren't we, Rachie? Rachel's mom owns a chandlers back in Maine."

Rachel stared furiously at Charlotte but didn't say a word.

"Well, I'm really not sure," the woman said.

"You said yourself you needed a bit of help," Charlotte insisted.

"Yes, but I don't think we …"

"Fine, have it your way," Charlotte said cattily.

"I don't want to cause any offence," the woman said anxiously.

"No, no," Charlotte said sullenly. "My bad – all my bad."

"Sometimes my friend can be a bit impulsive," Rachel said.

Charlotte manoeuvred herself out of the front seat dejectedly and went to sit in the back with the old man.

They heard a raspy cry coming from him a few minutes later, and Rachel and the woman looked back to see Charlotte with her hands around his neck.

"Sorry," she said, throwing her hands up guiltily in the air. "I just thought a little massage would help to unblock his lungs. They're all congested."

"Ah," cooed the woman. "That's a sweet idea – isn't it, Jackie? Don't be afraid, the nice lady just wants to make you better."

The man looked petrified. Charlotte put her hands back on his shoulders and began kneading the back of his ribs with her thumbs. He shuddered under her, but didn't make any other outward signs of complaint.

"There, you go, Jack-the-lad," his wife said soothingly. "You'll be right as rain in no time … Give us a nice smile, pet, huh?"

Charlotte massaged the length of his spine and down his forearms, patting his greasy hair with the tops of her fingers like raindrops. His mouth was tense and his eyes looked indignant, but she could see he was sort of enjoying the sensation. She reached into her bag and picked out one of her phials pouring a few drops from it into a cup she found on a shelf and mixing in some water.

"Drink this," she said, "it'll help."

He cocked one eye closed, looked hard at the cup and grimaced before turning away.

She reached back into her bag and took out the bourbon, adding an inch of it to the cup without letting his wife see. She winked at him surreptitiously.

Jack grabbed desperately for the cup and cradled it in his shaking hand a moment, sniffing the sweet alcohol compulsively before swallowing it back in one go with a grateful smile.

"I don't smell booze back there, do I?" the woman said.

"No," Charlotte said confidently.

"You're not drinking, Jack, are you?" the woman asked anxiously.

He looked fearfully at Charlotte, who shot him a reassuring smile and said, "No, don't worry, lady, I just gave him a bit of medicine for his cough."

"Ah, aren't you a dear," the woman said.

The man licked his lips, smiling happily to himself.

"I'll just give him another drop, if that's OK," Charlotte said.

"Do make sure there's nothing too strong in it," his wife said, "He's got a sensitive stomach."

Charlotte poured him another generous measure and lay her hand on his inner thigh, stroking it firmly.

His face broke into a blissful smile, and they drove on south towards the coast.

Ten

Drumlish turned out to be a disaster. The seas were unseasonably rough for early June. They hauled their nets three times and caught nothing. On the fourth attempt, the nets caught in the winch as they were feeding them out in the middle of the night, and they were forced to cut a whole length loose. They lost a few hundred euros worth of netting, then the ice machine shorted out so that even if they had managed to land a good catch, they wouldn't have been able to keep it fresh.

Back in the harbour, they transferred the one half-full crate of plaice into the rowboat and rowed to the pier. The fish were sloshing around in a pool of melted ice with a pair of oilskin leggings thrown over them to keep away the flies. Dónal jumped out at the slipway, and Con passed him the crate. He turned to carry it up to the pick-up and found Gráinne there leaning against the builder's scaffolding outside Bridie's bar, her fingers playing with the collar of her heavy woollen coat and shifting from foot to foot awkwardly.

"What are you doing here?" he said.

"That's nice, Dónal," she said sarcastically. "Very nice."

"Well?" he said.

"Always the same," she said bitterly. "It's always the same."

"It's been a bad night," he said.

He refused to catch her eye but nevertheless could imagine the glower that was set upon her face. He stared down at Con and Seáinín who were watching from the rowboat. They both nodded up at her when she looked at them.

"It's about him," she said finally, angling her head in the direction of the quay wall.

Dónal followed her glance across and saw Colm sitting between two crayfish pots, his knees hugged in close to his chest and his arms, bent at the elbow, flapping up and down rapidly.

"Colm," Dónal called.

Colm didn't answer. He was grinding his teeth from side to side. Dónal ran across and laid a hand on his shoulder. "What's up?" he said.

Colm shrugged Dónal's hand away in a spasm that came from deep inside him.

"Are you OK?" Dónal said.

Colm still wouldn't say anything, and Dónal looked to Gráinne, who just stared indignantly back at Colm.

Dónal sighed. "What are you doing here?" he asked Colm. "Were you waiting?"

"I just need you to leave me alone right now," Colm said in a monotone slur.

Dónal had taught him to say this whenever things got too much for him. Seven years earlier, when Colm had finally started school, Dónal had been worried about how the other children would treat him, and he'd given him this line as a defence, a protective shield to use whenever things were tough. Since he was very little, he had always sought out a quiet corner and crouched down into himself when he needed time alone, and Dónal had told him to go right on doing it, but maybe to add those words in case others didn't understand.

Colm had been sitting on the quayside for almost two hours, waiting for Dónal and thinking – his mind shooting through different ideas to distract himself, such as the fact that humans have only three colour receptors, while birds have four and shrimps have eight. He was trying to imagine what they could see that he couldn't: blue and red made purple, but what about blue, red and ultraviolet? But no matter how hard he tried, he couldn't push out the memory that flashed before him.

Dónal turned reluctantly to Gráinne. "What happened?" he said impatiently.

"I don't know if I'm more angry with myself or him," she said.

"Why? What happened?"

"We tried a new thing in class this week, an American thing – show-and-tell. The children all bring in something from home and tell the class about it …"

"Grab the oars and bring them up, Dónal," Con shouted over.

"Just a minute," Dónal said.

"I met Colm yesterday," Gráinne continued, "and he said he had something that he would love to show the class. I told him to come in today and bring it. I was happy that he seemed so keen. I thought it was one of those nice sticks he carves …"

Gráinne stopped and winced. Con and Seáinín had climbed out of the boat and were piling up the equipment on the pier.

"Take hold of the other end of this crate, Dónal," Con said. "We'll haul the lot up in one go."

"Give me a minute," Dónal called to him.

"Stop mucking about and get over here!" Con warned.

Dónal grabbed the prow of the rowboat and the three of them carried it up the pier. He was looking back anxiously at Colm the whole time.

"So?" Dónal shouted over to Gráinne.

"It wasn't a stick," Gráinne said plaintively. "It was … Taytos."

"Taytos?" Dónal shouted over. "So, what's the problem?! The children must have loved that."

"That's not all he brought," Gráinne said. "He brought your kitten too."

"Kittens?"

"He had them both in the same box, a cardboard one with holes for air and a newspaper in the bottom to keep it clean," Gráinne said, trying to keep her voice even.

"Yeah? I don't get it!" Dónal said.

"When he opened the box ..." Gráinne began, but then started to cry.

"What?" Dónal exclaimed. "For Christ sake!"

"Taytos had attacked ..." she began. "The cat's insides were all over ... It's belly ripped open."

"Oh God!" Dónal said, running over to Colm who had started to cry.

"I just wanted them to see," he whimpered.

"Taytos jumped out as soon as the box was open," Gráinne called over. "She kissed Colm, even tried licking some of the children. There was blood ..."

"Jesus!" said Dónal.

A car horn began blaring at the top of the pier, and they looked around to see Jimmy, the postman and voluntary lifeboat coxswain, getting out of his van and opening the double doors of the lifeboat shed.

"*Glaoch éigeandála*," he shouted down to them. "*Beagán siar ó dheas ó Charraig an Urra. Chonacthas tóirse slándála sa spéir timpeall deich nóiméad ó shin. An féidir libh teacht liom, nó an bhfiafróidh mé an bhfuil Corrigan i mBridie's?*"

The lifeboat crew was a voluntary one, made up of whoever happened to be around at the time. Neither Con nor Dónal had been called out in over a year; it was right they should go. The call didn't sound all that serious, just a flare from a yacht a mile or two off shore – probably an inexperienced day-sailor with more money than sense.

"We'll do it," Con said, before switching to Irish after seeing the slight twitch of annoyance on Jimmy's face, "*Táimid díreach tagtha isteach agus beimid réidh i gceann soicind.*"

Jimmy was of the older generation, still wedded to the language. It was either Irish or nothing. He looked to Seáinín, who also turned to Irish, saying he'd bring the crate of fish to the buyer in town while Con and Dónal went with Jimmy.

Dónal knelt down in front of Colm. "Are you going to be all right?" he said and turned to Gráinne. "Keep an eye on him for me."

He pulled on the lifeboat oilskins that Jimmy handed him and grabbed hold of the bright orange Zodiac, and together they carried it down to the water.

Within minutes they had primed the engine, run through the checklist and were off, roaring towards Uarra, bouncing over the waves, leaving a ploughed-up trough behind them.

Eleven

When they pulled up at the marina in the Isle of Wight, Charlotte had again offered their services on the trip across to Cork, but the woman had said it wasn't possible. She already suspected that Charlotte was a bad influence on her husband. He had perked up considerably on the journey south, which wasn't really a bad thing in itself, but it made him more voluble and demanding, and she had grown used over the months to his semi-comatose state. She had come to depend on his indolence and incapacity, and was irritated by the fact that he had begun telling his old stories again. Ever since Charlotte turned up, he'd been cracking his weary jokes, laughing at every stupid punch line that his boss had fed him over forty years. She had spent her life listening to these and would probably have divorced him long ago had not guilt set in after his creeping dementia began wiping his mind clean of everything a few years before. Now he was turning giddy again, unpredictable. It was the last thing she needed.

Charlotte wouldn't have admitted that there was an ulterior motive behind the attention she was giving Jack. She had convinced herself she was being kind purely for the sake of it. She had cast herself as the charitable heroine of the situation, and she found it deeply offensive that his wife hadn't been more appreciative of her efforts. The fact that her offer of help on the trip to

Cork had been dismissed outright was an insult, a slur on every-thing Charlotte stood for, in particular her Wicca beliefs. It was in breach of every natural law to refuse the hand of friendship when proffered in good spirits. Charlotte had tried explaining this, but the woman had just sniggered at the mere mention of witchcraft.

"Oh you are a hoot!" she had said.

This had infuriated Charlotte beyond words, especially con-sidering she could clearly see the woman dabbled in such matters herself. Charlotte had seen her stack of crab apple chutneys and bilberry jams on shelves in the rear of the van and knew straight away that she was some kind of nature guardian or wild forager. It disgusted Charlotte that the woman didn't have the courage to come out and admit it openly. She must have noticed Charlotte's pentagram, but she hadn't said a word about it. This was what was wrong with womenfolk today: they weren't prepared to stand up for their beliefs, to be open about their worship of the good fairies. Charlotte found it hard to tell all the different Wicca devotees, human goddesses and nature practitioners apart nowadays, but she could tell straight off that the woman dabbled. That much was clear.

"Don't take me for a fool," Charlotte had sneered. "I can see you're a forest gatherer. I could tell you were the minute I set eyes on you. You lot always have a problem with us American witches. What you need to realise is the tradition never died out, you know? Just because our Founding Fathers were Presbyterians does-n't mean the womenfolk lost their beliefs. We kept the old lore alive, and we don't like being talked down to by you lot. My peo-ple were descended from Goody Toole from Norwich … what do you have to say about that? Are you afraid I'm planning on edg-ing into your territory? Because it's not about that, sister. Me and my girl, we're just passing through. Travellers on the road."

The woman was too perplexed to say anything.

"What's wrong, cat got your tongue?" Charlotte said. "I'm glad we're talking turkey now, you and me. We're on the same wavelength."

The woman had looked anxiously back at Jack.

"I think we should give the old girl a chance?" he mumbled.

She stared back at him aghast, but managed to give some non-committal reply about giving the matter some thought overnight before making a final decision in the morning. She then grabbed Jack and steered him hurriedly to the clubhouse, leaving Charlotte and Rachel to find a room for themselves in a cheap boarding house two streets in from the seafront.

The landlady of the boarding house had come out on to the front steps as they approached, as if suspecting something was up and wanting to ward them off. Her greeting was frosty and became even more so when she noticed Charlotte's pentacle.

"What do you ladies want?" she sniped.

"A room," Charlotte said demurely.

"Are you intending to share just the one?" she asked in a sly, accusatory tone, as though she was already imagining the sordid rituals they might perform together.

"Yes, we'd like a double," Charlotte had said. "Two beds."

Rachel turned to Charlotte and asked timidly, "Would it be OK if I had a room of my own?"

Charlotte stared at her.

"Why?" she said. "I'm not made of money, you know. The universe is abundant and will provide for us all, but there's no need to go to excess. What's wrong with sharing?"

"Nothing, it's just ..."

"I don't snore if that's what you're worried about – I didn't last night, did I? And I don't fart much ... unless after a big bowl of onions or kidney ..."

"It's not that. It's just …" Rachel said.

"What?" Charlotte had blustered. "You're not thinking of bringing a boy back, are you? Forgotten all about poor Nathaniel so quickly?"

The remark hit Rachel like a body blow. A wave of both anger and misery swept over her, but she didn't have the heart to react. She just stared at the ground, realising how powerless she was. Charlotte took a step back and looked at her.

"What?" she said. "Is it the cutting?! Are you still cutting yourself?"

Charlotte yanked up Rachel's blouse, but the cuts had faded to a few faint pinkish ridges by now.

"Fuck off!" Rachel cried.

"Oh, I know what's up," Charlotte enthused. "I should have guessed. Teenagers – you're all the same! You probably want to … well, play with yourself a bit. That's OK. We're all women here. Seen it all, done it all. It's good to free the juices now and again. Your reproducing energies are your friends, I want you to remember that. Anyway, I'm planning on going for a few drinks after dinner, so you'll have the room to yourself."

A blush of fury swept up through Rachel from her belly to the tip of her head and she turned away. The landlady was staring at them wide-eyed.

"We'll take a double," Charlotte said breezily. "Non-smoking, if you please."

The woman handed them a key and sent them upstairs to a damp windowless room. Charlotte collapsed on one of the beds and sighed. She was relieved that things were beginning to work out at last. She could see where the road was leading her now, and it was exciting. Ireland was definitely the destination. She was already beginning to forgive Jack's wife for her inhospitality. It was only natural that witches would be suspicious of one another, after all; at heart they were traditionalists, determined to maintain the status quo. Charlotte realised it was up to her to be diplomatic and to try to adapt to local ways, like the way she had slipped the term 'if you please" into her speech just now, which she was inordinately proud of.

Rachel was sprawled out on her bed with her headphones on and her music turned up loud, trying to block Charlotte out, although it was hard, as she was humming and muttering to herself loudly.

"I was only trying to help," Charlotte said to no one in particular, her mood darkening all of a sudden as she thought further about Jack's wife. "That's what really sickens me. Offering our services for free, gratis and for nothing, and they just threw them back in our faces. That sort of thing hurts, you know? You could see she was jealous. That much was a clear as the nose on my face. She was so jealous! Of me, and I think of you too, Rachel dear, of your beauty, your youth. She hated that."

Rachel tried to tune her out, but it was hard. Charlotte was so overbearing. Rachel cursed herself again for having ever agreed to come away with her. She was just too unpredictable. Instinctively Rachel's fingers sought out her old scars and began tracing gently along the crests. She noticed Charlotte looking at her and turned away, growing angrier at herself for having got into this mess, for not making better decisions. Nathaniel had always said to be clear about what you wanted, to never go with the flow. Only dead fish did that, he used to say. Dead fish and lemmings.

They went out for a fish and chip supper later that night, neither of them saying much, and afterwards Charlotte had gone to the pub while Rachel went back to the room and cried herself to sleep. She slept fitfully until at around dawn she was woken by the sound of Charlotte's alarm clock.

"Wake up, sleepy head," Charlotte slurred. "Lots to do."

Rachel looked around her blearily. Charlotte appeared to be exhausted, as if she had gone to bed only moments before.

"Leave me alone," Rachel said.

"I mean it," Charlotte said. "We're pulling out – plans have changed."

"What?"

"I sorted it all out last night. Come on, get dressed, and I'll tell you on the way."

Rachel, too tired to question her further, pulled on some clothes, stuffed her things in her bag and followed Charlotte out, doubling back to leave money for the room on the reception desk as Charlotte hadn't shown any intention of doing it herself.

"Oh, aren't you the honourable one," Charlotte teased her when she caught up with her.

Rachel tried to query her about her plans, but Charlotte just kept walking determinedly towards the seafront. Finally Rachel grabbed her and demanded an explanation.

"We're going to Cork," Charlotte said. "It's all sorted. I met up with Jack last night for a few drinks. He apologised for his wife's behaviour, and he wanted me to apologise to you too on his behalf. He's a nice old goat, at heart. It turns out that a friend of his had a boat that he needs to have brought to Ireland, and he says we can take it."

"Really?" Rachel said cagily. "But we don't know how to sail."

"I do," Charlotte had assured her. "Now keep moving. We have to get going before the tides change."

There had been no time to discuss it further. Charlotte made sure of that. She slipped in underneath the marina fence, as the place was not yet open, and dragged Rachel in with her. They walked out along the line of boats, stopping at one that was conveniently moored furthest out. It was a beautiful yacht, a short, slim racer with a beige hull and the name Valhalla inscribed in neat black font along the waterline – a lean, stripped-back vessel with no brass or glass, or even any wood, except for two slender lengths of varnished cedar along the deck. Its hull, deck and galley were all extruded from a single piece of fibreglass like an aeroplane washroom or a shower suite in a cheap hotel. On deck, all that could be seen was a small blue outboard and its red fuel can, which Charlotte was already storing away in a locker to make room for herself in the narrow cockpit.

"Hurry, come on," Charlotte called to Rachel, who was still hesitantly considering things on the jetty. "There really isn't time."

Rachel had a thousand questions she wanted to ask but, too worn out to form a coherent sentence, she instead just shrugged and grudgingly made her way out to the boat. She knew a bit about outboards from summer trips with her father and offered to help start it, but Charlotte refused in a brusque manner, saying that it would be a crime to disturb the morning calm with such noise. Instead she began pulling out the sails from the fore hatch.

"You mean you're going to try sailing straight out of the marina?" Rachel said.

"Why not?"

"But why bother?" Rachel said. "Why risk it when the engine's there?"

"Just get over here and help me thread the sail."

They spent half an hour working in a light drizzle, attaching the mainsail and raising it, and then by a stroke of good fortune a light breeze arose, allowing them push off and sail straight out of the mouth of the marina.

Rachel asked Charlotte why the boat owner hadn't come to show them the ropes and see them off, and where and when had they arranged to meet up with him in Cork.

"Because it's five o'clock in the morning," Charlotte replied matter-of-factly.

"OK, but why leave so early?"

"I told you. The tides."

The rain grew harder, and Rachel tried to go below deck, but the main hatch was bolted.

"Where are the keys?" she asked, and Charlotte just shrugged. It was only then that Rachel allowed herself face the facts that had been rising in her mind. Something was not quite right here.

"We don't have permission to take this boat, do we?" she said with a sinking heart.

"It's not a boat," Charlotte said. "It's a yacht – a lithe, graceful racing yacht. You ought to show more respect."

"Have you stolen it?"

"No! Of course not," Charlotte said in a hurt tone. "I told you, Jack said we could have it. His friend wants it brought over to Cork for the summer season. But Jack had wanted to talk to him first to see what he thought about letting us do it. He was sure his friend would love the idea. I planned to wait and meet them all for breakfast, get some pointers and all that, but then I thought about that evil cow, Miss Bitch-face herself. You know how she is? What was the point in waiting if that wench was just going to stop us? I guarantee you, she'd find some way of screwing it up. I presume you noticed she's on the dark side? Well, the thing I realised is that she probably dabbles in black magic. In fact, I'm sure of it. That's what's at the root of the whole thing. And although my magic is strong, it's white magic – no match to the crack she's peddling."

"Oh God!" Rachel cried.

"What? She's evil. I wanted to protect you from that."

"We've stolen a boat," Rachel muttered dejectedly.

"It's a yacht! And we haven't stolen it. We're doing someone a favour, that's all. You've gotta believe me."

"You're insane!"

Charlotte lashed straight out, slapping her across the cheek.

"Don't you dare!" she said. "I warned you, don't you …"

Charlotte walked away a few paces to calm herself, while Rachel sunk to her knees with her head in her hands, muttering to herself under her breath. "Oh God!"

After a moment, Charlotte swung around saying, "I'm ashamed of you, you know that? You're as ignorant of the real world as you are of the Wicca world. I'd understand if you weren't up to speed on Wicca matters – you've been away from it a while after all – but your ignorance of your own world is unforgivable. It's about time you started looking around you, girl, really looking around you."

Rachel sighed. The rain was pounding down at this stage. She yanked at the main hatch until it came off its hinges, then slunk down below deck.

"The world works on a trust-and-receive basis," Charlotte shouted after her. "That's the secret you gotta learn. Does a bird bitch and moan when it gets up in the morning? No, it sings! It knows it needs worms to survive and that it'll find them. That's what I'm talking about. It's how the world works, on a need by need basis. You needed to be rescued from your dumb daily stabbing routine, and I came along. Now, we need to get to Cork, and so this opportunity presents itself. Everyone's a winner. We all share what we have; that's how the world works, or is supposed to at any rate. Jack and his friend have done us a favour, but I'll bet you we'll end up returning it five-fold."

"Bullshit," Rachel called up.

"What? What's wrong with you, girl?"

Rachel said nothing.

"They need the boat brought to Cork," Charlotte reasoned.

"So, why not just wait and let them give it to us?"

"I told you, the black witch! Have you not been listening?

Anyway, Jack wasn't sure his friend actually intended to bring it to Cork exactly – just somewhere in Ireland. But I bet you they'll be glad in the end. Cork is special; that's what I think, and I haven't even been there! And what's more, Jack agrees. He says his friend works too hard. He never takes a break. That's what the yacht was for, his retirement, but he just won't let up. What do you reckon he'll come over to Cork and see a whole new way of life? He'll end up thanking us, I promise you. I have a good feeling about this."

"Jesus!"

"I wish you were more open, Rachel," Charlotte said. "I mightn't have invited you along if I thought you were so stitched up. You remind me of your mother."

Rachel stuck her head up through the hatch. "We're going to end in jail, you know that?" she said wearily.

"Rubbish," Charlotte countered. "Granted, the man might be a bit pissed at first, but you'll see …"

"We're in serious trouble."

Charlotte just laughed. "I can tell you one thing for certain," she said. "Jack won't let him go to the cops."

Rachel guffawed. "Why? Is he a good wizard? A sugarplum fairy or something?"

"He just knows that it would be in his best interest not to make a fuss, let me put it that way."

"What do you mean?" Rachel said suspiciously.

"Well, let's say I did him a little favour last night. Gave him something to remember me by. I doubt he'll want his wife to know."

"What?" Rachel said suspiciously, and then gradually realising from the smug look on Charlotte's face. "Oh God, no!"

"What? I was just giving him pleasure. You can't possibly be against that … helping an old man. That's our role in life, Rachel, to help out when and where we can. The problem is everyone is

too busy to see it nowadays. That's why I left my job. I was literally being eaten up by it. I spent two years in the Federal
Detention Service, helping former inmates get used to life in the
outside world. You'd see them coming out, determined to stay
clean, to keep away from whatever it was that had put them
inside, but eventually they'd slip back. They'd always slip back. At
one time I had eight of them sleeping on my floor. It was like a
puppy sanctuary or something. But it was the only way I could
be sure they'd stay clean. That's my style, to take a hands-on
approach to things. If you don't like it, you can lump it."

The first part of the journey was the trickiest as they had to keep
out of the way of container ships in the English Channel. There
were numerous tidal influences, sandbars, opposing winds and a
frightening amount of traffic, but they took it very slowly and
managed to make reasonable headway by keeping in near the
coast and occasionally making sudden last-minute changes of
course and allowing themselves drift with their sails into the wind
until they were out of harm's way. Rachel spent much of the time
lying on deck looking over the prow watching out for rocks, as
Charlotte admitted she had never learnt to read charts properly
because of her dyslexia. By early afternoon of that first day, they
had reached the Devon coast, where the waters became suddenly
choppier and Rachel began to feel a bit queasy. Theirs was the
only yacht to be seen now, and although the isolation was disqui-
eting, the extra space made things less stressful. The boat handled
well, its smooth hull riding easily through the waves. Overall,
Charlotte proved to be an adequate sailor – she was glad that so
much of what she had learnt as a twelve-year-old in Chesapeake
Bay had stayed with her. It was a hard slog, constantly beating into
the prevailing wind, but the gusts were fairly moderate, and the
swell was hardly noticeable for long stretches. Once they rounded

Land's End and left the English coastline behind them, the wind picked up, and they kept to a steady seven knots until early evening when they had the pleasure of a perfect sunset off the Cornish coast. When darkness fell, Rachel wanted to drop anchor, but Charlotte insisted she wasn't tired and would keep going. In the end, Rachel went below deck and slept fitfully to the clinking of shackles overhead and the slurping of water splashing against the hull. She awoke to find they were just passing out of English waters, according to Charlotte, who had no real way of knowing where she was. They spent the day sailing across the Celtic Sea until they caught sight of the coast of Waterford that evening.

They dropped anchor on the second night because of the increased risk of rocks, and Rachel spent the following morning, once again, lying on her tummy keeping an eye out ahead as they rounded the southern tip of Ireland. When they came upon a spectacular band of soaring cliffs, Charlotte reckoned that they must have reached County Cork. She said she could feel it in her bones. But since the wind was strong and they had no charts for this area, they decided they would keep on going until they saw a harbour with a clear channel into it. Hopefully by then the wind would have slackened.

Both of them grew to rather enjoy the journey. They were entranced by the beauty of the landscape; the sheer vibrancy of the headlands plunging into the Atlantic, the purple sheen of the limestone cliffs towering above and the heather-clad mountains aflame with tiny purple blossoms that reminded Rachel of Nathaniel's suits. There were white blotches of sheep scattered on the inclines of each peninsula and stone-walled fields trailing down to reed-bearded morsels of land that ran straight into the sea – like sacrifices to appease a hungry god, Charlotte said. The headlands ran on seemingly for ever, a series of hulking shapes lined up like pale mauve dominoes retreating into the distance, all of them slowly being digested by the waves like a snail eating through a leaf.

Around mid-afternoon, Charlotte saw a pod of dolphins coming in from the west.

"Oh my God!" she screamed at Rachel. "Look, for God's sake. Look!"

Rachel looked.

"It must be a sign!" Charlotte gushed. "What do they want? What do you think they want?" She was rushing around the deck wildly. "What? Tell me, what?"

Rachel was excited too but was somewhat put off by Charlotte's excessive reaction. She tried focusing her attention on the dolphins themselves. They were so graceful, exalted. They sparked a long-forgotten memory within her; something Nathaniel had said the evening of the accident. It was when they were lying on the floor after the movie, eating the last of the popcorn, and Melanie had made some comment about the oddly shaped staircase that Rachel's mother had designed for the house.

"Are you going to include kooky touches like that when you're an architect," she said, "just to mess with the minds of the folks who get to live in your houses."

"She's not even sure she's going to be an architect," Nathaniel had said. "She's doing biology."

"I am?" Rachel had said, reaching over to him.

"Sure," he said. "That's exactly what you'll do. Marine biology."

He said it with such confidence that it was as though he had always known it. And although Rachel had never considered it before, something about the way he said it made it seem real to her. She could picture herself out on a research vessel somewhere studying marine life.

The moment was lost as Lek had said, "Isn't that just about studying plankton orgies and dolphins copulating and stuff? If you do it, my advice is get yourself a first-rate wetsuit and keep away from the tiger sharks."

"Why *not* spend your life learning about dolphins copulating?" Nathaniel had said defensively, and Rachel suddenly realised that it was actually he who wanted to study marine biology. He had never talked much about what he was going to do after school before. An image suddenly came to her of the two of them going off to college together to study, and maybe working side by side out on a research boat, discovering things, just the two of them, and at night peeling off their wetsuits and hopping into bed together. Tears flooded Rachel's eyes at the thought of it and she let out a sob, not only for Nathaniel but for everything: her life, her friends, all the things she had left behind. Thinking back over that evening, she remembered Lek passing Nathaniel another beer and warning him that new research revealed some unsavoury aspects about dolphins' propensity for gang rape. Everyone in the room had scoffed at the notion – Lek was liable to make things up when drunk – but he insisted he was telling the truth.

"I read it in *Science,*" he cried. "Don't shoot the messenger. All that jumping out of the water is supposed to be a sure sign that some poor female is down below getting it from every guy in the pod. Those classy jumps they do are like a post-coital two-fingers to the poor girl down below. What gets me is all those happy-clappy moms and dads snapping photos of jumping dolphins – they're actually recording a rape scene."

Nathaniel had been outraged and tried defending the dolphins, but he'd been too drunk to make a proper effort. That was always the problem with Nathaniel; by midway through the night, he'd be no good to anyone. Rachel and he had an idyllic relationship up until around 11 p.m. After that it was just embarrassing. He'd always be really apologetic in the morning, genuinely so, and no matter how wrecked he was, he'd somehow manage to get himself up and dressed, and would appear eager to do whatever they'd planned for the following day, bike-riding or hiking or whatever. Rachel was aware that she'd never really confronted the problem or even really allowed herself admit he had one. One thing was certain, if he'd been sober, there's no way he would have hit the first deer. It hadn't come racing out of the forest towards them; it had been standing stock still in the middle of the roadway for quite some time, just watching them. Rachel had spotted it from far off and presumed Nathaniel had too. It was the fawn she had seen hiding in the forest watching its mother. Nathaniel must have been too drunk to notice.

Rachel suddenly felt light-headed, unsure whether she was going to cry or laugh, but in the end a wild, tragic laugh came as the thought of a dolphin committing rape in front of boatloads of happy tourists filled her mind. She was determined to block out thoughts of Nathaniel and was about to tell Charlotte Lek's dolphin theory when her attention was suddenly caught by the appearance of a wonderfully agile blue-grey torso of a dolphin soaring out of the water beside her. Its huge shimmering flanks whipping up and over before pounding back down again, leaving the water rippling like shook foil. A shout of pure emotion came from her in spite of herself, a surge of elation and relief that banished everything else. She looked around to Charlotte, who was just in the process of pulling her jacket off and frantically undoing the buttons of her shirt. Rachel was about to shout to her, to ask what she was up to, but the urge to look around in case another dolphin jumped was too great. When she looked back towards Charlotte, she noticed that she was now down to her bra and had her jeans half way down and was yanking at her boots trying to kick them off.

"Don't just stand there!" Charlotte cried, "They need our help. They're calling to us. Can't you hear them?"

"Huh?"

"Come on, quickly, help," Charlotte said, freeing herself from a boot and pointing towards the water. "They're calling us."

She didn't bother pulling the rest of her trousers off, just bent her knees and dived straight in.

"What the hell …?" Rachel yelled after her.

She jumped below deck and pulled out two life jackets, throwing them out to Charlotte who was by now screeching with the shock of the water. The dolphins had disappeared the moment she splashed in.

"Come back," Charlotte was screaming at them. "Come back, please!"

She managed to grab one of the life jackets and was treading water and looking around her desperately, dipping her head underneath occasionally and calling to them. Her teeth had begun to chatter. She and the yacht had begun to move apart the moment she left it. The current was strong, and Rachel was not experienced enough to know how to counteract the drift or to manoeuvre the yacht back around. Charlotte was beginning to realise she had lost the dolphins, and she turned reluctantly to swim back to the boat, but the current was stronger than she anticipated, and it began hauling her in the opposite direction.

"Go about," she screamed through chattering teeth to Rachel. "Go about!"

Rachel knew more or less what was meant by this but had never actually done the manoeuvre herself. She pushed the rudder away from her as far as it would go until the boom swung across. It was a messy turn, and the new course didn't bring her any closer to Charlotte. She tried adjusting the jib a bit as she had seen Charlotte do and aligning the rudder, but it didn't make much difference. Unless Charlotte was able to swim faster than she was doing now, it was unlikely she could beat the current.

Rachel realised this and dropped the main sail as quickly as she could, pulling out the engine and screwing it frantically to the backboard with blood dripping from her fingers where she had scraped them on a clasp. She shivered involuntarily at the sight of the blood, but focused herself and pulled the ignition chord a few times. The engine caught, but then spluttered out. After checking the fuel line, she realised it was kinked, but even after she had straightened it, the engine still wouldn't start. When she looked up again she saw Charlotte had drifted further away and her strokes were getting weaker.

"Keep swimming Charlotte!" she called, racing down below deck and ransacking the place until she found flares. She read the instructions quickly and fired one up into the sky.

Twelve

Dónal spotted the yacht on the horizon and called back to Jimmy to let him know. It was an elegant vessel with clean lines silhouetted against the grey sky and a bare mast that arched athletically back, making it look more like a designer's sketch than an actual yacht. It was a change from the usual fat cruisers that turned up here in the summer, helmed by finicky city folk dressed in Helly Hanson gear and docksiders, who regarded the surroundings with a mix of bemusement and sentimentality and who meticulously laid out white fenders along the length of their gunwales to ensure they never got too close to the place. It was nice to visit rustic ports like these, as long as no grubby trawler or semi-perished tyre hanging from a quayside actually came in contact with them. Dónal spotted the life jackets bobbing in the water a little way off and pointed them out to Con and Jimmy. They radioed back to the coastguard station to say the yacht had been sighted and that there was possibly a man overboard.

When they reached the boat, Charlotte was still treading water with frantic resolve, clinging on to both life jackets and staring deliriously up at them.

"You came!" she shouted with a beatific beam. "You really came! I knew you would, and I promise you I will now fulfil my side of the bargain."

Her teeth were chattering so much that the men found it hard to make out what she was saying. She had evidently lost her bearings a bit.

"Are you all right there, love?" Con called down to her, while Jimmy was edging the zodiac in closer.

"Have no doubt," she chattered, "I won't forget my promise."

Jimmy lent out and grabbed her hand, heaving her up to where Dónal could catch her and swing her in over the gunwale. They wrapped her in a blanket while Jimmy took her pulse. She didn't seem too badly off; no serious signs of hypothermia. Dónal pulled the lid off a can of self-heating soup and handed it to her. She sat staring down into it in silence as the lifeboat turned towards the yacht.

"Charlotte? Are you OK?" Rachel shouted when they got near enough.

Charlotte didn't even look up. She was lost in her own world.

"She's fine, I reckon," Con called across. "We'll bring her in to shore and have her checked out just in case. Can you follow us in?"

"I can't start the engine," she shouted.

"Can you sail her?"

"No," Rachel said.

"Why not?" Con said.

"I don't know how."

Con shook his head. "I'll get the boy here to come help you. He'll sort it out. I need to get this woman back to shore."

Con brought the zodiac alongside, and Dónal jumped across.

"Does she have any clothes?" Con said, pointing to Charlotte.

Rachel gathered up the jacket, shirt and trousers that Charlotte had shed and handed them across to Jimmy, who began straight away to dress her, brusquely, as you would an uncooperative toddler or a rigor mortised corpse.

155

"We'll meet you at the pier," Con said, swinging the zodiac away. "Radio me if you have any problems."

"I don't have a radio," Rachel called.

Con idled the engine. "You don't have a radio?!"

"I don't think so," Rachel said.

Con shook his head. He opened a hatch underneath his bench and pulled out a day-glow orange bag and tossed it on board the yacht, then sped off towards land.

"So, what's wrong with this engine?" Dónal said when they were left alone.

"Don't know."

"Has it got fuel?"

"Think so."

Dónal followed the fuel line back to the canister beneath the bench and shook it. It was half full. He pulled the ignition chord a few times, but there was no response. He unscrewed the fuel valve and blew into it, then screwed it back and tried again, but it still wouldn't start.

"We can sail," Rachel said.

I thought you couldn't sail," Dónal said.

"I can't, but you can," Rachel said.

"No, I can't."

"You can't sail!" Rachel exclaimed. "But you're part of the lifeboat. What good is that!"

Dónal sighed. "Can you just stay quiet?"

"Sorry?" Rachel snapped.

"Just stay calm," Dónal said, staring at the engine, trying to work out what to do. All he really wanted was to get back to Colm and sort out the Taytos problem. It wasn't a good sign. Colm had been making great progress settling into himself over the last year. He was less anxious now than he used to be and he seemed like he might almost be ready to engage with the world on his own terms. This incident with Taytos didn't sound good. Dónal felt the pressure jars begin to swell, but he wouldn't let them. He focused his attention on the problem at hand.

"It just seems odd," Rachel said. "That's all."

"What?" Dónal said distractedly.

"That you can't sail."

"You know what I think is odd?" Dónal snapped, "That you're out here without a radio."

"Easy now!" Rachel said. "Easy, Tiger, I know you're all caught up in the Great Hero role, rescuing us and all, but … Well, I don't want to burst your bubble or anything, I just thought that you guys would know how to sail. My mistake."

"Look, I need to work on this engine now, OK?" he said.

Rachel found herself feeling a mix of anxiety and elation. The fear and relief had made her agitated, like she felt before a race. There was something about Dónal that provoked her – his stubbornness and the way his rough, square jaw seemed to chew over a problem. The idea of being rescued by such a man was appealing. Being rescued by anyone was exciting, but particularly someone with a touch of Celtic hero to him.

"What's in the bag?" she said, pointing at the thing Con had tossed over.

Dónal frowned and pulled a knife out of his pocket to tinker with the engine screws, scraping oil residue away and tightening them.

"You guys probably carry brandy, don't you?" Rachel asked capriciously. "For medicinal purposes."

He turned to her and sighed. She continued to stare at him straight in the eyes.

"Have you got a screwdriver?" he said wearily.

She looked at him petulantly out of the side of her eye. "How would I know?"

"Well, this is your boat," he said. "Now stop cod-acting and please just show me where you keep your tools."

"I don't know, I told you. I don't know!"

"Look, lady," Dónal said, "I'm just trying to help."

Rachel began to cry.

Oh Christ, Dónal thought. "What's wrong?" he said. "I'm sure this whole thing must ..."

She turned to him, raising a hand, and he thought she was about to slap him, but instead she touched his cheek, stroking it lightly. Neither of them said anything for a moment. Then she reached up on her toes and kissed him harshly on the lips.

"What ...?" he said.

She smiled coyly and brought her arms down around his waist, saying, "You're not really a lifeboat man are you?"

"Sure, I am," he said. "We all are."

"Thanks for saving me," she said and reached up and kissed him again.

"You're welcome."

"Just hug me, please," she said, and he stepped closer and hesitantly put his hands around her. She lent her head on his shoulder, and he pulled her to him again, tighter this time. Without thinking about it, he bent down and kissed the cleft of her lip. They locked eyes for a moment.

"Will Charlotte be OK?" she said, pulling back.

"The woman?" Dónal said. "Was she in the water long?"

Rachel shook her head.

"What was she doing there anyway, with her clothes half off?"

Rachel sighed. "Do you really want to know?"

He nodded.

"Now?" she said, grasping his belt.

He edged a little closer to her and brought his hands up under her T-shirt, rubbing them together to warm them when he felt the goose pimples rising on her skin. Rachel lent in to him, not allow-ing herself consider what she was doing. For the first time in a long while, she allowed herself forget everything. She took his arms and led him below deck, and they fell on to one of the berths together.

"Is she secure?" he asked, looking around him.

"What?"

"The yacht. Is she anchored fast?"

"I think so," she said. "I dropped an anchor front and back, and they seemed to hold."

"Let's hope you're right," he said, pulling a Kevlar sail over them. The mad scientist and the pressure jars had gone.

Thirteen

Charlotte was dropped at the room in town that was used as a clinic once a week, and the nurse was called to give her a full examination. Growing immediately concerned just by the mere look of the urine sample and the initial results of the blood tests, the nurse wanted to keep her in for a few days, but Charlotte wouldn't agree to it. She insisted on being allowed leave straight away, and in the end the nurse had no choice but to let her go, telling her that she was sending her blood to the county hospital for further tests and she must return in a few days to get the results.

With this agreed, Charlotte left the clinic and made her way straight back down to the harbour to look for Rachel, but there was no sign of her or the yacht there.

She was just deciding what she should do next when a tall fresh-faced boy of about seventeen, with scuffed boots and a donkey jacket, came up to her.

"I'm Colm," he said, raising and dropping his raised fingers in a hello gesture.

She had no idea how unusual it was for him to approach someone unbidden and most particularly to look someone straight in the face as he was now doing. The moment Colm had seen Charlotte, he knew that she wasn't someone he ought to recognise. He was certain that he'd never seen her before, nor anyone like her. She may have had identical features to a hundred other people in Reek – Colm was the wrong person to tell whether she did or not – but certainly there was no one else around who walked and dressed like her. And what's more, he could see a slight glimmer from her; nothing really worth mentioning, but interesting nonetheless.

"I think you're the person my brother went to rescue," he said. "I'm wondering why he isn't back. I'm not worried so much as just wondering."

"Me too," she said.

He smiled. There was something strusual about her that Colm liked. Strusual was his term for things both strange and unusual – invariably some of his favourite things. His sister Máiréad said the word was redundant since both terms meant the same thing. Not to him they didn't. Shopping baskets were strange but not unusual.

"I'm rolling rocks," he said.

"Are you?"

"I wouldn't lie about a thing like that for pissing sake."

"Right," she said.

"But he never did."

"Sorry?" she said.

"Write! He never did write."

"Oh, I see."

"Said the blind man, You're a liar said the dummy."

"I didn't catch that," Charlotte said.

"As the monkey said to the man with no hands."

"OK, OK," she laughed, catching on, "that'll be the last."

"As the cobbler said to his apprentice."

"Enough already. I can't stand it any more."

"As the farmer said when he saw the round egg."

"What are you up to?"

"As the mathematician said to his apprentice."

She laughed again. "Can you keep this up all day?"

"As the wall said to …"

"No seriously, stop," Charlotte said, trying not to laugh.

Colm was proud of the reaction he was getting. He decided on the spot that funny phrases suited him better than curses.

"Sure, it's only a mere trifle," he said, "as the priest said pissing on the sponge cake."

Charlotte made no reply, thinking silence was the safest course of action. She noticed the way his thin arms moved independently of the rest of him: stretching above his head, over and back, grabbing one elbow with the other hand, then bringing them forward and stroking his chest or rubbing the delicate hairs on the back of his neck, all the time moving, flowing.

Without saying anything more, Colm took Charlotte by the hand and led her along the lane back to the farm house, through the yard and out over a five-bar gate into a back field. There were about seven very large rocks arranged in a rough circle in the far corner beside the hedgerow.

"Do you like them?" Colm said.

"The rocks?" Charlotte said, surprised. "Yeah, they're interesting, I suppose."

"I put them there," he said proudly.

"You? They're huge!"

The rocks must have weighed over a ton each.

"There were two," Colm said, "and I thought there should be more."

"How did you get them here?"

"One-two-three push! One-two-three push," he said. "A relatively simple programme, as long as you can count to three and are willing to sweat a lot. Anyone can do it, I think. It's slow though, very slow."

"Must be."

Colm nodded seriously and looked out to sea.

"It's a sacred circle," she said, "like in the old days."

"No, it's not," he said, shaking his head vehemently. "No way!"

She was about to insist, but noticing his eyes looking out to sea, she followed them and saw the silhouette of *Valhalla* appearing around the headland; its lines as elegant as the cut-out shapes of a child's mobile or a prop in a shadow-puppet show.

"They're back," she cried, pointing. "That's the boat your brother is on."

"He rescued you," Colm said proudly.

"He did."

She set off back towards the harbour, and Colm followed her as far as the yard. He considered going down to meet Dónal but thought it was more important to correct the misconception that his stones were a sacred circle before anyone else made the same mistake.

"It's not a circle," he called after her from the gate, and when she had disappeared around the corner, he went to the barn and got out a roll of fencing wire that had been left over from the summer before when Dónal and his father had refenced the fields up on Cnoc Ciarán. He dumped it into a wheelbarrow and wheeled it out into the field, trapping one end under a rock and winding the rest clockwise around the outside of the stones until a rough pentagon was formed. It went around three times before the roll ended. He went off looking for more, but there were only scraps remaining and, eventually, he had to make do with ripping apart the old chicken run his father had made and using the rusty, scrunched-up fencing from it as the internal wall of the pentagon. This took a while as it all had to be unsnipped and flattened of its creases first, then dragged across the field and arranged around

163

the inside of the rocks. He had been hoping to start collecting stones to fill in the gap between the two layers of wire, so that a solid wall would be formed, but he needed cement for that, and he still hadn't resolved that issue.

He sat down and gave some more thought to the cement problem. On the positive side, at least he now knew that the hardware shop had what he was looking for. Somehow he needed to find a way to get over the account problem. For all he knew, his father might well have had an account in the shop; he might have many even, but since he didn't really understand what an account was, he didn't know how to go about accessing it. He could ask the shopkeeper, but he didn't want to have him laugh at him again. No, the only way was to go in with cash, or a cash equivalent, and buy the cement straight out. He knew that delivery wouldn't be a problem: the truck that delivered gas cylinders to the house often carried building materials from the hardware shop. No doubt they would deliver them right to the yard once he had found a way of paying for them.

He was still worrying over these matters when he looked up and noticed the familiar sunken shoulders and stooped head of Dónal coming across the field towards him. The strusual woman and another girl were with him. A far stronger light was coming from the new girl, but Colm knew enough by now not to say anything. He had no problem making out that she was female – he could always tell someone's gender unless they went to great efforts to hide it.

Dónal dropped down beside him, relieved to see Colm looking more relaxed.

"How are you doing?" he said. "Are you getting on OK?"

"As the bus conductor said to the cripple," Colm replied.

"Seriously. You OK?"

"Just so, so, as the tailor said to his seamstress."

Dónal looked at him and smiled. The only way of breaking the cycle was not to respond.

"You see, it's not a circle!" Colm said to Charlotte over Dónal's shoulder. "I told you it wasn't."

Charlotte looked around her at the stones all knitted together now into a solid doughnut that looked more circular than ever, but she didn't say anything.

"Any sign of Taytos?" Dónal asked.

"She thought it was a circle," Colm complained.

"What was?" Dónal said.

Colm pointed behind him towards the bottom of the field.

"Where did those rocks come from?!" Dónal said, staring down at them in amazement.

"From me," Colm said.

"Did you have Páid Scárthain dump them there?" Dónal said.

"No!" Colm said horrified. "I brought them. It took me for ever – or at least a few weeks – pushing them."

"Are you serious?" Dónal asked.

"I pushed them with my mouth open," Colm said. "That helps a lot. You can get more air into your lungs."

"But … how? With winches or pulleys or something?" Dónal said.

"Just a wedge sometimes to get over a mound," Colm said.

"Why?"

"Every man to his fancy and me to my Nancy," Colm said, "as the farmer said when he kissed his cow."

"No, seriously, Colm. Why?"

Colm shrugged and changed the subject, "Gráinne says we have to go get Kittens."

"Does she now?" Dónal said.

"He's still in the classroom. In the box. Still all bloody."

"Who's Kittens?" Rachel asked.

165

"A pet," Dónal said.

"Gráinne says we should bury him," Colm said. "The children would like that."

"How did he die?" Rachel asked.

"Not now," Dónal warned.

"His belly was ripped open by my fox," Colm said.

"Has Taytos not shown up?" Dónal said.

Colm began to wring his hands.

"Who's Taytos?" Rachel said.

"The vixen," Dónal said.

"Can we bury Kittens over the cliff?" Colm asked.

"What do you mean?" Dónal said.

"Like, say a prayer and throw him over," Colm said.

"No!" Dónal said.

Colm's hand wringing grew faster. He could normally control it, especially in front of strangers, but it had been a difficult day, and he couldn't seem to find the will to stop himself.

"You certainly can not," Charlotte interceded. "Cats hate water. It would never rest easy – might end up haunting you."

"Oh," Colm said with interest, his hands stopping instantly. He was right about this woman – she was a good one. He half thought she might be one of the people in the hot air balloon, but he wasn't sure.

"We need to find a sacred spot to return him to the earth," Charlotte said.

"Oh," Colm said.

"Know of any?" she said.

Colm shrugged.

"This is County Cork, after all," Charlotte said. "There must be hundreds of sacred sites."

"This isn't County Cork," Dónal said. "It's Kerry."

"What?" Charlotte said.

"We're in Kerry. Reek is in County Kerry."

"It is?" Charlotte said. "But I thought we were in …"

Rachel looked at her, shaking her head in exasperation.

"Don't you start, young lady!" Charlotte snapped at her, before turning back to Dónal. "Well, surely you must have holy places here too?"

Rachel turned around to look at the view, tuning out of Charlotte's talk. Now that there were other people around, it was easier to cope with her various inanities and bluster. The short time she'd spent with Dónal had given her a welcome break and taken her mind off her own self-absorption. He was as different from Nathaniel as anyone could be, and that was definitely a good thing. It was the only way she had been able to kiss him. If his mouth had resembled Nathaniel's sprightly, equivocating one in any way, she couldn't have managed it. In the end, they had made love beneath the sails, although she hadn't really wanted to, but it hadn't been as bad as she thought it would be, and she was sort of relieved to get it over with. She wasn't sure what had come over her in the boat; but somehow she had found herself with an irresistible desire to engage with someone. It was most likely the adrenalin surge that comes from cheating death and her over-whelming gratitude for the rescue party. They probably had women throwing themselves at them the whole time, Rachel rea-soned. She hadn't actually imagined that Dónal would respond so eagerly – it was mainly due to him that it had gone any further. He managed to get her clothes off so quickly. His skin, pasty and bloated in the dim light below deck, wasn't particularly attractive. In fact, he looked like a laboratory specimen, and she had some last minute doubts about going ahead, but in the end it was his face that clinched it – his intriguing eyes, dry chapped lips and stubborn cheeks. He looked so different from the soft-skinned boys at home. The sea swell was intense and the boat was riding uneasily on the anchors which made the whole experience a bit farcical. Rachel had to make a conscious effort not to vomit, and at one point she had tried pulling away from him, but he looked so demoralised that she hadn't the heart not to go through with it. He had saved her life after all.

Afterwards, when Dónal had managed to get the engine started and they were motoring back towards the harbour, he had asked her to tell him about herself, and that was when they both realised how little they had in common.

"Running," she had said, when he asked her what she would be doing now if she were at home. "A year ago I would have been having fun with my boyfriend – just hanging out, probably begging outside Denny's or Starbucks."

"Begging?" he said.

"Yeah, sure," she said.

"You're a beggar?" he said.

"What's wrong with that?" she said. "Do you think only the poor should be allowed beg? Only lepers and cripples?"

"You mean busking?" he said. "You busk?"

"No, begging!"

Dónal looked at her, and Rachel realised she probably would never be able to explain the situation to him.

"People just give us change and stuff," she said.

"Why?"

"Because we ask them," she said. "We ask them nicely. Really polite. We might do a trick for them or something in return, but it's not expected. My friend juggles, and one time I sang a Southern spiritual for this old lady. She gave me the words and told me how she wanted it sung, then gave me six bucks."

"But you don't need the money?"

"No, not really, but it's nice to have. People remember when they were young and how cool it was to have a few bucks for ice cream or coffee or whatever. We liven up the street, make people smile. So, tell me about you, you're a fisherman, right? When you're not out saving people's lives. Sounds sort of heroic. It's certainly a beautiful place for it."

"Huh," Dónal said dismissively and fell silent.

Fourteen

Rachel was conscious that she needed to sort things out with Charlotte. They needed to decide what they were going to do about the yacht, but Charlotte seemed reluctant to focus on the problem. Dónal said he had to go to the school to collect Kittens and that they ought to make contact with Jimmy at some point as he would need their details for the incident report.

"Bridie has some rooms upstairs if you're looking for a B&B," Dónal said.

"Sure, we're fine on the boat," Charlotte assured him, "although I do want to stretch my legs a bit first. Can we come along with you. Get a sense of the place – find our bearings."

"There's not much to see," Dónal said, shrugging, "but you're welcome to come to the school if you want."

Colm ran to the barn to put the wire snippers away and then followed them down the lane to the coast road towards town. It wasn't long before Charlotte began to get excited about what she saw around her – gnarled whitethorn bushes, hayricks, turf sheds, standing stones – all sparked gushing exhalations, especially the holy well beside the road sign and a fairy fort that was just visible beyond the sand dunes.

"Oh my God, this place is awesome!" she cried. "It's like it's been designed by God especially for holding ceremonies. We could bury your cat anywhere at all."

"I don't think so," Dónal said sternly.

"Sure," she said. "Look, even over there. Isn't that a totem stone?" She was pointing at a tall length of rock with ogham carvings on it in a field in front of someone's newly built bungalow. "This is going to be great, Colm. We will give your little kitty a send off like he never imagined. We need to start planning the whole thing right away."

Colm didn't know what to make of this, but he liked the fuss she was making over Kittens.

"What do you envisage?" she said. "Prayers? Rituals? A symbolic sacrifice? Or gifting perhaps?"

"I want Kittens to be happy," he said. "I want his heart to be open and fully alive, I want him to shine."

When they reached the school, they could find no sign of Gráinne, but the cleaning lady showed them to the box which was still in the classroom, lying more or less where Colm had dropped it. It hadn't begun to smell yet, but Kittens had turned stiff as wood. The cleaner said that Gráinne had suggested holding the funeral the following day just after second class – if that was OK with Dónal and Colm. They nodded, and she went on to say that Gráinne had mentioned that since the priest would be making his weekly visit the following day, she thought it would be a nice idea for him to say a few words too.

"Certainly not," Charlotte cried in horror.

They looked at her. Colm enjoyed the intensity of her reaction and decided he would take his cue from her. She was finding it hard to contain her revulsion at the idea of a priest butting in on the fabulous ritual she was planning, but she realised she had to be careful not too appear too dogmatic and so smiled wanly and turned away to admire the children's paintings on the walls. It was hard to remain calm as the idea of doing a ritual in a sacred site in Ireland was just so exciting. She loved rituals and got so few opportunities to perform them: a genuine animal death ceremony in a remote Irish community – it was more than any Wicca could hope for.

"*Cé hí seo?*" the cleaner asked suspiciously.

"What? What's she saying?" Charlotte said, turning on her heels accusatively.

"She's asking who are you," Colm said.

"A friend," Charlotte interceded in a bright voice, before Dónal could explain. "I'm merely a concerned friend … And it struck me that considering it's a wild animal we're dealing with, I'm not sure the presence of a priest would be appropriate."

Diplomacy wasn't something that came naturally to her, but she was doing her best.

"Yeah," Colm agreed. "No priests. Definitely."

"Poor lad," Charlotte said, adopting a solemn expression and laying a hand on Colm's shoulder. "It must be very hard on him. Brave soldier! He's right, you know, priests and the wild animal kingdom ought never to come together. They can be overcome by the pagan forces. I've seen it myself. I was involved once a long time ago with a healing ceremony for a husky dog up in Alaska and, my God, it was intense. They surround themselves with all sorts of sprites and daemons. I'm not sure your holy man would be up to it, or even safe."

"I think Father could handle …" the cleaner began.

"That poor husky," Charlotte said, cutting her off. "She was the best in the pack. Her name was Bonsai. Once, she even rescued this guy I knew, Trapper Carl. Carl was out checking his traps way far out in the plains and somehow didn't see the patch of dodgy ice. I reckon he had booze taken – he normally had. Anyhow, he fell through the ice, and if it wasn't for old Bonsai marshalling the pack and pulling him out, he would have died there and then. Guaranteed. It was 35° below. Bonsai became more important than all the rest of us after that, more important even than me, and I was Carl's girl at the time. I suppose the truth was that I was mainly only there to cook and clean for him, and warm his bed at night – I had never actually saved his life, which put me way down in the pecking order. After the incident, he insisted that Bonsai be allowed sleep in the house on cold nights. I told him it was asking for trouble, but would he listen to me? Would he hell?

"You see, old Bonsai was more wolf than dog, so it was inevitable things would turn bad. The first night she stayed in the house I didn't sleep a wink. I was afraid to, in case she got it into her mind to attack us both – or at least me – the first moment she could. She wasn't a bad bitch; it was just in her nature to hunt, to kill. All night long she glowered at me until finally, around dawn, I just couldn't keep my eyes open any longer and I fell asleep. An hour or so later I woke and immediately checked all my fingers and toes for signs of blood. I was about to turn over and go back to sleep when I noticed the cat wasn't beside the stove where he usually lay. I got up and looked around, but there was no sign of the poor critter. No sign at all. He had been in the house when we locked up and now he was gone. Vanished! Carl insisted he must have climbed up the chimney, but why would a cat do a thing like that? Anyway, I checked the roof in the morning and there were no marks. I spent a few hours calling him, but he never replied. At one point I happened to take a look into Bonsai's eyes, and that told me everything I needed to know. I could see as clear as day what had happened. Bonsai had eaten the poor thing. I could see it clearly – she was racked with guilt. I tried telling Carl, but he wouldn't believe me. He said I was just jealous. It took three days, with Bonsai sleeping in the room with us each night, before I finally managed to prove it. But I sure did, in the end. When the poor cat's collar turned up in a mound of dog shit in the yard, I brought Carl straight over and stuck his nose into it."

"She had eaten it?" Colm exclaimed.

"Yep."

"And left no trace, not even a drop of blood?" Colm said.

"Nothing. She must have licked it up clean. The perfect crime."

"Wow."

The others were too stunned by the unexpectedness of this epic story told at gunfire speed to know what to make of it.

"Anyway, that's not the point," Charlotte continued. "Poor Bonsai got sick that evening and kept getting sicker, until by the end of that week we ended up burying her with the mashed up bones of the cat still inside her. The ceremony was something else! I'll tell you this much: there were some seriously intense energies spinning around. Oh yeah. For a while I thought they might even end up getting the better of me. It took all my powers to keep it together. Trapper Carl was completely freaked. Winds started whipping up around us, slamming doors and blowing the sled chains ..."

"I'm very sorry," the cleaner managed to intervene, "but I need to get back to my work here. Can you just take the box and come back tomorrow, around 11 a.m.?"

"Uh, right," said Charlotte in an aggrieved huff.

Rachel was afraid she was about to turn stroppy and warned her, "Don't, Charlotte, please don't."

"I'm not saying anything," Charlotte said. "Just thinking about the whole idea of Ireland of the Welcomes. The Céad Míle Fáilte – isn't that what you guys say?"

Rachel steered Charlotte out of the school before she could say any more. Dónal took the box, and they headed back towards the pier. Rachel tried again to persuade Charlotte that they needed to discuss what they were going to do next, but Charlotte was more concerned with finding a suitable hazel tree to use for making dowsing rods.

"We need to have a talk," Rachel pleaded. "Urgently!"

"Yes, of course, dear," Charlotte said, sighing stoically and looking indulgently at her. "Go right ahead."

"In private," Rachel said through gritted teeth.

"Well, I don't know, dear. Colm and I have a lot of preparing to do before the morning, and if we're to find a good burial spot I'm going to need to make some dowsing rods to track for energies."

"This won't take long," Rachel insisted.

"Whatever!" Charlotte said resignedly and turned towards Dónal and Colm, saying, "It seems we have to go now, I'm afraid, but what are you doing later? How about you both come over for dinner on the yacht?"

"Bollicky bollicks," Colm said, remembering he hadn't been keeping up his practice, "that's sounds fucking great."

The three others stared at him.

"Shitting douchebag, what's up?" he said.

"What do you think you are doing, Colm?" Dónal asked.

"Huh?" he said. "I'm practising, like you told me."

"Practising what?"

"Cursing."

"I never told you to curse," Dónal said.

"You fucking-well did."

"I just told you it was something people did," Dónal said. "You can't use words like that in front of just anyone."

"But you said …!" Colm whined.

"Please come to dinner," Charlotte said to smooth the waters. "I can't promise you haute cuisine, but we'll certainly rustle up something. It'll give us a chance to plan everything out for tomorrow."

Dónal was too perplexed to make any reply, and Colm was determined not to say another word until he had sorted out what was wrong with Dónal. He was only doing what he'd been told, after all. Dónal had definitely told him that cursing put people at ease.

"Well?" Charlotte said.

Neither of them knew what haute cuisine was, and they found the idea of being invited on to a boat at night to be, at best, bizarre. Boats were work vessels; bars were for meeting in. After a moment, Colm decided he liked the strusualness of it and, although Dónal wasn't so keen, he couldn't think of any excuse to refuse, so they both agreed. It was better than spending another night at home.

As soon as Dónal and Colm were out of earshot, Rachel turned on Charlotte.

"What the hell are you thinking of?" she screamed.

"What's wrong with you?" Charlotte said.

"The boat!"

"I keep telling you not to call it that," Charlotte said.

"Look, Charlotte, we've stolen something. This is serious. We've got to sort it out."

"I refuse to discuss the issue if you insist on using inaccurate terminology. It isn't stolen and you know it. What's the use of me explaining these things to you if you don't even listen. I'm trying to teach you here, and you're giving me nothing back. I realise it's not our yacht, of course I do. And yes, we will have to get it back to its owner at some point. I realise that. God, what do you take me for, an imbecile?"

Rachel said nothing, just stared. Charlotte looked out to sea and sighed. She adopted her most magnanimous, indulgent expression.

"I'll tell you what I'll do," she said, "I'll call the yacht club and see can I get in touch with Jack; bring him up to date on the whole situation. How would that suit your ladyship?!"

"You mean, Jack really knows?"

"Of course he does," Charlotte said. "I told you that."

"OK, so ring him," Rachel said. "But now. Do it straight away."

"Certainly," Charlotte said, "it's just that I don't see any phone around."

Sure enough, there was no sign of a phone at the pier. There might have been one inside Bridie Brennan's pub, but it was shut.

"There'll be one in town," Rachel said.

"We can go see if you like," Charlotte said. "It'll give us a chance to stock up on things for dinner. I was thinking of falafels with feta salad. What do you think?"

They walked back into town, where Rachel triumphantly pointed to a rickety glass and aluminium phone box on the main street, but Charlotte said that she had no change – in fact she had no Irish currency at all. Rachel shook her head in exasperation and took out twenty dollars of her own.

"That's not going to get you very far here child," Charlotte said. "They use pounds."

"Actually, they use euros," Rachel snapped back and strode across the road towards the tobacco-smeared window of Daly's Hardware & Bar, in the hopes that they might change it for her. She pushed in through the double doors into the darkness inside.

Charlotte took the opportunity to sit down on a low wall and take a slug of bourbon to steady herself. She could feel the familiar tiredness creeping up on her. She was definitely growing weaker. Clinging to a life jacket in the Atlantic was not what the doctors had in mind when they advised her that a trip to Europe would do no serious harm. They were adamant that she oughtn't to exert herself, and she worried now about what the incident might have done to her health, her kidneys in particular. To avoid focusing on the issue, she tried doing her breathing exercises – the most important thing was to keep the lungs oxygenated, they had said – but she had hardly got through the first round before Rachel came back out with a fistful of coins and began pushing Charlotte towards the phone box.

"Now, for God's sake, ring him," Rachel said. "Please!"

"Sure," Charlotte said, fixing a smile back on her face. "I'll sort the whole thing out. You wait there and catch some sun while I make everything hunky dory."

"You sure you have the right number for the yacht club – the right code? The shopkeeper said to put a 00-44 before it."

"I have made phone calls before, you know," Charlotte said, shuffling off towards the phone.

Rachel sat down to wait. Even in the few hours she had been here, this place had begun to make an impression on her. She was taken aback by the ruggedness of the landscape and particularly by the tiny boats they used for fishing. Dónal worked in some of the wildest waters on the ocean, in ancient wooden trawlers that looked somewhat medieval. He was doing the same thing his ancestors had been doing for generations, hunting fish and maybe growing some potatoes and cabbages in the spring. There was something almost romantic about it. Life here seemed slower, simpler and somehow more genuine than at home. The reason Rachel and her friends went begging was to reintroduce a grain of reality back to their lives. Her closest contact with anything elemental was the pistil of a crocus which was tattooed above her pelvis. It was blue and red and corresponded in colour to a tiny honeybee Nathaniel had tattooed on his ankle. She wondered had the cutting been connected to that too – a way of feeling something real.

Charlotte returned less than ten minutes later with a fixed, though somewhat chastened, grin.

"Good old Jack," she said. "We've sorted everything. He's going to bring his friend over to collect the boat as soon as he can."

"When?" Rachel said.

"Well, there's just a little problem in that Jack's wife has got ill. Very ill. She didn't take well to the stress of the whole situation. It's regrettable, but to be honest, it doesn't surprise me. This is what happens when white magic comes up against dark."

Rachel stared at her suspiciously.

"Did you do something to her?" she asked.

"What? Now, suddenly you believe I have magic powers or something? Well, there's a surprise."

"Tell me you didn't poison her," Rachel said.

"God, Rachel! Of course not. I did nothing … or at least nothing active. It's just the laws of the universe – when light comes up against darkness, the darkness always suffers. Think about it, if you bring a candle into a dark room the darkness goes, but can you bring darkness into a light room?"

"What are you on about?!" Rachel cried. "Just tell me what Jack said."

"He thinks he should stay and keep an eye on his wife for a few days. When she's strong enough, they'll both sail over with *Valhalla*'s owners. It'll probably be in about a week. He says it might be better if we weren't around by then. He managed to convince his friend not to contact the police, but he didn't take the whole incident as well as I hoped, and Jack reckons it would be better if we didn't meet face to face."

"So what do we do?"

"Well, I don't know about you, but I intend catching up on my yoga. It's been killing me that I haven't had a chance to practise since we left the States. You don't stay as young and nimble as me without caring for the body, you know."

Rachel sighed and walked on ahead.

They spent an hour trying to buy food for dinner, peering into every tiny cubby-hole shop looking for something edible, something other than sun-bleached boxes of Corn Flakes and bruised brown apples. A tiny pork butcher's with a counter of cracked tiles had only a tray of blood-pudding and a crate of smoked rashers on offer. When Charlotte asked whether he had anything else, the butcher pointed to a bucket of trotters in the corner. The vegetable shop consisted of a single metal rack with some malformed turnips, parsley and clay-smeared parsnips. In the single-aisle grocery shop, they paced up and down, scanning the shelves for anything worth putting into the metal basket that the shopkeeper had proudly handed them. Finally, they admitted defeat, and Charlotte announced that the only way they were going to be able to provide dinner was by going out foraging on the seashore.

Fifteen

When Dónal and Colm arrived at the boat that evening, they found it glowing gently with a hundred flickering lights. Charlotte had bought three large packets of night-lights and put each one into a beer bottle she had found at the back of Bridie's and smashed the top off. Down below deck the clammy, resin-moulded galley had been made to look ethereal, with candles glinting through brown and blue bottles. Laid out on a wonky trestle table was the food Charlotte and Rachel had managed to assemble. It looked like nothing the boys had ever seen in their lives before.

"Sorry about this," Charlotte said, when she saw them staring. "Your town doesn't seem to go in for much in the way of real food. Unless you happen to like something called Denny's steak'n kidney pie in a Frisbee tin, you're out of luck. What the hell is that about? I wanted to make falafels until I found they had no chick peas. Not only that, but they had never actually heard of them. Then I found there was no feta, or any other kind of cheese at all, except for something called Dairy Lea, which came in evil aluminium triangles. This place is worse than Alaska for food. In the end I had to take the triangles for want of anything else, but I have to warn you they're inedible. Like bath sealant. The shopkeeper had only a vague idea of what an avocado was. He refused to believe a zucchini was a vegetable, and when I asked for peppers he said he only had salt. I tried asking for a load of other stuff, but he said that it was a 'self-service shop' and he preferred if I got things myself. 'What *things?*' I said to him. 'You don't have any things.' I learnt that the nearest natural yoghurt is forty miles away, and that I'd have to see the chemist if I wanted olive oil. I mean, for Christ sake, how do you guys survive?"

Colm was staring entranced at the dishes on the table. He had never seen anything like it before. There were four plates, each arranged identically into something that resembled a Miró painting or, at least, like Miró rendered in plasticine. In the centre there were hard, waxy, yellowish brown balls, and above them an arc of dark green paste, speckled with nibs of white. To the left was a blotch of orange-red pebble-dashing, and down the bottom were ectoplasmic shapes arranged on a translucent yellow background. Colm was awe-struck.

"I stormed out of the man's shop," Charlotte went on, "but we realised his was the biggest shop in town, and so Rachel had to go back in and get what she could. This sorry spread is the best we could do, I'm afraid."

"What is it?" Dónal asked anxiously.

"I hope you guys aren't lactose intolerant, are you?" Charlotte said.

They stared at her in incomprehension.

"I guess not," Rachel said.

Colm pointed towards the balls. "What are they?"

"Aren't they great?" Charlotte said. "Rachel said I was letting my artistic side get the better of me, but I knew you guys would just love it."

"Are they actual balls?" Colm said.

"Those beauties are my own personal version of temari zushi – and the best thing is there's no meat in them! You wouldn't think it, would you?"

"What are they?" Dónal asked again.

"Temari zushi. In Japan they use thinly sliced sashimi-grade fish or butterflied shrimp, but I've adapted it to my own secret mix, which includes tinned sardines, banana, peanut butter, orange juice and those aluminium triangles – I'd normally have used Camembert, but what the hell. Rachel made the orange and red stuff – isn't it gorgeous? Turns out, she's a whiz in the kitchen. Aren't the colours just wonderful? It's actually just a salad really, but she chopped the carrot and apple and walnuts so finely and added oats and nutmeg. Hope you like it. And those funny shapes at the bottom – a bit like eyeballs – they're periwinkles we picked on the strand. They looked so good, I didn't bother cooking them, just marinated them in lemon juice for a while. You eat them with popcorn – Ecuadorian style."

Colm was getting increasingly into the idea of weird shaped food. "What about the paste?" he asked.

"That, you'll have to taste yourself," Charlotte said. "Go right ahead, try some."

Colm looked at her apprehensively.

"Go ahead, put some on the popcorn, it won't kill you."

Colm dipped a cloud of popcorn into the paste and a haze of dust rose up from it, like when you kick a puffball in a field. He grimaced at first and turned away so as not to sneeze, then laid the popcorn on to his tongue and swallowed back.

"Good isn't it?" said Charlotte. "It's my very own secret seaweed dish."

Colm and Dónal just stared down at the table in wonder.

"Sit down," Rachel said, "tuck in!"

"Aren't we going to say grace?" Colm asked.

Dónal shot him a frown.

"Do you want to?" Charlotte asked.

Colm shrugged.

"Maybe Rachel would like to bless the food," Charlotte said. "You can use your wand if you like."

Rachel glowered at her.

"Her what?" Colm said.

"Her wand," Charlotte repeated. "Rachel has a beautiful wand – carved from a young plum tree, *prunus japonica*, Show them, Rachel!"

Rachel glowered again.

"Really?" Colm said.

"No, Colm, I don't," Rachel said.

Both Colm and Charlotte looked crestfallen; Charlotte far more so. She looked suddenly weary and alone.

"Oh, I see," was all she could summon herself to say in a deflated tone. "So, you actually didn't bring it with you? I thought you were just pretending."

She took a moment to compose herself, then pinning a smile back on her face, she got down on her knees, and said, "Well, I better do it so … Oh Mother Earth and blessed sun and river's rain, we hail you for giving us these fruits of forest and of field, please nourish and nurture us as we cherish you."

She got up, careful not to look at Rachel.

"Now tuck in," she said, brightening again. "We've a lot of planning to get through."

Dónal pushed some Kevlar sail aside and sat down. It was odd to be back here again, fully clothed. He shot a glance at Rachel and she looked away. Colm perched himself on a plastic-covered mattress and began flicking his fingers, from thumb to littler finger. Rachel looked at him, trying to work him out. There was something timeless about him – an intruiging mix of boy-child and wizened warrior.

"You're flicking?" she said.

"I know," he said.

"It helps him settle," Dónal said.

"Do you fidget?" Colm asked her.

"What?" Rachel said.

"Fidget?" Dónal said.

"Or flap?" Colm added. "Or flick? Or jiggle? Or bounce? Or rock? Or sway?"

"I suppose," she shrugged.

"Or, how about play with the change in your pocket?" Colm said. "Or click a pen in and out repeatedly? What about if I scattered a box of paperclips in front of you?"

Rachel laughed. She liked the way his mind worked. "It would be hard to resist playing with them, I have to admit."

Dónal stared at the food, wondering how he was going to put any of it into his mouth. He looked over at Colm and noticed him shimmying his hips against the bunk to loosen his jeans, then pulling his zipper down halfway. Dónal was just about to say something, when Colm reached under his boxer shorts and plucked out a coiled pubic hair.

He held the hair up to the candle and asked, "What do you call one of these, again?"

"Colm!" Dónal said.

"What?" Colm cried.

Dónal just stared.

"At least it's better than your nipple hair," Colm said defensively. "Dónal's nipple hair shoots straight out like a goat's *meigeall* – what's that in English, Dónal?"

"A goatee," Dónal said wearily.

"Yeah, well, we are like one of these, in a little locket around the neck of Reek pier," Colm proclaimed, waving his strand of hair.

"What?" asked Charlotte.

"Well, this boat is tiny, OK? And we're cramped inside it, like in a locket. But the locket isn't around a neck, it's in the sea, tied to the pier. So we three are the lock of hair in the locket," said Colm.

"But we're alive. Isn't hair dead?" asked Rachel.

"This can't be dead," said Colm, pulling at it, "because if I straighten it, it curls up again."

"Unless it died curled up, like the fingers of an old hag," said Rachel.

"There was an old woman near us who was a hag," exclaimed Colm. "Páid Loinsigh's mother. I heard that she killed the calf of a white bull and drank its broth and then slept for three nights on its hide. Taytos never liked her. She'd slink around …"

Colm fell suddenly quiet. Taytos still hadn't turned up, and he didn't like to think what might have happened to her. A tear rolled down his cheek.

"What's wrong?" said Rachel.

"Just …" Colm said. "Nothing."

"He's worried about Taytos," Dónal said.

"It's nice to be around people who care about animals, isn't it Rachie?" Charlotte said. "People can be so cruel. In London we saw pictures of Japanese fishermen massacring sharks and dolphins – corralling them into an inlet and then butchering them all with these vicious wooden-handled sushi knives. The water ran red with blood. It's appalling …"

Charlotte fell quiet, and nobody said anything for a while, until eventually the silence was broken by sniffles as Charlotte began to cry. Everyone looked at her. The tears came very slowly, as if she were desperately trying to hold them back. She was exerting enormous effort to stem the tide, but it was no use. She had that inwardly focused look that you see in *tai chi* masters or a baby filling its nappy.

"What's wrong?" Colm asked.

She just shook her head.

An awkward silence fell over them all. Without her bluster, they all became aware of how odd this whole situation was, how strange it was to be sitting together in this yacht, and how little they had in common. They turned to her as one and stared, hoping she'd recover herself soon.

She felt their discomfort and opened her mouth to say something, but no words came. It was too late for that now. She had resisted saying what needed to be said for so long that it was as if the words had atrophied inside her. Somehow she had to convey to them the fact that she was ill. Very ill. The news would probably leak out from the nurse at some point soon anyway. She had been ill for a long time now, but it had been getting gradually worse. She could feel her energy vacillate wildly from volatile to phlegmatic. Her left kidney had failed months ago, and she could tell the right one was about to go. It was time for a transplant. The doctors had wanted her to have one months before, but she knew there was little point: the rest of her organs were in such a mess it was unlikely to take, or at least, not for long. It had been explained to her that she was being kept alive by a cocktail of drugs that could only stave off the inevitable for a certain length of time.

It wasn't a tragedy. The illness had brought her the compensation money that had made this trip possible. In her letter to Rachel, she had written that the money came from a pay-out for a fall in a bowling alley, but that wasn't entirely true. The truth was that it came from a drugs company trial that went wrong. She had been taking part in a controlled trial of a new medicine, and they had made a mistake with dosages. It had weakened her kidney.

No wait, that's not entirely true either. This was no time for more half-truths. Yes, she had taken the drug trial and it had caused kidney problems, but in fact it had only exacerbated a more serious condition she had inflicted on herself when she was still binge-drinking and taking drugs. She had pushed her body too hard, had her stomach pumped once too often. The doctors had warned her that even if she never touched another drink or drug again, she wouldn't make a full recovery. Her immune system was shot. She would be prone to pneumonia and other viral attacks. Since then, she had given up most drugs and cut back a lot on her drinking, and that was probably what had kept her alive until now.

The clinking of cleats against the mast brought her back to the present and, looking up, she noticed the three of them staring at her. She smiled awkwardly. Colm reached out and patted her.

"We have dolphins here," he said brightly, "and no one tries to butcher them with Suzi knives or any other sort. Although we weren't very nice to seals in the past. My granddad used to clobber them with clubs, but now, not so much."

"Sometimes we all do things we regret," she said through her tears, upending the contents of her bag and lining up the various items across the table as though looking for something. The others kept quiet, staring at her in silence. "We can't help ourselves – often times it's not us, it's the hurt inside that's doing it. We take something to make it feel better, to make it go away, and that then has its own repercussions."

She fell silent again, but no one said anything. They had no idea what she was on about, but could see from her eyes, from the beads of sweat on her upper lip, that it was important. She had picked out her three tiny brown phials and lined them up together like bowling pins.

She wanted to tell them what had happened, about the drugs, how somehow it had all gone wrong, or all gone right in the end, depending on how you looked at it. She certainly never meant to be on this yacht, in this place, at this time. That much was certain. She hadn't even expected to be alive still. When she learnt about the illness and her chances of recovery, she had taken stock of things and realised that all she really wanted to do was see her niece one more time. She hadn't laid eyes on her for fourteen years after all; not once in all those years since that horrible evening when she had conked out in her sister's living room while babysitting her. She had woken with a start when the paramedic had injected something into her, to find Lucy and her husband staring down at her as though they had no idea who this creature was. The paramedics had tied her to the stretcher as if she might be dangerous, when in truth she was just an auntie who loved her little niece and was wrestling with a drug dependency. They took her away, and she hadn't seen Rachel since.

It hadn't surprised Charlotte all that much that Rachel hadn't remembered her when she turned up on her doorstep. In a way it was good; it meant "the incident" – the whole sudden leaving-taking in a haze of blue ambulance lights – mustn't have made too big an impression on her. Secretly Charlotte had always hoped that this would be the case. Lucy mustn't have referred to the incident while she was growing up, and for that, at least, Charlotte was grateful. Rachel must surely have asked for Auntie Sha now and then, but over time she would have forgotten. Charlotte didn't resent this; children's minds were like that, malleable.

As it was, returning to her sister's house was the best thing to ever happen to Charlotte. Finding her beloved Rachel in need of help had kick-started things, or ignited a tiny pilot flame of spiritual insight that hopefully could be stoked up during whatever time remained to her in life. Finally, after all these years, she was no longer completely impotent; she had rescued the one person in this world she cared most about; had saved her from her stabbing fits. That was impressive in anyone's book. The fact that she had turned up at the divinely ordained time and swept Rachel from danger was almost miraculous … clearly an incidence of sacred concurrence, or at least a manifestation of Owen Meaney's *no-coincidence*.

Of course, if she had been a real witch, she could have been more subtle about her actions, but it was hardly her fault that the divine entities above skimped on her powers. It ought to be a lesson to them not to be so miserly in the future. They had certainly underestimated her. She had now proved that she was made of the right stuff; that she had real potential, if only they were wiling to invest in her.

She was becoming an instrument of the angels and hoped that her remaining months on earth would be a period of consolidation, of gradual transmutation as her full powers came on stream – a potentially frightening period of apparitions, disembodied voices, guidance from disincarnate beings and dark chasms to be faced. She would undergo a process of divine reconstruction in a metaphorical alembic; her neural pathways would be recalibrated to allow for her increased divinity. It was exciting – she might even be on the cusp of enlightenment. Imagine that! It was this thought that had kept her awake all night in the cell of Concord's police department. The facially topiaried warden thought she was on drugs and had made her undergo a test.

"Unless you have a drug that detects the presence of divine transcendence, you'll find I'm clean, clean as a bright new washing machine."

And she was too. The lab found traces of a whole cocktail of drugs flushing through her, but they were all legal, prescription drugs for which her hospital back in Charlottesville was able to fax through documentation – all of them striving to keep her remaining kidney functioning while stabilising the other organs.

Unfortunately, no sooner was she released from police custody and put on the Greyhound back home than the certainty about her new powers began to wane, and with the first seeds of self-doubt came the old impotency that she had felt all her life. She realised that she had no more access to wisdom than she ever had. Either it had all been a big mistake, a temporary delusion, or else she had been found wanting somehow by those above and been excluded once again. Either way, the shutters into the magic realms were firmly closed against her. She contracted a fever as soon as she got home and was taken straight into the drug company's private hospital. She spent two weeks there, and although the fever tricked her into thinking her omnipotence might have returned and that her soaring temperature was part of a necessary tempering process, no sooner had she been discharged than she realised she was just plain old Charlotte again. She went home and settled back into her life of yet more tests and treatments, all the while negotiating the final terms of her compensation settlement with the lawyer for the drug company. That was, of course, until she'd got news of the report of Rachel's athletic success and she came up to New Hampshire to find her.

Sixteen

Dónal, Colm and Rachel had waited a moment for Charlotte to finish her point about the things we do that we later regret, but as she lapsed into silence again and retreated deep into herself, Colm turned to Dónal and asked him why people in the area had only ever killed seals and not dolphins.

"We needed their oil for lighting, I suppose," Dónal said. "Dad said we never ate much of the meat. I'd say dolphin would be tastier though."

"Dónal!" Colm said, horrified.

"What?" Dónal said. "They're just big bloated sea pigs, lardy lumps that leave a trail of destruction behind. You should see the state of the nets after they've mangled the fish in them. It costs Con a fortune in repairs. As far as I can see, they're as dumb as any other grazing animal."

"We saw some on the way here," Rachel said.

"They're a lot of them around here," Colm said. "Even one or two friendly ones who follow the trawlers in and out and let people swim right up close."

"Really?" Rachel said keenly.

"Yeah," Dónal sighed. "It's mostly tourists who swim with them – I tell them a trip to a pig sty would be a lot warmer."

"No, you don't," Colm said. "That's what Con says. You're just trying to show off."

Dónal shrugged and picked at a periwinkle.

"There's one dolphin who just hangs out at the mouth of the bay, waiting for passing boats," Colm said. "He reminds me of a bored collie chasing cars. He's just fidgeting, I suppose he can't help it."

"But aren't they so beautiful?" Rachel said.

"No more than any other animal," Dónal said.

Charlotte rose her head again and turned back towards them, wiping her eyes. Colm and Dónal looked over at her. Rachel kept her eyes low; the less contact she had with her aunt the better. Charlotte had to cough loudly to provoke her into looking up, and when Rachel's eye's rose, the mix of derision and contempt in them was enough to make Charlotte wince. How had things gone so wrong? She knew that teenagers could be impetuous, their feelings ricochetting from love to loathing in an instant, and that a teenager's contempt was never all that it appeared to be. Nonetheless, over the last few days, things had been so fraught between them that Charlotte was beginning to have doubts about the whole thing. She knew that any sacred journey must include precipitous stretches, unforeseen challenges, periods of uncertainty; yet by the time they were on the yacht, she wondered had she taken a wrong turning somewhere, been blown metaphorically off course. She was at her lowest ebb when the dolphins had appeared – a sign from above, no doubt about it. They had revived her, shown her the way forward, enticing her into their world. She knew her body was unlikely to take the strain of an Atlantic immersion, but this was no time for holding back. She had to be courageous, to believe.

It had been a harsh and frightening immersion, but it had instantly washed away all uncertainty. When she laid eyes on the rescue team, she clearly saw the divine path the angels had been laying. They would deliver her to where she needed to be. Despite not having the greatest propensity for prescience, she could always tell when something important had come into her life. It was her one intuitive gift: recognising incidences of divine intervention. She was better at it than any seer or witch she knew: she never missed the sight of a robin crossing her path or a spider leaving its web dangling at just the right angle. She gave thanks to the Mother Goddess, but also to herself for trusting, for finding a path through. These stout Irishmen would lead her forward, that much was certain. She and Rachel were in safe hands now. All she had to do was …

"It's funny," said Colm, looking around him. "I like this locket, but I've never wanted to be locked up before. I think it's really good to keep out of places where they try and lock you up."

His remarks were, as they often were, seemingly apropos of nothing.

"I know I'm doing good when I'm still not in one," he went on. He was looking at Charlotte as he spoke, as though sensing she was mired in some trough and eager to winch her out. "Sometimes I get so happy and then so sad, flipping back and forth just like that, that I think maybe this time I'll have to go away; and that's OK, if I really have to. I went to a few doctors before, didn't I, Dónal? They had bad breath and stains on their trousers. I think they were very tired. They were trying to help, but really they were, well, not very good. One said I was unbalanced and he wanted to give me drugs, another willowy woman with orange chin hair said I was sexually confused – like those periwinkles that are both male and female. She said it would make her happy if I went to see a friend of hers who was either also sexually confused or knew how to make people and periwinkles stop being confused. Then, there were other doctors who just came up with words to describe me which I didn't understand and they wouldn't explain. So, I learnt them off so that I could tell other people what I was: neurologically imbalanced; socially malad-justed; potentially quasi-suicidal. It's good to know the words for what you are, but I'm not sure if they really helped much. I'm still me; me being me. I think I'm just finding a way of being comfortable with all that. I think that's it …"

He rubbed his nose with his fist a few times, considering if there was more to add, then placing a hand on Charlotte's knee, he asked,

"Why were you crying?"

She looked up at him with a start. "Oh, I don't know," she said. "I'm just confused. And those Japanese fishermen. It's so cruel what they do to the sharks and dolphins, don't you think?"

Rachel got up and cleared away the plates, replacing them with four saucers on which were laid out razor-thin slices of orange cut across the sections into individual dials which were sprinkled with cinnamon.

"We should start planning things for tomorrow," Rachel said. "Have you guys decided where you want to bury the cat yet?"

They stayed up half the night discussing the funeral arrangements, agreeing to meet up again at the school the next day just before eleven o'clock break. Charlotte was so excited she hardly slept, and first thing in the morning she was back at the school looking for books on the history and archaeology of the area. She wanted everything to be just right.

She had convinced Colm to dress up for the occasion. She asked Dónal to do the same, but he'd refused. Colm had wanted to know what sort of costume Charlotte had in mind, and she suggested something traditional: a druid or warrior, perhaps. It would add to the sense of occasion, she said, and the children would certainly like it. He had asked Máiréad to help him, but she wasn't keen; she thought it might be sacrilegious and refused.

When he begged her she relented a bit, but her suggestions for what would work were so unimaginative he would have been better off alone.

In the end he had made up some old sandals himself out of rope and bits of leather he cut out of an old saddlebag. He planned to wear this with black pyjama bottoms that he frayed around the bottoms and an old tunic of Máiréad's, but the tunic had polyester in it which made his skin itch, so he ended up going bare-chested.

When Rachel saw him arriving at the school next day, his blond ringlets draping down his chest and his stomach taut and rippled like a beach at low tide, she was taken aback by quite how mythic he looked, how much the costume suited him. She worried about what the teachers would say about his appearance, and she suggested getting a cape or a blanket or something to put over him. He was reluctant at first, but he decided to trust Rachel. He set off back down the road to the parochial house, which was the nearest house to the school, and asked Rosie, the priest's housekeeper, if she happened to have anything suitable. Rosie was an amateur dramatics nut and always loved the idea of dressing up. She went upstairs and rooted around in the bedrooms until she dug out an old Pentecostal mantel that had been put aside for darning. It had once been elaborately decorated with gold and silver stitching, but now the embroidery was so frayed that a tangle of tinselly braid swelled around the edges, making it hard to discern its exact shape. Rosie brought it out into the front yard and beat it a few times to clear it of dust and moths, then she laid it carefully on his shoulders. It was purple – his favourite colour – and suddenly gave the costume a whole other dimension. When the wind blew, the threads spooled about, bouncing in the breeze. Colm adored it. Its frizzyness gave it a strange ethereal aspect, as though it might not be fully present in this dimension, but was vacillating between here and somewhere else.

When he got back to the school yard and Charlotte set eyes on him, she screeched with delight. This was going to be fun. Gráinne looked horrified when she saw Colm and was clearly taken aback by what this whole ritual was turning into, but she had already promised the children that they were going to bury Kittens and it was too late to back out now. She had been warned about the Americans by the cleaning lady, but the older woman was even more outlandish than she had been told – it wasn't her appearance so much, a dumpy, jovial woman with ruddy cheeks, but the feral gleam in her eyes. The younger one seemed more biddable – she was pretty with high cheekbones and a straight back. There was something unsettling about the way Dónal looked at her, as though he knew her in some way.

Sensing Gráinne's doubts about the whole situation, Charlotte took control, gathering everyone together at the school gates, working out the order of things, who should be up front and who could be trusted to walk behind to keep an eye on the smaller kids who might trail behind. The burial site Charlotte had chosen was almost a mile away. Gráinne tried not to think too much about what was happening and focused instead on making sure all the children had their coats on and were lined up in a neat file. When everything was set, Colm stood out in front with the shoe box held aloft, and Dónal and Charlotte lined up behind, followed by Gráinne and the children. At Charlotte's signal, they set off in an orderly parade towards the burial grounds, with Charlotte uttering incantations into the wind as they went.

"Let the Lady of the Lake join the saints of Reek," she intoned, "bestowers of sovereignty, weavers of magicks, makers of the sacral sword, healers of the wounded King and nurturers of our feline friends, come upon us now. We beseech the waves and the woods to light this path for Kittens our friend's *ex egis* the earth across …"

They walked along the centre of the road, careful not to step in the cow-shit that was splattered along much of it, and when they got to the Black Spot corner, Gráinne made sure to keep the children in tight to the verge. A Norwegian camper van and a car full of Koreans passed them, the drivers of both slowing down and staring while the passengers rooted out their cameras.

Once the parade reached the burial ground, Charlotte led them over the stile and through the knee-high meadow of thistles, dock leaves and ragwort to the spot she had chosen early that morning with the help of her dowsing rods. It was an early pagan ritual site now abandoned and overgrown, apart from a narrow trail leading to a ruined church. They all gathered around Colm, and Charlotte asked him would he like to nominate someone to say a first prayer on behalf of Kittens, and without even thinking about it, he called on Rachel. She looked at him in panic and then stepped up uncertainly to the shoebox.

"O Lord God," she began, "hear our prayer, eh … as we gather, um …"

"No, no," Colm cried. "Not a church prayer. Something special. Something Kittens would like."

Rachel stared hard at him. "But, I didn't know …" she began.

"You'll be fine," Charlotte coaxed her. "Just let the voices of the druids rise up through you."

Rachel winced, but managed to stifle a withering remark and to her surprise realised that some ideas were coming to mind. There was something about Colm that made her want to help, made her put aside her reservations. He leant in towards her and whispered something in her ear, and she smiled and nodded. He had asked her to think of the most foolish thing she could possibly say.

"Love is a horse," she began, throwing a glance his way. He seemed pleased. "Love can be ridden … It is for you … Just like the cats. The horse and the cats we love you for ever."

"Bravo!" Colm said, clapping.

Gráinne, Dónal and the children just stared at her, but Rachel didn't care. She shot Colm a conspiratorial look, and he blushed.

"The horse and the cats we love you for ever," she repeated.

Charlotte then led the procession right around the perimeter of the burial grounds, steering them away from the twelfth-century church ruins to a hidden corner in which an old carved stone stood leaning against a weather-worn limestone trough. She was almost sure that this was the most energy resonant point of the site, but since her dowsing skills were never all that good, she couldn't be certain. She'd just have to hope for the best. Fortunately, dowsing was something that you could cheat at a little and still convince yourself that you were pretty good at it. They planned to say a few prayers here and then set light to Kittens on a miniature funeral pyre made from fuchsia wood that Dónal had been sent out to gather that morning.

Gráinne clustered the children around her, as Charlotte threw her arms up into the sky dramatically and began to preach.

"O Lady and Saint of Reek, in bonnet and golden mantel we would have thee with us for all time in the realms of the lower world and the spirits beyond. Hark well what is sayen, thou are not the Morrighan, Chooser of the Slain. Hark that the moment of death be upon us now, Fair One."

To add emphasis to her words and to ensure the children didn't get bored, she had arranged for Colm to do a series of movements while she spoke. A death-dance, she had called it. She had begged Rachel to join him, but she had refused, yet now as she watched Colm begin to strike his simple stretches and bends, Rachel found herself softening. He was putting such intensity into each movement that it seemed churlish not to help him out. She stood beside him with her knees bent and her arms outstretched and copied him as he bent forward touching his toes, falling to the

199

ground like a cat and rolling over. They repeated this movement twice before standing up again and stretching, balanced on one leg. The children were delighted. Dónal had hold of the shoebox and was holding it above his head in the direction of the sun.

"As red as the blood," Charlotte continued, "as white as the snow, as long as the winter's night on solstice eve is no compare to Kittens' goodness, to how his sword it did shine for truth and light, and his whiskers, they did penetrate the world ahead …"

Charlotte was impressed by her performance. She had rarely officiated at a burial before, and she never imagined it would come so naturally. The words appeared on her tongue as though they were being channelled straight from a divine source. She had read everything there was about pagan sites, but had never actually visited one before.

A minibus of Americans and Germans pulled up outside the site and began clambering over the entrance stile with much ooplas, crikey's and *forsicht*'s. They looked at Colm and the rest and were immediately captivated. They began making their way towards them, powering up their Nikons and Canons as they went, but their guide, spotting the distraction, somehow managed to position herself in front of them and began heading them off. She was determined to keep them on track, to give them a quick tour of the church before herding them back on to the coach and to the next destination – most probably a souvenir shop or lavatory stop. She was nervously checking her watch and pointing pleadingly towards the ruins, and gradually most of them obliged and turned around. It was as though their job was to please her and not the other way around. As soon as she had corralled enough of them around her, she launched straight into her spiel about the crumbling Romanesque arch overhead. Some of them were still more interested in what Charlotte and the rest were up to, craning their necks to see what was going on with the boy in the cape and the other with the shoebox, but the guide kept them under control, brandishing her umbrella as both a pointing rod and herding stick.

". . . of lesser note would be the Charlemagne-influenced peripheral oratory," she intoned, "an approximation of the later Graeco-Roman elaborations documented by Eckart in 1863. While the nave's perimeter buttress is evidently of cruder carved stone, there are really no grounds to believe the site dates from any earlier than the Romanesque period ..."

Charlotte stopped her incantations suddenly with a horrified expression on her face. She swung around towards the tour guide.

"What did you just say?!" she shouted indignantly across to her. "Did you say there were no grounds for believing the site is early? That's hogwash, and you know it."

The tour guide looked over anxiously.

"Go blow it out your buttress!" Charlotte yelled at her.

"Excuse me?" the guide said squeakily.

Charlotte went marching across to her.

"I'm sorry, but you and me both know that's horse shit," she said. "I tried to let the rest of your spiel go, but I can't stand here and listen to you peddling crap. My fellow countrymen deserve to know the truth. And what the fuck have buttresses got to do with anything?"

She turned to the tourists. "Sorry, guys, but you need to know you're being sold a crock of baloney here ... What this lady isn't telling you is that people have been worshipping here for four thousand years. There was a pagan site right there where you're standing – a passage where the sun entered like a penis on the solstice to impregnate the earth and ensure a good crop. The reason this place exists at all is because of that boulder right up there on the hill. See it? It's heavily quartzed, right? See the way it's glinting? It's in a direct line of sight with that standing stone just above that mound there by the shore. It marks out an energy line. Dowse it and you'll see for yourselves."

Two of the group pointed their cameras at the stone and clicked.

"Don't shoot it, for God's sake!" Charlotte cried. "Feel it! Feel it in your bones. Most of you are probably part Irish, yeah? Well, this is your heritage. It's the same for you Germans; we all have Celtic blood in us at some point. These are your ancestors I'm talking about, for Christ sake. Feel it!"

The guide tried to regain control of her group, but Charlotte was just warming up.

"I'm not blaming your guide; she's only telling you what she's been told herself. Her main aim is to get you to the next craft shop with time to spare. That's were she makes her money, and I've no problem with that. I used to be in the game myself, giving tours of the old antebellum houses of the South. The tips were the best part. What I object to are the lies."

"Excuse me," the guide harrumphed. "I mean really, Miss ..."

"This site isn't fucking Christian!" Charlotte spat at her.

"Charlotte!" Gráinne cried at the use of the obscenity.

"Sorry, kids!" Charlotte said, throwing her palm guiltily to her mouth and adopting a goofy contrite expression. But nothing could stop her now. She was fighting for truth. "Just look around you. This is as pagan as you're ever going to get. It was co-opted by the church. What you've got to remember is this place is associated with Brigid, yeah? The goddess of poetry, and for the Celts there was no difference between poets and shamans. Poets are prophets, see? Songs are magick. The word enchant means to sing, for Christ's sake! So what you're seeing here is a nexus, something like an early chamber of transmutation. The poet or shaman stood about there – right there where that fat lady in the oxblood Gore-Tex is ... Yeah, you, lady – you're standing right on top of the power point of this whole site. Can you feel it? Can you feel all that druidic potency? The poet would have been dressed in bird-feathers. And if he was performing a *tarbh fheis*, a type of augury reading, he would be gorging on a chunk of raw flesh torn from the bull he had just killed. This is all true, just ask your guide; she can't deny it. But they never tell you this; and you know what, that makes me sick."

"What happened next?" one of the Americans asked.

"Well, while he was gorging on the raw meat, the others would recite incantations over him. He'd be in trance, you see? They'd all be in a bloody trance at this stage, out of their tiny minds, helped by booze and mushrooms."

A middle-aged man in shades and a John Deere cap guffawed loudly.

"I'm serious, man!" Charlotte cried. "Just ask your guide; she knows. This shit is all documented."

"Well?" the man asked.

The guide coughed nervously and said, "*Tarbh fheis* rituals are known to have occasionally taken place in pre-Christian Ireland, and indeed perhaps into early Christianity."

"What about the drugs?" he asked.

"Intoxicants may have been ingested," she said reluctantly, "but the annals are vague, and most particularly, the reference to bird-feather apparel is disputed by certain sources."

Charlotte smirked. "So there you go," she said, waving her arms triumphantly. "I've got to get back to something here, but you guys, enjoy your stay in Ireland. Just make sure you're being told the truth. If you're going to be fleeced in the gift shops, make sure you get your money's worth at the sites … Yeah? Have a nice day."

The guide gathered up her charges and steered them sheepishly back to the bus.

"Now where were we?" Charlotte said as soon as they were alone. She noticed that Gráinne was gathering the children together and preparing to lead them away, horrified at the unorthodox history they were getting to hear. Her main concern was that they might bring it up when the priest next visited and that she herself would get blamed.

"But we've only just started," Charlotte cried.

"That's quite enough," Gráinne said. "The children have seen and heard quite enough already. You should be ashamed of yourself."

"Tell them, Colm," Charlotte cried. "Tell them we haven't got to the best part yet. We're going to light the funeral pyre soon."

"Yeah! And throw Kittens on," Colm said. "Charlotte says we'll get to see its soul leaving the body."

"Well, not actually see it," Charlotte corrected, "but you'll hear it for sure. At some point you'll hear a mini explosion, a popping sound as the brains expand in the skull and burst. In Indian ritual it's considered the point at which the soul departs. It'll be fun, I promise."

But the children didn't get to hear any of this. Gráinne was already marching them back towards the stone stile, away from danger.

"What do we do now?" Rachel said deflated, looking around the empty field.

"Why, finish our work, of course," Charlotte said. "It's their loss if they miss out."

Colm's shoulders sagged, and he looked around him anxiously. Without the audience he suddenly felt a bit foolish in his cloak and bare chest. Turning to Dónal, he said, "Strelka coming on."

Strelka was short for Strelka Puppy Syndrome, a term he had coined to describe a sense of disorientation that he imagined was similar to the feeling that the puppy of Strelka, the Russian dog sent into space on Sputnik, must have felt when it was sent as a gift to John F. Kennedy. Colm had been intrigued by what the puppy would have thought of the sudden transfer from a sterile cage in some grim Soviet laboratory under the care of vodka-breath apparatchiks to the lawns of the White House where she was cuddled in the fug of Jackie's Chanel No. 5. Colm wondered whether the puppy could have some degree of genetic memory, passed on by her mother, of the journey into orbit – of being shot through a limitless black expanse at ten thousand miles an hour, watching her home and kennels and favourite bone racing further and further away until suddenly, after eighteen earth orbits, she came crashing back down into the Caspian sea.

That was how Colm felt. Everything suddenly lost perspective. He looked around him and wondered where he was and what he was doing here, standing in the middle of a field with a priest's cloak on. These people were his family and friends, but they did-n't understand him. Taytos had understood him, and she was still missing. His mother was missing too, though she had never understood him much. She had accepted him, and that was some-thing, but not the same as being understood. Nowhere near the same. He wanted to be understood, or at least, to understand him-self a little better. Like Beatrice had helped him do. Stelka and her puppy probably had no idea who or what they had become – it's what comes from being a pioneer.

"Can we go home now?" Colm said dejectedly and began grinding his teeth.

"What about the burial?" Charlotte said

"Who cares," he said.

"But we have to do something," Charlotte said.

"OK, but can I do what I want?" he said.

"Sure," Dónal said.

Perking up a little on hearing this, Colm turned around and

led them back down the road the way they had come. A wind picked up, raising froth on the sea and hurling it up at the cliff face, frightening a lone puffin out of its nook. The last two remaining currachs that were kept on the pier, more out of nostalgia than for any practical use, were rattling on a timber rack – since the trawlers had come in two decades ago, the currachs were only ever used for regattas and fair days. They had no real place in the modern world.

As the wind gusted, the rusted black and white road sign pointing towards Reek quay at the four-road crossroads looked as if it might finally snap off its bracket. They followed Colm along the old track, its thin layer of tarmac almost obliterated by the fat strip of moss running up the centre, dotted here and there with dandelions like periscopic cat's-eyes.

Colm slipped his hand into Rachel's.

"Thank you for coming," he said, and she smiled.

"It's an odd place," was all she could think to reply.

"It's mainly a place people leave from," Colm said. "That's Reek's claim to fame. During the famine, thousands headed to America from here, and then a hundred years later they set off again, when those islands you can see out there were cleared of people. My mum's mother came from the smaller of the islands. And, of course, a thousand years before that the first person to ever go to America from Europe set off from just down there."

"Christopher Columbus?" Rachel asked.

"No! The man that mountain is named after – Saint Brendan. You see those tiny black boats – the canoe-like ones. He sailed one right across."

"When?"

"About a thousand three hundred years ago."

"You're kidding?" she said.

"No, seriously … he wrote an account of it all," Colm said.

"But how?!" she said.

"On vellum," Colm said. "That's very thin calf skin."

"No, I mean, how did he get to America?"

"Oh," Colm said, shrugging. "He just went."

He slipped his hand from hers and walked slowly across the field to the cliff edge, bringing the shoebox back up over his head as he walked, while quietly explaining to Kittens that his body was now going to drop deep into the sea, but that he shouldn't be scared and should continue making his way across the bridge of glistening lights and through the tunnel into the bright realm on the other side. He told him to be sure to look out for the spirits of kitten-friends who'd be there to guide him. Then, he raised the box up behind him and hurled it straight out to sea. The others came running, reaching the edge in time to see it splashing into the mercuric water.

"Sometimes you need to get battered around a bit to be freed up again," Colm said. "I think Kittens hadn't fully accepted he was dead – he needed a bit of a shock to the system. That was the equivalent of a 220v shock, I reckon. It'll send him straight home."

They stood for a while staring into the churning sea before suddenly becoming aware of the chill and moving on. There was nothing more to be done now except to get in out of the cold, and they turned to go their separate ways – Charlotte and Rachel to the yacht, and Dónal back to the school to see Gráinne. He needed to talk to her. He had been doing some thinking and realised that things couldn't go on as they had. Even if his mother did turn up soon, she couldn't be expected to keep running the house for ever, and Máiréad had been dropping hints about moving up to Kildare to live with Ciarán her boyfriend in one of the army houses before she got married. Her initial plan had been to wait until after the wedding to move in with Ciarán, but she was less keen now to hang around the house as housekeeper to her brothers and father. The arrangement had always been that Dónal would be left the house and farm and that he'd take care of his parents. It was time he began to face up to his responsibilities. And, of course, there was still the problem of Colm. Dónal was happy to have him at home, but eventually he was going to have to find a place for himself in the world. There was a lot ahead for Dónal, and he would need some support. It made no sense to be fighting with Gráinne now of all times. They had been going out for too long – there was no point in rocking the boat, and it certainly wasn't fair to play around with her feelings.

Seventeen

Colm had gone straight back to his boulders after the funeral. He needed to work out the cement issue. He began gathering small stones from the field in a wheelbarrow and mulling over how he could get the money he needed for supplies. His mind twirled around in circles trying to come up with a plan, but this only made him agitated and he had to resort to hooking up the hose in the yard for some relief. It was either that or disassemble the house's electrical circuits again. Both things had got him through bouts of worry in the past. They were often the only thing that worked, that calmed his mind. It was the malleability and vigour of water that was so great, and the way it gurgled and glugged and cast off brilliant diamonds into the air like electricity.

He brought the hose into the back yard and began twirling great lassoes of water around his head, perfecting their shimmering multicoloured parabolas and flinging rainbows up so that they almost reached over the house. He knew he was just wasting time, but he found it hard to stop once he'd started. It felt too good. All kinds of water appealed to him, from the sea to dew, to spit, but his favourites were those that he could control, make do whatever he wanted them to: showers, taps and hoses in particular. The only type he didn't like was frozen water. He disliked snow and hated ice with a passion ever since he had slipped and banged his head on it one winter. He suspected ice from then on; thought it might be out to get him. He couldn't understand why people would want to put it in drinks. It caused frostbite if you weren't careful, and even if you were careful, it numbed your tongue. Ice and all its variations were to be avoided. He had decided that there would definitely be plenty of water in the house he was building – a fountain, for one, and perhaps a cascade too if he could work out the engineering of it. He had found a roll of half-inch piping that he could use to connect up to the supply in the yard; all he was missing was a pump. It was going to be an underground dwelling with a fountain right outside the door, although he hadn't told anyone that yet. The ring of stone would serve as the outer wall – he loved the idea of a house with only one wall. The only thing visible from outside would be the ring of stones with sods of grass laid on plywood as a roof. Inside there would be one large room. All he needed was a living space with a bed in it and a circuit of electrical sockets going around – a wall-mounted ring circuit with spurs dropping down to socket boxes that had transparent front plates on them so that he could see the wiring at all times. He would be happy there.

He had just managed to convince himself to turn off the hose and was reeling it back up again, carefully pinching out any kinks, when he saw Rachel coming along the headland past the house. The glow of light shining from her body had brightened, and he blushed at the sight of it. Seeing light from anyone was always a confusing experience. Rachel's light was special, the clarity of it and the diversity of its colour range. But he decided to keep it to himself for the moment – he really didn't want to embarrass her.

She waved at him and turned to come over. Colm ground his teeth and put a hand above his eyes like a visor. She was one of those glinting ones, he realised: hard to look at straight on – a muted, scaled-down version of those NASA images of imploding stars.

"The light coming from you is ..." he began, unable to prevent himself.

"Sorry?" Rachel said.

"Right, I'm putting the hose away," he mumbled.

"This place is soaked," she said, looking around her.

He nodded agreeably. "Yeah, I need cement."

Rachel looked at him quizzically, and Colm explained about his problem getting building supplies. He even told her all about his underground house although he had told no one else about it yet. She loved the idea. It reminded her of the mud buildings that she and Nathaniel had helped build at a workshop in the woods.

"Why don't you use mud instead?" she asked.

He gave it some thought, before shaking his head and saying, "I think there's enough mud in the ground already without adding any more. An underground mud house is basically a rabbit warren and I don't like rabbits."

"Could you barter for the cement?" Rachel suggested.

"Huh?" Colm said.

"Like, you know, give the man in the shop something else instead of money."

"Like what?" Colm asked, intrigued.

"Well, what would he like? Sometimes back home I sing or dance in return for a cup of coffee."

"I don't think that would work here," Colm said with conviction.

"Well, what do you have that the man might like?"

Colm pulled out a few sticks that were carved with intricately swirling shapes.

"These?" he said.

"Did you carve them?" Rachel said.

He nodded.

"They're beautiful, but I think he might want something more valuable."

Colm looked around the yard.

"Hens?" he said.

"No, I don't think they'll do."

"Cows?"

"Maybe," Rachel said. "Are they yours?"

Colm shook his head.

They both fell quiet for a minute. Rachel was looking at him out of the corner of her eye. He was intriguing. There was no single category that she could easily place him in. He was unlike anyone else she had ever met. If she had known the term strusual, that might have done.

Rachel said after a moment, "How about getting a job?"

Colm thought about it for a moment, "Like what?"

"I dunno, leaf-blowing or something."

"Leaf-blowing?" Colm cried. "Blowing leaves? Why would I blow leaves?"

"Do folks not blow leaves here?"

Colm couldn't stop himself from laughing. It was such a ridiculous concept. He was laughing so hard he couldn't answer and just shook his head.

"In the fall?" Rachel continued adamantly. "With a leaf-blower?"

"A leaf-blower?" Colm said when he'd managed to compose himself.

"Yeah, a machine, for blowing leaves."

Colm burst out laughing again. "You're pulling my leg," he said.

"No," she said, beginning to laugh spontaneously along with him. "How else do you gather up leaves?"

"Can you see any trees here?" he said looking out at the barren green fields. "And even if we had any, why would we want to gather the leaves? Are they valuable? I know you get sugar from trees in America, but ..."

Colm stopped dead, noticing that Rachel had begun to cry.

"What's wrong?" he said.

She looked away, shaking her head and wiping her eyes. "Nothing."

Colm watched the tears rising up inside her. He could imagine them squeezing up through her tear ducts and could see her trying to fight them back just as Charlotte had done earlier, curving her shoulders forward like sticks caught in a stream. Her light had dimmed significantly.

"What's the matter?" he said.

She shook her head. How could she ever explain? It was partly the fact that she just realised that she hadn't laughed in so long – not since they had been kicked out on to the motorway in England, and that had been more out of despair than anything – but mostly it was the way he had looked at her. It was as if she caught a glimpse of her own light reflected back at her from his eyes. She had forgotten so much about who she was, or at least, who she had been. Seeing the look in his eyes prompted her to remember that she had once shone. Those years with Nathaniel when she had felt a constant warmth glowing inside her seemed so long ago now – an impossible dream.

She thought back to the morning dips in the lake with her dad and mountain biking with Nathaniel at weekends and just hanging out with her friends – it all seemed so idyllic. How had she drifted so far from there, so far from the Rachel she had been? When Colm looked at her, it reminded her of Nathaniel and of her parents, of how they used to see her before things turned sour, before her parents adopted that constant – and infuriating – piercing expression of concern. All she ever saw in her dad's eyes now was anxiety, and perhaps just the merest remnant of the light she had once inspired – not enough to cling on to, not enough to guide her back to where she'd been. That, more than anything, was probably the reason she had followed Charlotte. In her eyes, Rachel saw some strange mutant form of light: a fanatic, frenetic luminescence, more a strobe than any kind of reassuring beam that might guide one home. It was hardly dependable, but better than nothing.

"Why do you look at me the way you do?" she asked Colm suddenly.

He just stared at her, fright passing across his face. "Huh?" he said at last.

"You look at me as though … I dunno, your face relaxes."

Colm blushed. He began to say something, but it came out as a stammer and he stopped himself. His face was creasing and stretching as though he were having to force the words out, to squeeze them through a grinder.

"Sometimes … sometimes, I find it hard to say the thoughts that are, eh …" he said, pushing the words out with tremendous force. "Dónal tells me I should have things ready to say. Like scripts I could fall back on. Like the way when tourists come here and read from their phrase book when they want something."

The volume of his speech diminished as he talked, until he eventually ground to a halt, or at least Rachel couldn't hear him any longer.

He paused, breathing deeply and in a moment tried again, "I wish I had the phrasebook now. It's OK as long as I know what I want to say. It's just hard when you get caught in detours, in unexpected …"

He fell quiet again as he saw Rachel staring at him. He wondered whether she was about to laugh at him, like the kids in school used to.

"You think I'm a *liúdramán*, don't you?" he said sadly. "My mum calls me that, when she's drinking. She used to be proud of me – reading so early and knowing all my sums. Now she …" He paused, steeling himself to go on. "When she rings her sister she says things to her about me, and I feel like getting sick. Fidgeting or stammering doesn't mean you're thick or anything, it's just …"

He gulped. Rachel was captivated by the intensity with which he was trying to communicate. "It just means you're trying to express the feelings inside," she said. "Trying to balance the inner thoughts with the outside world."

Colm looked up at her in surprise. "Yeah!"

Rachel pulled her T-shirt up and looked down at her belly. Colm followed her gaze and saw the map of low red contours on her skin.

"What are …?" he said, startled.

They were mostly healed by now, but the words were still visible.

She pulled up her trouser leg and showed him the cat's cradle on her calf.

"Who did that to you?" he asked.

"Me," Rachel said. "I was trying to … to say stuff, I guess."

Colm looked at her for a long time and then said, "Why?"

"I dunno, Colm. I was sad and it made me feel better. I sort of wanted to distract myself – to punish myself maybe too. Every day I cut myself a little more. It was like a diary."

"That's how fidgeting is," Colm said. "A message board of how I'm feeling, except I only half want people to understand."

"I get you," Rachel sighed.

"And you put a blade into your skin," Colm said tracing his finger along the ridges. He was visibly moved.

"Every day. It was the only way to release the tension. It was quieter than screaming and didn't attract so much fuss."

"Why did you stop?"

"Charlotte came."

"Oh."

"Yeah, she saved me."

Colm put his hand back on her belly, and she winced not out of pain, but the memory of it.

"I've just thought of something!" Colm announced. "A brain-wave."

"Yeah?"

"You know the way you're good at cutting?" he said nodding towards her scars.

"Uh-uh," she winced.

"Really good, from what I can see," he gushed. "Well, would you help me with something?"

"With what?" she said warily.

"Something that would bring us money."

Rachel raised an eyebrow.

"First off, how do you feel about jellyfish?" Colm asked. "About cutting jellyfish."

Rachel couldn't help laughing again; a proper belly laugh.

"I'm serious!" Colm said. "There's these people in Dublin who want jellyfish bits. They'll pay well."

She was thinking that she ought to tell him that she was not going to be around for much longer, but that if she was she would gladly have helped. Instead she said, "Will you do me a favour first?"

"Sure!"

"Bring me swimming with the dolphins."

"Really?" Colm said.

"Sure."

"Well, there's just one problem. I think you should know, I don't like cold water – I mean freezing water. I'm fine if it's above 8 degrees Celsius."

"That's fair enough," Rachel said.

"I don't like ice cream either, because milk is 98 per cent water. Or sky ice cream, which is snow. Or pretty much anything frozen. OK?"

"I can understand that," she said.

"Really?" he said.

"Well … yeah!" she said.

She noticed his eyes were unsettlingly clear. Their sheen reminded her of the water at the end of the jetty where she and her father swam at home. When he looked at her, it was with his entire focus; it was unconditional.

"Would you be prepared to try an ice cream," she found herself saying, "if I made one with your favourite things in it?"

He hesitated and began flicking his fingers back and forth. "Maybe," he said. "Would you be prepared to accept it, if I didn't like it? Would I have to pretend to like it so as not to hurt your feelings?"

"I don't see why you'd have to do that," she said.

"OK then," he said contently.

"Let's go swimming," she said, "and we can think more about it."

"The dolphins don't come in close to shore until early evening. If you like we could go up to Cnoc Ciarán first? There's something I want to show you there."

"Fine by me," Rachel said, getting up and following Colm out of the farmyard and up the hill behind their house to a track that led towards the mountain.

As Colm strode purposefully through the gorse toward the brow of the hill, he shouted back to her, "You are going to love this; it's my favourite place."

Rachel found it hard to keep up, and she was about to call out to him to slow down when they reached Colm's stone shelter, the

217

tiny cell of corbelled limestone built either by shepherds a few decades before or pilgrims hundreds of years ago. Colm spread his arms out majestically, as though the view was entirely his. Rachel was overcome by the expanse of sea stretching out like an iridescent bolt of tweed towards the horizon. It reminded her of one of Nathaniel's overcoats, the blue-green one he wore ice-skating. The wind coming in off from the Atlantic breathed the land to life, setting the stone walls murmuring and whistling through the five-bar gates – sounding a different tune on each rung. Everything seemed more alive up here, from the quivering heather under foot to the tiny streams that gurgled through the boggy ground.

Colm walked along the brow a bit to the glinting boulder that Charlotte had pointed out from the burial ground, and he looked down towards the sea and the remains of a stone fort teetering on the edge of a sheer precipice beneath them: a crumbling Iron-age relic covered in lemon-grey and ochre lichen and surrounded by ferns and brambles. At one time, it must have stood out exalted around a network of fields pulsing with stock; now it was forgotten and ignored. Each year Colm noticed more of it tumbling into the sea. Soon it would be just a memory – three thousand years of struggle, survival and salvation confined to a few photos in old guide books. It was too remote, too precarious, to be a proper tourist destination. There was no easy access for a coach, and even a moderate gale could send tourists hurtling over the edge. Its name was Dún Mór, after Mór, the daughter of the Celtic sun god and wife of the sea god, Lír. To Rachel it looked like the skeleton of some great sea creature that had been hurled up on to the cliff by a giant wave. Its outer defences were like a ribcage of three horseshoe-shaped ramparts, and at its core was a hub of stone cells, like a trefoil knot or a gnawed skull, which sparkled mysteriously as the sun set shards of silica alight.

"Imagine how brave they must have been," Rachel said, looking down at it. "Barricading themselves in there, right up against the sea, with nowhere to run to."

"There was danger on every side," Colm said. "Wolves and bears in the mountains and wild tribes roaming the countryside. Also from the sea there were Vikings and Visigoths looking to rape and pillage. There's no fresh water inside the walls, so eventually the locals would have had to come out and fight."

"Your ancestors," Rachel said, disturbing a lizard as she sat into a plum-purple cushion of heather and absent-mindedly crumbled a sliver of rock debris with her fingers, revealing crystalline fragments that glinted the colours of petrol.

"You're fidgeting," Colm said, pointing at the bits of rock.

She laughed. "Sort of," she said. "I was just thinking how beautiful it is, how much my dad would love it."

"It always makes me feel good," Colm said. "Sometimes, too good. I get so excited up here that I have to stay a while longer, until I calm down again. If people saw me they would think I was mad. Or *madder*."

"You're a little unusual, Colm – but you're not mad," Rachel said, planting a kiss lightly on his cheek.

"It's like all my cells begin spinning in different directions," he said blushing. "I feel it coming up from the earth, or maybe down from the sky, I dunno. Eventually it becomes a loop with so much love that it's hard to breathe; so then I have to stand up and breathe deeply … one, two, three, breathe in – hold, hold, hold – and then breathe out. It's in case I faint and no one would know where I was, or else maybe all my cells could spin so fast that they'd come apart like blood samples in a centrifuge machine."

"You know how much I would adore to feel like that sometimes, Colm?" Rachel said. "Even for just a short while."

Colm shrugged.

"I haven't felt anything in so long," she said, looking out over towards America. "But I used to. I've just forgotten how."

"Maybe cutting was a way of setting your cells spinning."

"Something like that," she said. "Looking for signs of life."

"I saw a crayfish pot being torn apart just down there a few days ago, and it made me think that sometimes you have to get battered up a bit to be free again."

Rachel stared at him, thinking. "You know what, Colm," she said at last. "The rest of us get time to learn all this stuff as we go along, to accustom ourselves to it, but it's like you were born old, you know? Like you didn't come in with a blank slate. It must get confusing at times?"

Colm said nothing. No one had ever put it like that before. He was just glad that today he seemed more or less able to say what he wanted to say. Occasionally it would wash over him that he knew what he ought to tell people, but the right words would never come. Today was easier.

"Often I feel I'm underwater," he said after a pause. "I hear voices in the distance, but I can't understand what they're saying, and because I don't understand, someone comes and laughs, and that's the signal for everybody to start laughing."

"Neither of us has a clean slate any more," Rachel continued, as much to herself as to him. "I wish mum and dad were here. I think I'm going to have to start over."

She reached down and kissed him again.

He looked at her, bending backwards and saying, "Hey, no leaf-blowers."

Eighteen

Gráinne had come out of class at lunchtime to find Dónal waiting for her again behind the lavatory block. He told her that he needed to talk, but she insisted that they wait till evening, so they could discuss everything properly. He turned away and headed home, and on his way he spotted what he thought was a large sheep or a small donkey rolling on its back up on the cliffs. The animal was in silhouette and indistinct. As he watched it, it suddenly rose up on its hind legs and remained in that position for some time. Dónal was intrigued. He made his way across the sand dunes towards the cliffs, noticing as he drew nearer that the figure was not in fact an animal, but Charlotte dressed in a woollen cloak and circling her arms and legs in slow, uneven ellipses, as if she were giving complicated directions in slow motion. Dónal had never seen anyone move like that before – he couldn't imagine why they would want to. He clambered over the last stone walls to get a better look, just as Charlotte lifted her gaze and saw him. She was breathing slowly and deeply, making gurgling noises in the back of her throat like a diver under water. Unfurling her pelvis slowly, she repositioned herself perpendicular to the earth and smiled inwardly.

"You're a bit of rat, you know that?" she said when he drew near.

Dónal could see that she had been drinking.

"What?" Dónal said.

"Sneaking up on me like that," she said.

"What are you up to?" he said.

"What does it look like?"

"Directing traffic," he said.

"It's yoga, for God's sake!" she cried. "Maybe not very good yoga – I'm out of practice and I've had a bit too much of this." She threw a bottle of brandy towards him, "Want some?"

Charlotte and Rachel had been arguing again. She had wanted to explain to Rachel about her illness when they had returned to the boat. Somehow, before she had even begun, she said something to irritate Rachel, and they ended up squabbling back and forth, before Rachel stormed out, saying she was going to see Colm. It finally dawned on Charlotte that far from being a help to Rachel she was now increasingly becoming part of the problem. She had only ever wanted to help, but it felt more and more like she was dragging Rachel down. It was clear that Rachel was worried about the yacht, and perhaps she was right to be. Taking it might not have been the best thing to do in hindsight, but in her heart Charlotte still felt she had acted honourably. All she ever wanted was to guide Rachel back on track, and she was in no doubt that she had at least helped to do that to some extent. Maybe now was the time to step back. She had become little more than a punch-bag for the girl, and while every teenager needs a punch-bag, Charlotte wasn't sure she wanted to be it. She had become a surrogate for Rachel's scarred belly – somewhere to express her frustration, to release her tension. That's how Charlotte saw it, and she wasn't prepared to let it go on, to become the focus of Rachel's new habit. It wasn't healthy.

As if to stress the fact that their time together was coming towards an end, Charlotte had collapsed on deck just after Rachel had stormed off. A series of stabbing pains ripped through her stomach, and she only just managed to reach the gunwale in time before retching over the side. The fact that it was a syrupy, dark mess of congealed blood convinced her of what she had long suspected: that indeed time was running short, the illness was taking hold. She had been expecting it all along – if anything she had been given more time than she had hoped for. Her angel helpers must have wanted her to complete the mission first. She had always known that her role in Rachel's future was a temporary one. She had never been so hubristic as to consider herself magnificent enough to heal another human on her own. It was up to Rachel now to take responsibility for herself, and it was likely she'd do it better and faster without Charlotte's interference. Hopefully someone else would come along to steer her through the worst bits, but either way Charlotte knew that she had to let go now. Of this she had no doubt, and she suddenly began to set about her preparations with a sense of clarity that she would have cherished had she not been in such pain.

She quickly scribbled a note to Rachel and left it on the galley beside the sink. First grabbing a bottle of brandy from the storage locker, she then made her way off the boat and up towards the cliff, walking out along the track until she found a particularly beautiful spot looking over the Atlantic towards the New World. She made herself comfortable there, on a golden slab of sandstone, and began drinking the brandy. It didn't take long for it to numb the pain, and she began to feel a whole lot better – admittedly only a temporary reprieve, but a welcome one nonetheless. She decided to do some yoga to prepare herself for what was to come and had been happily lost in this when Dónal came upon her.

"What are they?" Dónal asked, pointing to two iron bars lying on the grass beside her.

"Scaffolding poles," she said dismissively.

"I can see that," he said. "What are they doing here?"

She looked at them hard and then at him for a moment; she seemed to settle on something.

"I don't know," she shrugged. "I found them on the way up and just took them with me. I don't really want them, do you? I think they're from Bridie's pub – you know, where the painting is being done?"

"I know where they're from," he said, looking at her strangely. He was unconvinced.

"I just thought they'd be useful," she said with a shrug. "Take them if you want."

Dónal looked at them and then at her.

"Wanna see a cool yoga move before you go?" she asked him.

Dónal shrugged.

Charlotte was feeling surprisingly good. It was the feeling she got on those rare occasions she ever felt clear about anything. Clarity had been one of the scarcest elements in her life, and it felt somehow unfair that it would suddenly come on so strong. *Could they not have managed to sprinkle it more evenly over my life?* she thought. It was almost an insult to shovel out such an abundance so late in the game. Bastards.

"You've never seen yoga before, have you?" she said, shaking her head in disgust. "That's horrifying. How can you live like that! Just pass me the bottle, and I'll show you something special, something you won't forget in a hurry."

He shrugged and passed her the bottle. She drank back a mouthful, quick enough to make her wince, and then sucked her breath in to dull the pain.

"You'll like this, I promise. It's called Dandayamara-Dhanurasana," she said, digging into her bag and pulling out a length of rope, then shifting her weight to her right leg. "Now if I was any good I wouldn't need the rope, but …"

She rose her left leg out behind her and bent it at the knee, then threw the rope over her right shoulder and looped it around her foot and pulled upwards, pausing now and then to get her balance. "In English it's called Standing Bow Pose. See the way I'm like a bow being pulled by an archer? You should try it, it's fun."

"Do you always drink when you do yoga?"

Charlotte glanced at him dismissively. "If I was really good, I could bring the foot right up to the crown of my head, and I wouldn't even need the rope. Iyenga could do that. I wish I had one of his books here to show you. In India some of the really old yogis can get the soles of their feet right flat against their heads – even with the foot flexed. Mad huh?!"

Dónal didn't know what to say. He stood up to go.

"What's your hurry? Have another drop of brandy," Charlotte said, bending down carefully on her right leg like a stork and passing him the bottle.

He refused it.

"You sure?" she said, looking at him ruminatively. "There's definitely a bit of rat in you. I can see that now. I mean it in a good way, of course. I think rats are so brave. Every other animal on earth would make a better scavenger than them. You know they can't vomit? They eat mostly shit and poison, yet they can't vomit. It's kind of heroic, huh? You and Colm, you're both kind of brave – for different reasons though. He shouldn't be here, but you, you suit the place. I always think it's tragic when you see someone born to live a different life to the one they're in ..."

"I didn't think ..." Dónal interrupted.

"No, the rat never does," she said. "It's better that way. The point is that life is a gift, but what happens is often unbearably tragic."

She put both legs back on the ground and reached out for the scaffolding bars and handed them to Dónal.

"Take these down with you, OK?" she said. "They shouldn't be up here."

He took them from her, throwing one over each shoulder.

"'You're a good rat," she said. "But you've got to decide which to believe in: the bit about life being a gift or a tragedy. Shall I give you a clue? Remember that we're all in a river, even the rats, and there's a waterfall approaching. Just remember that. And while you're doing that, will you do me a little favour?"

"What?" he asked. Her eyes had turned dark, and Dónal became a little anxious.

"Will you leave me alone now?" she said.

Dónal grudgingly turned around and walked away.

She called after him, "You're a good rat, OK?"

Colm and Rachel came down from the mountain and took the road through town and out along the coast to a stretch of shore-line where dolphins could often be seen. It was a particularly deep stretch of sea where shoals of mackerel occasionally passed and lobsters had once been abundant until the fishermen wiped them out a decade ago. About a quarter of a kilometre on the far side of town, just past the souvenir shop with the over-sized car park, a spade-faced boy with cargo pants and an over-abundance of front teeth approached them, raising his Red Socks cap to get a better look.

"Rachel?" the boy asked hesitantly. "Is that you?"

A look of fear passed across Rachel face's. He looked too young, too naïve, to be a cop, she thought, but you could never be sure. He was definitely American, and even sounded like he was from New Hampshire. If they were sending someone the whole way over here things must be bad.

"It's Jake," the boy said. "Cameron's brother, remember? Your mom built our house."

"Oh, right, Jake," she said, relieved. "What are you doing here?"

She was desperately trying to place him. She wasn't sure she had ever even met him in Cameron's house, although the more she thought about it, there had often been a figure lurking in the background – normally engrossed in some computer game.

"Summer vacation. What about you?" he asked.

She didn't reply. Suddenly the story about him feeding his teacher crushed glass came back to her.

"Did you …?" she began.

Maybe he guessed what she was going to say, because he quickly stepped back to reveal his companion, a mousy-haired girl in a grey cotton tank top.

"This here is my girlfriend, Briony," he said. "Briony, this is one of Cam's friends, Rachel. Isn't that weird – what are the odds, huh?"

"Gee," said Briony.

"We've just come from Bunratty Castle," Jake gushed. "Have you been? It's awesome. They do a full medieval banquet with Riverdancers and a fiddle player and this sort of ye olde type food. Briony and I got smashed on mead in Durty Nelly's beforehand, and when the minstrel-guy called us up on stage, I almost barfed on his winkle-pickers!"

Rachel managed a tight smile.

"Who's your friend?" Jake said pointing to Colm.

Colm had his eyes firmly planted on the ground and was busily counting his fingers. Rachel looked at Colm and put a hand on his shoulder, but he didn't look up. "This is Colm," she said.

"Hi, it's Jake – Jake Grouter," Jake said extending a hand forward.

Colm turned away from them, muttering, "I've got to check on some periwinkles."

"Woh! What up with him?" Jake said watching Colm shuffling off. "Seems like one bubble short of plumb."

Rachel was looking with concern towards Colm and wasn't aware of what Jake was saying. He gave Briony a reassuring squeeze.

"Real sorry about what happened to Nathaniel," he said. "Cam was really messed up about it … He's going out with Katy now, y'know? You heard what happened to him, yeah? Getting kicked out of St George's, like twice, for pissing in the pool – *doh!*"

He and Briony collapsed into gales of laughter at this.

"Look, I've got to go," Rachel said.

"Oh … right," Jake said taken aback. "You don't want to go for a drink or something? There's a bar back in town that does a mean Irish coffee. It's full of old critters speaking pure Celtic or whatever."

"I really have to go," Rachel said.

"Well, make sure you check out Bunratty. I thought it was going to be a total yawnathon, like serious slumber-fest – but, grando mistako!"

Rachel walked off towards Colm. She stopped after a few feet and turned back, about to call out to Jake, to ask him whether he had actually given his teacher coffee with crushed glass in it, but then she realised she didn't care. None of it mattered any more.

She looked around for Colm, who was sitting outside the souvenir shop surrounded by Aran jumpers, shillelaghs and fridge magnets in the shape of scheming leprechauns. He was leaning against a turf-basket full of inflatable dolphins, staring at the passers-by, actually looking up from the ground and staring hard at their faces for a change. He was trying to find ways of telling them apart. It oughtn't to be all that difficult, he reasoned; everyone else seemed able to manage it. There must be some key or knack that he hadn't yet gathered. One of the reasons he felt so uncomfortable at school was because Gráinne used to get him to hand back the copy books to the class as a way of involving him more with the other children. She never seemed to realise that he found it next to impossible to put the names to the right faces. He would break into a sweat each time, trying to remember who was wearing what clothes, or whose voice he recognised, or memorising where people usually sat. He invariably would mix things up, and half the class would have to swap their copies back and forth between them. Colm had asked Dónal a few times to explain the problem to Gráinne, but it seemed she couldn't grasp it. She simply didn't have the imagination to conceive that someone might not be able to recognise a person's face.

On looking over towards Rachel now, Colm had no problem spotting the lustre from her. She was unmistakable. He saw the two Americans walking away, and looking at the girl he wrinkled his nose, wondering why Americans were so fond of liver-coloured clothes – not the wonderfully vibrant dark purple of fresh liver, but the pale, grainy, grey tones of cooked renal organs that they chose for their T-shirts and hoodies.

Colm got up as Rachel approached.

"Let's go find these dolphins," she said, and they walked out further along the coast hand-in-hand, turning down along a boreen behind one of the stretch bungalows with movie-screen windows that were gradually replacing the old farmhouses, and along the headland to a small inlet where Colm said he had seen people swimming with dolphins in the past. There was no sign of them there now.

"Are they often here?" Rachel said.

"At this time of year, yeah, especially in the evening," Colm said. "I think they come in for shelter after feeding. Some are really friendly and hang out here for months or even years."

They sat down on the warm sand and looked out to sea.

Colm jingled his keys busily between his fingers, and Rachel felt in her mind a vague, but distinct, sense of being drawn to her right, towards him. It was as though Colm had opened a valve which drew her inextricably in, like how early astronauts when opening the catheter to pass urine could feel the hungry tug of space, of absolute vacuum, pulling at their innards. Through him she felt herself connected to something bigger, just as the astronauts were hooked up directly to the void via their urinary tract. It wasn't quite the connection of hummingbirds and angel's trumpet, or zero to one that she had felt for Nathaniel, but there was definitely a resonance. Had Colm been asked, he might have described it as akin to that between popcorn and periwinkles. A combination that one would not at first think would go together, but somehow does. It struck Rachel that it was no wonder people were a bit wary of Colm; he had access to something unknowable, and when he let his shields down, you could get some sense of what life was like for him: the incessant bombardment of rapid-fire sensual assault he constantly absorbed and pinged off in other directions.

"Do you think water is alive?" he asked her, but before she got a chance to reply, a dorsal fin appeared and a dolphin suddenly breached.

"Oh my God!" Rachel cried.

"A lardy pig," Colm said with a grin.

"Isn't it beautiful!" Rachel said.

Colm nodded.

"Can we go in?" Rachel said.

Neither of them had a swimsuit, and they stared at each other for a moment. Rachel often swam naked at home in the mornings, but she didn't know whether it was OK here. Colm rarely swam despite his fondness for water, but he had never understood why people would cover themselves anywhere, especially in the water. He looked around him again to check no one was around and began shrugging off his Breton smock and jeans.

"Normally people wear wetsuits here, but the water should be OK by now," Colm said, wading in.

Rachel pulled off her summer dress and panties and followed him, cursing as she stubbed her toe on a stone, and then giggling as some sucker insect wriggled around her ankle. The water was cold, but not unbearably so. It deepened quickly, lapping against her thighs, making her shiver and cry out. Colm had never seen a woman naked before, except for his sister when she was little. He turned around, awestruck by the sun playing on the rise and fall of her golden body. She noticed a trace of concern flicker across his face, and she approached him and took his hand.

"Are you OK?" she said, reaching out and taking his flicking fingers, feeling their intensity coursing through her, like the coiled power of a trapped butterfly.

He nodded and smiled, marvelling at her open-pored, pumice-like skin, her tight, light-bulb shoulders curving down to small breasts that rippled as she moved and the surf-like back-curl of the hair between her legs.

"What's that?" Colm asked, pointing at a delicate strand of blue and red marking just above her pelvis.

"It's a pistil, from a crocus," she said. "My friend Nathaniel got a honeybee, and I got this to match."

"It's nice," he said. "Really nice."

To change the subject, Rachel placed her hand on his stomach, which had the texture and form of a pale ceramic basin, with his bellybutton as the plug hole. She said, "You're not all that hairy, are you?"

"No," he said, looking down at himself curiously. "It's because of the O-gene – the gene that gave cavemen their square jaws and hairy, stumpy bodies; this place has more of it than anywhere else in Europe – but I didn't get it. I'm the exception in that too, the freak."

Rachel suddenly cried out as an enormous grey torpedo came grating against her leg. She looked behind her in time to see the dolphin swerve around and come at her again from below. Slowly and gently it approached her feet, then backed off and swam away.

"Oh my God!" cried Rachel. "Did you see that?!"

She and Colm could still make out its vague form disappearing into the murky water. All awareness of the cold had left them by now.

"Do you think it'll come back?" she said.

Colm just laughed, and they both swam out after it, swimming side by side, pausing occasionally to dive down and circle around each other in the water, checking each other out like the dolphin had done. Before they knew it, they were joined by two more dolphins, their enormous silky-smooth bodies pock-marked with old wounds and scratches. One of them looped below, forming a figure of eight. Colm could clearly make out its blowhole and, when the angle was right, even see deep into its eyes. Bits of sand glimmered in the water, mixing with bubbles that rose from the seaweed below. Colm couldn't imagine why he had never thought of coming to swim here before. He had always just presumed it was something tourists did, and it had never occurred to him to try it himself. His researcher friend, Beatrice, had talked a lot about the dolphins, how sensitive their sonar was, how they could gauge almost everything about you, down to the structure of your bones and layout of your anatomy, even what you had for breakfast, before you even saw them coming. That was why pregnant women were advised not to swim with them, as sometimes the dolphins got so excited by the new life that they inadvertently caused harm.

The water was mostly slate grey, and only in the few sandy patches were they able to see any distance below them. From snatched glimpses here and there, they gathered that there were more than three dolphins. It was hard to tell how many, but there was a baby which had lost its right fin and had just a knot of cartilage jutting out where the flipper should have been. There were two dolphins who showed most interest in them – perhaps these were scouts for the others. They circled Rachel and Colm a few times, drifting to the surface to take some air, then sinking back down again. Colm remembered something Beatrice had told him about how dolphins originally lived on land before deciding to take to the water millions of years ago. He liked the idea – that they had given up his world for their own. At some point the water suddenly fizzed with the sound of a faulty fuse. One of the scouts had begun to call, making a fizzy clicking noise, a warning perhaps, as they all instantly sped off, fading into the grey-green depths like pale ghosts.

Colm looked around him at how Reek must seem for them when they breached momentarily for air: a ring of green hills and purple cliffs, with the decrepit block of lighthouse clinging to Reek Head and Cnoc Ciarán rising up behind, before curving back down to a maze of fields that ran towards the shore road, past Long's farm and Bridie's bold carbuncle at the pier. It was all Colm knew, this bay carved out by a retreating glacier 20,000 years ago. For the first time, it felt constrained, and Colm suddenly envied the dolphins being able to come and go at will. The bears and woolly mammoths that had arrived here after the last Ice Age had long ago moved on, and now it was just his people and a few lean rabbits clinging to the scant earth, joined by whatever motley band of tourists found their way here in summer. He suddenly understood why his mother had had to leave, to get out and find somewhere she could breathe for a while.

Charlotte was glad she'd given the scaffolding bars away. She took another sip of brandy and bent back into salutation pose just as a cormorant brushed in off the sea, swooping low overhead. She traced its path as it spooled through the air and dived downwards after some flicker of dashing silver it spotted in the sea. She had had the dream often enough to know what was expected of her, but the details had been left a little scant. At first she thought she was meant to walk straight into the water, without weights or anything, just give herself up to it. She knew she had enough resolve, acceptance – but she'd borrowed the scaffolding bars just in case. Now she knew she would mount no resistance. It was life that was the struggle; death had always appealed. She understood it – existence without human form; freedom from an awkward body and limited mind. In spirit she would be who she always wanted to be, who she had been up until that awful journey through the birth canal – an experience she would certainly not be repeating again in a hurry. Overall, she was happy enough that she had endured a life on earth, but it was not something she was eager to repeat. No. There would be no more voluntary enlisting; if she were coming back again she'd have to be drafted – and even then she might try escaping over the border to the spiritual equivalent of Canada. There had to be a Canada in the realms beyond; every universe needs its Canada. It was the meagre-mindedness, the limitation of life that she found so wearisome – the lack of knowingness, of potency. Being human would have been fine if there wasn't so much frailty involved. It was an experience she was more than glad to wash off her in the cold waters of Reek Harbour. This was the moment she had been waiting for for so long after all. She was proud of the fact that she had never gone through with it on any of the many previous occasions. And there had indeed been many: ever since she first realised as a teenager that she didn't quite belong. The fact that during her drug binges she had always stopped short of taking that extra step was something she was proud of. She knew that cutting life short before one's guides called one back would have repercussions on the far side. She understood now why she had been made to wait around for so long – for Rachel, of course. She wouldn't have been there in her hour of need, and that had been, without doubt, her finest moment. She only wished she could be there when Rachel finally realised all she had done for her. Was it conceited to yearn for the muted glory of the moment when she would be called forth triumphantly by Rachel and her team of guardian angels to approach the pedestal and collect her gloriously scented bouquet of gladioli and white lilies, shyly curtsying, while hugging her niece to her breast and bestowing kisses all over her beautiful head? Afterwards, she imagined they would gorge on lobster and champagne and paint the town red. It was just unfortunate that it couldn't happen while Charlotte was still alive. It would have to wait for the next realm, and things were never quite as real, quite as tactile, there.

Charlotte imagined the process would be set in motion the moment when Rachel got to read the letter she had left her in the yacht. It laid everything out, apologising for the night of the blue flashing lights and hoped that the fortune she was leaving her from the drug company payout would be some compensation. It was just bad timing that Charlotte was being called back now. She felt sure she could have reached a resolution with her niece with just a bit more time, but the way of the white witch had always been one of humility and selflessness. Her work here was done. No doubt she and Rachel would meet again on the other side, and they would laugh and kiss and love about it all. Indeed, they would, no doubt about it.

Charlotte got up unsteadily to her feet, took one last sip of brandy and hurled the bottle away. She put her thumb out in front of her to get ready for spinning, which she had always been good at, ever since a Sufi from Santa Fe had taught her the trick of overcoming dizziness by keeping her gaze on her thumb as she spun around. It was a trick the old mystics in Syria used, according to the man, to allow them keep going for hours on end. Charlotte began slowly to spin around, and it felt surprisingly good, as though an outside force had taken hold of her and sucked her into a typhoon, neutralising her pain. She was feeling a bit giddy, and her heart was pounding madly in her chest. She felt wonderfully free sailing over the rough ground, gradually edging towards the cliff. She didn't look down; she didn't want to know exactly when she reached the precipice. She wanted it to be a surprise.

Colm's fingers were beginning to wrinkle, and he was considering turning back to shore when he heard clicks and squeals announcing the return of the two dolphins, swerving and sashaying with delirious abandon. One of them had something in its mouth – a gelatinous greyish mass with thick tendrils hanging from it. Colm wasn't sure what it was at first; it looked like a jellyfish, but more solid and striped with thick brownish lines and a band of purple nodules at its mouth.

"What is it?" Rachel asked.

"I think it's a cuttlefish," Colm said, suddenly recognising the tubular shape of its body. "It's a type of shellfish with its shell on the inside. It tastes horrible."

Colm fell suddenly quiet as he noticed the dolphin had curved around him and come right up to Rachel's stomach, where it paused for a while. Rachel was utterly captivated. The dolphin approached to within a metre of her face and stared at her, turning to one side so that it was looking directly at her, eye to eye. She felt it was looking right inside her – not just into her body, but into her mind. It was a disconcerting feeling. Rachel hadn't allowed anyone this close since Nathaniel. In fact, one reason she had warmed to Colm was that she recognised in herself his own reluctance to make eye contact – it made her feel less alone. The dolphin kept staring – pouring its large grey eye into her – and she felt something begin to shift inside. She found she couldn't look away, although she wanted to. It was as if she could sense a shutter begin to open in the recesses of her mind, and the minute she became aware of it, she began to panic. But the dolphin wasn't ready to let her go. It somehow managed to distract her by swivelling its grey-bauble eye, which had a mesmeric quality, like those nurses who take your blood while keeping your focus far away. Suddenly, when it was too late to close down her thoughts, to switch focus, the dolphin turned and swam off, diving down out of sight. Rachel found herself confronting a hammer-blow of realisation. A memory loomed into the forefront of her mind, an image that she had done her best to expunge. She desperately wanted to pull the shutter back down, but it was too late.

"They're gone!" Colm cried looking around him. "And they've left the cuttlefish behind."

He looked over at Rachel and noticed she was crying.

"What's wrong?" he said, swimming over.

She began to cry louder and Colm put an arm around her and helped her as she lurched back towards the shore. She was too upset to even notice he was there. She just stood on the sand shivering until Colm got his smock and gently began to pat her dry, then pulled her dress over her head as she collapsed down on the sand, staring out to sea.

"Dónal says I should always try to talk about what's upsetting me," Colm said, dressing quickly and sitting down next to her to keep her warm. "It helps."

Rachel knew she ought to share what was on her mind, but it was hard. It had been hidden for so long; she was afraid.

"There's something …" she began, gasping for breath.

Colm just looked at her, his eyes wide.

"It's about my boyfriend – the accident?"

She told him about the party and the trip home with Nathaniel and the deer on the road, and he took it all in, nodding. It was the exact same story she had told everyone else, except for one thing. She added one salient detail that she hadn't been able to face before: when she noticed the fawn in the woods, she had cried out to Nathaniel about how cute it was, but he hadn't bothered looking.

"Look, look!" she had cried. "It's adorable."

But Nathaniel didn't seem to care. He was too drunk to care, so she stretched her arm across to point at it and had blocked his view for a second, or a few seconds perhaps. She presumed he had already seen the doe on the road. It had been standing stock still straight ahead looking at them for a quarter of a mile.

Rachel now managed to get these details out to Colm in frantic stops and starts. When she was through, she fell on to his chest, and he hugged her to him, rocking her back and forth as much for his own reassurance as hers. He couldn't think of anything suitable to say, so he just swayed with her until her sobbing died down. Eventually, when she had the courage to look up, she noticed that his eyes were so free of censure and full of compassion that she began to cry again.

"They're off again," Colm said, touching a finger to her cheek. "As the dog said after being deloused by the vet."

Rachel smiled in spite of herself.

"A smile," said Colm. "The rest won't be long now, as the fox said when his tail was cut."

"What rest?" Rachel asked, in spite of herself.

"As the insomniac farmer said to his plough-horse."

"What?"

Colm shrugged.

With the weight of secrecy suddenly lifted from her, Rachel was overcome with elation. It was as though Colm and the dolphins had conspired to bring it about. She leant forward and took his hands in hers and kissed him on the lips. He jerked his head back, concentrating as though trying to guess the flavour.

"It's OK?" she said, reaching her hand up to his cheek and stroking it.

"Yeah," he said, his lips parted, and she bent forward again slowly and kissed him longer until he rolled over giggling.

"Is it really OK?" she asked.

"It's OK," he said. "I don't know about the *really*."

He rolled back towards her and brought his lips again to her mouth. She stuck her tongue out and licked them as though applying lipstick, then she parted his lips and licked in behind them, making him shudder.

"You sure you're fine?" she said.

"One more grind like that, and we'll have to get engaged, as the clutch said to the gear."

She wrapped her arms around him and they lay back on the sand.

Nineteen

Ensuring the church didn't get their hands on Charlotte's sandals and woolly cap proved quite an ordeal. These were the only remnants of her left by the time Rachel found the note on the yacht and roused Dónal and Jimmy to go looking for her. Dónal had a fair idea where she might be, and he took the Zodiac round the headland towards the cliffs, but the waves had carried her far off by then. She had landed not in the water, but in a heap on the rocks below; and the waves had picked her up and smashed her forwards a few times, pulling her back and forth so that she was pummelled a bit before a larger wave came and took her away.

The priest was at the pier when Dónal and Jimmy got back, and he had wanted to lead them to the church to say a prayer, but Rachel was determined this wouldn't happen. She yanked the fertiliser sack in which Jimmy had stuffed the sandals and cap from the priest's hand and marched towards Bridie Brennan's, entering the pub hand-in-hand with Colm and slapping the sack on the counter.

"Pints!" she had called out, as though possessed. "Pints, for everyone."

The priest had followed her to Brennan's along with Dónal and Jimmy, but he soon realised she wasn't going to change her mind, and he slunk away. Rachel was hammer-beaten with shock;

a gradually mounting sense of loss piled down upon her, but with it came an equal and opposite feeling of release, of relief. She had burst into tears when she found Charlotte's note, crying like she hadn't done since she was a baby. It had felt amazingly good, just to get it out of her. The note was stuffed inside the blue dinosaur with a big arrow drawn in pencil pointing towards it. When Rachel found it, her stomach began heaving in and out in desperate gasps until she had vomited only inches from where Charlotte had, earlier in the day. It suddenly became clear to Rachel all that Charlotte had done for her and she felt so … so, blessed.

"Pints!" repeated Colm proudly. "Dirty fucking pints of beer!"

Bridie began to stack them up, and, as though scenting it on the breeze, people began to filter in, hearing rumours of action, the makings of a good night, perhaps a session, a wake, even. Con and Sheila came first, followed soon after by Seáinín and Ulrika, his Swedish student. They all shook hands formally with Rachel, commiserating with her, and with Colm too because he was standing right there beside her. Colm squeezed each hand firmly, like a man, and looked hard into everyone's eyes.

"I have something to say," he said to the gathering. "It's about Charlotte, or not so much about her, as about something she had. Something cuttlefish have too, by the way. And jellyfish, come to think of it. And that's: power, voltage, light."

Máiréad came into the pub, looking taken aback to see Colm not only in the pub but actually talking to people, holding forth.

"Cuttlefish spray ink to confuse their enemies," he continued. "That's what Charlotte did. That's what I liked about her. The way she could change colour, depending on who was around, like cuttlefish squirting tiny drops of dye under their skin to blend or clash. If they want to hide, they can, and if they want to glow like a thousand Christmas trees, they can do that too; 'cause, you see, their reflector plates beam back colour brighter than ever. That's how they communicate, like technicolour billboards. It's how Charlotte was. She was great, and now she's gone."

Colm paused, considering for a second, then simply repeated, "She was great and now she's gone," and fell quiet, looking around him, happy that he'd captured what he wanted to say.

Rachel kissed him. "Thanks, Colm," she said.

"They remind me of you too," he said to her quietly.

"Who?"

"Cuttlefish," he said. "The way they can't see all their beautiful colours themselves. They can only see polarisation, but not colour … Do you have any idea how bright you shine?"

Rachel felt herself about to cry again. She got up and headed out to the passage where the payphone was bolted to the wall beside the lavatory. She knew she had to ring home to let her mum know about Charlotte, and she wanted to get it done while she was still sober. She began feeding coins into the slot, but each time she dialled the number she was cut off. Bridie had given her a pocket full of change from the register, not knowing what she wanted it for, but as soon as she noticed what Rachel was doing, she came bustling out from the bar and insisted Rachel use the private phone in the back room.

Rachel was just preparing herself to ring again when she suddenly noticed an animal in the corner.

"Christ Almighty!" she yelled, "What the hell?"

There was a fox in the corner, curled up in a ball, its cinnamon-black tail masking most of its body. It was staring straight at her. Bridie came rushing back in to find Rachel frozen to the spot.

"It's only Taytos," Bridie said.

"Shit," Rachel said. "What's it doing there?"

"She arrived an hour ago looking bedraggled, so I fed her some milk and crisps and settled her by the fire."

"Have you told Colm?"

242

"Not yet."

Colm had heard the shout and came running in. He was already picking Taytos up, cradling her to his cheek.

Rachel knew she better make the call before she lost her nerve, and she signalled Bridie to steer Colm and Taytos out towards the door. Rachel managed to get through first time from the private line, and her mother answered straight away.

Rachel breathed in to steady herself. "Hi, it's me," she said.

"Rachel?" Lucy replied, after a pause, the single word infused with so much – hurt, love, resentment, regret.

Rachel steeled herself. She hadn't been in contact since Nathaniel's funeral. They had attended as a family, mother and father standing solidly behind her, buttressing her grief. But Rachel found their concern infuriating, and next day she just had to escape. It could have been anywhere; it just happened to be Charlotte who had offered a means. She had packed a bag and gone. The selfishness of the act felt appropriate in some way, offering a degree of twisted relief.

"Where are you?!" Lucy asked across the Atlantic.

"It's OK," Rachel said, trying to keep control.

"It's not OK, not near OK," Lucy said with a note of panic. "What's she done to you?"

"Who?"

"Charlotte, of course! What has she over you?"

"Mom! This is nothing to do with ..."

"With what?"

"I just had to get away."

Lucy sighed. "Will you please tell me where the hell you are?"

"I needed some time."

"I don't understand. What's going on?"

"Look, it doesn't matter. There's been an accident," Rachel said.

"Are you all right?"

"Not me – Charlotte …"

"What's she done now!"

"She hasn't done anything! She was sick. It turns out she's been very sick."

"Charlotte?!"

"Yes!" Rachel felt the tears rising. She didn't know if she had the strength to go on.

"So? She's sick?"

"Mum, can you please just let me finish."

"What?"

"I just need to say this!"

"What?" Lucy said again, with slightly less bitterness.

Rachel had been about to explain the whole thing, about flying to London and the yacht and somehow ending up here in a bar on a crumbling pier on the furthest western point of Europe, but after a few false starts all that came was, "I'm sorry."

It was little more than a whisper, and Lucy made no reply.

"I'm sorry, I said," Rachel repeated louder.

"You're sorry?" Lucy said, playing for time, trying to feel the forgiveness that she knew she ought to. It wasn't coming; the wound was too deep. It had grown calloused over the years. It wasn't enough that Charlotte had gate-crashed her childhood, had demanded all the attention with her constant crises and ostentatious birthday presents; she then had to put her daughter's life at risk with her reckless drug use, and now fourteen years later she comes waltzing back to steal Rachel again at the very moment she's at her lowest ebb. Some things are hard to forgive.

"Yeah, I am," Rachel said, realising that she really meant it. "For everything."

"It broke me – you leaving."

"I had to."

"I felt so …"

"I didn't mean to hurt …"

"Why did you do it, then?"

"I didn't *do* anything."

"You know what I mean!"

Rachel shrugged into the phone.

"With her!" Lucy cried. "You went with her."

"She just turned up with plane tickets." Rachel wanted to explain further, but that was all that seemed to come.

"I wanted to help, you know."

"I know, Mom."

"I know, Mom," Lucy repeated sarcastically. "Your father and I, we both did."

"I know!"

Lucy just exhaled, then rallied with a sudden thought. "Is Charlotte there with you now?"

"No, that's why I called. There's been an accident …"

"What now?!"

"Mom! Can you just listen!"

Rachel began to explain as best she could about the yacht, about Charlotte diving into the water, and about what Charlotte had said about the drug trial that went wrong. And as she talked she could feel her mother's defences receding a little, her hurt ebbing just a fraction, and her breathing begin to calm. She was conscious of her mother's mind spooling back to a life that she had never known, of the cogs of her memory rewinding through time to the realisation of past hurts from before Rachel was even born.

Back home in White Mountain, New Hampshire, Lucy was shaking her head in bewilderment as Rachel told her about Charlotte leaving the note and heading up to the cliffs. "Melodramatic as ever," she muttered. "Always the theatrics."

"It was kind of brave too," Rachel said.

Lucy sighed, considering for a while before saying, "Sort of fitting, anyway."

"She left you something," Rachel said pulling a piece of paper out of her pocket which had been folded up inside the dinosaur's little backpack along with her own note. It was a sketch of Charlotte's hand drawn in pencil, the right hand, the one that had been shackled to a chair the last time she and Lucy met. Suddenly Rachel wished her mother was there with her so that she could give it to her, so that she could look her in the eye as they talked.

"It's a drawing," Rachel said, flattening it out with one hand, "and underneath it are the words, 'For my only sister'."

"Poor Charlotte," Lucy said distantly.

"It was inside a dinosaur, a blue one. I don't know if she wanted you to have it too."

"Is there a funeral?" Lucy said, trying to control her voice.

"Not really Charlotte's style, I reckon."

"Guess not," Lucy said. "So, are you coming home?"

"I don't know," Rachel replied, suddenly feeling lost. "I just don't know."

"Are you OK, Rachie?"

Rachel considered the question a moment, before replying, "There's a house here that I want to help build."

"A house?" Lucy exclaimed.

"Yeah. A friend of mine is building a house."

Lucy sighed again. "How did it get to this? I have no idea what's going on in your life."

"I know," Rachel sighed.

"I want to."

"Yeah."

"So?"

Rachel considered for a moment, before finding herself saying, "How about you come out here for a bit?"

"Where?"

"To Reek. It's in County Kerry. I think you'd like it."

"Are you serious?"

"Sure, I could do with the help. We sort of need an architect."

SOME OTHER READING
from

BRANDON

Brandon is a leading Irish publisher of new fiction and non-fiction for an international readership. For a catalogue of new and forthcoming books, please write to Brandon/Mount Eagle, Cooleen, Dingle, Co. Kerry, Ireland. For a full listing of all our books in print, please go to

www.brandonbooks.com

THE TRAVEL BOOKS OF MANCHÁN MAGAN

Angels and Rabies: A Journey Through the Americas

"[Magan's] writing is unashamedly sensual and he has an engagingly confessional narrative voice; his adventures are as poignant as they are hair-raising." *Sunday Telegraph*

"Frightening, funny and lovable." *The Sunday Times*

"His writing is intimate and immediate, perceptive and humorous." *Books Ireland*

ISBN 9780863223495

Manchán's Travels

"Often humorous, at times hilarious, Magan... has an evocative and elegant turn of phrase." *New Statesman*

"Mad, brilliant and often hilarious." *The Irish Times*

"Magan has a keen eye for the hypocrisies of elite urban India and artfully evokes the 'fevered serenity' of the Himalayas." *Times Literary Supplement*

ISBN 9780863223686

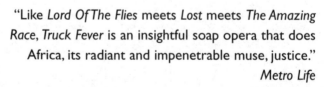

Truck Fever

"Like *Lord Of The Flies* meets *Lost* meets *The Amazing Race*, *Truck Fever* is an insightful soap opera that does Africa, its radiant and impenetrable muse, justice." *Metro Life*

"An excellent writer, has a wonderful talent for transporting the reader into the heart of every experience. He is an intelligent observer of people and places, and his writing is sensitive and engaging. *Truck Fever* is a great read." *Sunday Tribune*

"*Truck Fever* is travel writing at its hair-raising finest." *Evening Herald*

ISBN 978086322389

JOEL THOMAS HYNES
Down to the Dirt

WINNER OF THE PERCY JANES FIRST NOVEL AWARD
LONGLISTED FOR THE INTERNATIONAL IMPAC DUBLIN LITER-
ARY AWARD

"A great novel that never surrenders to peace of
mind." Dermot Healy

"A new and distinctive voice, unique in the fierceness of its feeling."
Alistair MacLeod, author of *No Great Mischief*

ISBN 9780863224300

LARRY KIRWAN
Rockin' the Bronx

"Larry Kirwan writes with all the charm of his music.
This is *Angela's Ashes* for a new generation."
Thomas Keneally, author of *Schindler's List*

In this big, passionate novel the Bronx is burning in
1980–82, Bobby Sands is dying, John Lennon is being
stalked, the Reagan Revolution has begun and AIDS is
about to be identified. But life goes on in the immigrant bars of
Bainbridge Avenue as Sean arrives from Ireland looking for his girlfriend,
Mary, and finds a lot more than he bargained for. Danny McCorley is a
new type of gay hero – a hard-hitting, book-loving, immigrant
construction worker with a shadowy past.

ISBN 9780863224188

ROBERT WALDRON
The Secret Dublin Diary of Gerard Manley Hopkins
A Novella

A bold exploration of the years one of England's
foremost Victorian poets spent in Ireland, of his
torments, ecstasies, fears and loves.

"Waldron's depth of insight makes him an author to
watch." *Publishers Weekly*

ISBN 9780863224096

MARION URCH
An Invitation to Dance

The extraordinary story of a dancer who scandalised the world; a thrilling epic, packed with passionate romance and incident from Ireland to India, from London to Spain, Paris and Munich, from the USA to Australia. This compelling, dramatic work of historical fiction recounts the astonishing life of Lola Montez, a daring young Irish woman who took on the role in life of a Spanish dancer.

ISBN 9780863223839 Hardback; 9780863223952 Paperback

THOMAS KABDEBO
Tracking Giorgione

"The scale is enormous, the thrust of the narrative vivid and precise... A brilliant story of ideas, and also a story of personal love..." Mary O'Donnell

"An intriguing and unusual tale... an absorbing read." *Historical Novels Review*

"Thomas Kabdebo's novel is elegantly written with a lightness of touch that makes it a pleasure to participate on the journey to recover Giorgione." *Irish Catholic*

ISBN 9780863223945

EMER MARTIN
Baby Zero

"An incendiary, thought-provoking novel, like a haunting and spiritual ballad, it moves us and makes us care." Irvine Welsh

In an unheard of country, each successive Taliban-like regime turns the year back to zero, as if to begin history again. A woman, imprisoned for fighting the fundamentalist government, tells her unborn child the story of three baby zeros – all girls born at times of upheaval.

ISBN 9780863223655

NENAD VELIČKOVIC
Lodgers

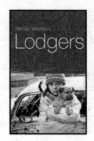

"Nenad Veličkovic offers a beautifully constructed
account of the ridiculous nature of the Balkans
conflict, and war in general, which even in moments of
pure gallows humour retains a heartwarming affection
for the individuals trying to survive in such horrific
circumstances." *Metro*

ISBN 9780863223488

AGATA SCHWARTZ AND LUISE VON FLOTOW (eds)
The Third Shore Women's Fiction from East Central Europe

The Third Shore brings to light a whole spectrum of
women's literary accomplishment and experience
virtually unknown in the West. Gracefully translated,
and with an introduction that establishes their
political, historical, and literary context, these stories
written in the decade after the fall of the Iron Curtain are tales of the
familiar reconceived and turned into something altogether new by the
distinctive experience they reflect.

ISBN 9780863223624

DRAGO JANČAR
Joyce's Pupil

"Jančar writes powerful, complex stories with
unostentatious assurance, and has a gravity which
makes the tricks of the more self-consciously modern
writers look cheap ... Drago Jančar deserves the
wider readership that these translations should gain
him." *Times Literary Supplement*

ISBN 9780863223402

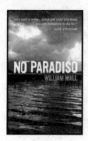

WILLIAM WALL
No Paradiso

"In addition to the author's alert, muscular style, his painlessly communicated appreciation of obscure learning, his vaguely didactic pleasure in accurately providing a sense of place, many of these stories are distinguished by a welcome engagement with form . . .
In their various negotiations with such tensions, the stories of *No Paradiso* engage, challenge and reward the committed reader."
The Irish Times

ISBN 9780863223556

DAVID FOSTER
The Land Where Stories End

"Australia's most original and important living novelist." *Independent Monthly*

"A post-modern fable set in the dark ages of Ireland. . . [A] beautifully written humorous myth that is entirely original. The simplicity of language is perfectly complementary to the wry, occasionally laugh-out-loud humour and the captivating tale." *Irish World*

ISBN 9780863223112

BARRY McCREA
The First Verse

"An intoxicating tale of a young man drawn into a bizarre literary cult... A clever satire of literary criticism, it's also a coming-of-age (and coming-out) tale, a slick portrait of 'Celtic Tiger' Dublin and a compulsive thriller."
Financial Times

"Entertaining, smart, and very, very readable. *The Irish Times*

"An audacious, kaleidoscopic blast." *Sunday Business Post*

ISBN 9780863223808

John Maher
The Luck Penny

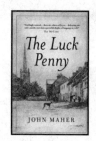

"John Maher confirms himself as one of Irish writing's bright stars with this meditation on death... [A] superbly executed story about bereavement told through characters that intrigue from the first... *The Luck Penny* is an outstanding Irish novel for the wider English-reading world." *Sunday Tribune*

"An expertly crafted, tender tale of grief, language and land... A richly rewarding read." *Metro*

ISBN 9780863223617

Douglas A. Martin
Branwell

"A tender, tragic portrayal of a doomed artist." *Publishers Weekly*

"Martin avoids the temptation of plunging headfirst into the gothic, instead conveying Branwell's psychic turmoil in simple, stripped-down sentences ... [He] sparsely fills in the outlines of Branwell's dissolution, a suitably phantom account of the man who painted himself out of his own family portrait." *Village Voice*

ISBN 9780863223631

Evelyn Conlon
Skin of Dreams

"A courageous, intensely imagined and tightly focused book that asks powerful questions of authority . . . this is the kind of Irish novel that is all too rare." Joseph O'Connor

"Astoundingly original . . . a beautiful novel, which will move you by its courage in delving into controversy and its imaginatively spun revelations." *Irish World*

ISBN 9780863223068

THE NOVELS OF MARY ROSE CALLAGHAN

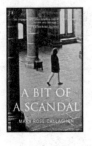

A Bit of a Scandal

"Mary Rose Callaghan hits the nail on the head every time in this sharply observed novel set in the zany world of semi-Bohemian Dublin a generation or two ago. That shabby city of gas meters, broken pay phones, lasagne and cheap wine, is recreated as never before. Young people pursue their heart-breakingly emotional, side-splittingly absurd love affairs in dilapidated bed-sits and seedy pubs, settings that seem as far away as the Middle Ages – which are also evoked, cleverly, in the novel. This is a real tour de force." Éilís Ní Dhuibhne

ISBN 9780863223884 Hardback; 9780863223969 Paperback

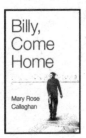

Billy, Come Home

"The slim, moving novel depicts the life of Billy Reilly, a schizophrenic man whose gentle nature and fragile psyche are no match for life in modern Dublin... Without becoming mawkish or preachy, Callaghan delivers an effective indictment of society's failure to care for a vulnerable minority." *Publishers Weekly*

ISBN 9780863223662

The Visitors' Book

"Callaghan takes the romantic visions some Americans have of Ireland and dismantles them with great comic effect . . . It is near impossible not to find some enjoyment in this book, due to the fully-formed character of Peggy who, with her contrasting vulnerability and searing sarcasm, commands and exerts an irresistible charm." *Sunday Tribune*

ISBN 9780863222801